SOMEONE SPEAKS YOUR NAME

LUIS GARCÍA MONTERO

Someone Speaks Your Name

Translated from the Spanish by Katie King

SWAN ISLE PRESS

CHICAGO

Luis García Montero is a Spanish writer whose work includes poetry, novels, essays, song lyrics, and literary scholarship. He spearheaded a literary movement in Spain known as the Poetry of Experience and is head of Spain's Instituto Cervantes.

Katie King is a journalist, media executive, literary translator, and translation scholar. She has collaborated with García Montero for more than a decade.

Swan Isle Press, Chicago 60628

Edition © 2022 by Swan Isle Press
©Luis García Montero
©Katie King

First Edition
26 25 24 23 22   1 2 3 4 5
ISBN-13: 978-1-7361893-4-4

Originally published as *Alguien dice tu nombre* ©2014 Alfaguara (Penguin Random House-Grupo Editorial).

An excerpt of *Someone Speaks Your Name* was first published by *World Literature Today*, Volume 89, No. 3 & 4, May-August 2015.

Epigraphs:
From "París, postal del cielo" by Jaime Gil de Biedma, *Las personas del verbo* (Editorial Lumen, 1982).
From *Encerrados con un solo juguete* by Juan Marsé, (Seix Barral, 1960).

Excerpt from "Le Cygne" by Charles Baudelaire, *Fleurs du mal* (Poulet-Malassis et de Broise, 1857).

Library of Congress Cataloging-in-Publication Data
Names: García Montero, Luis, author. | King, Katie (Katherine M.), translator.
Title: Someone speaks your name / Luis García Montero ; translated from the Spanish
    by Katie King.
Other titles: Alguien dice tu nombre. English
Description: First edition. | Chicago : Swan Isle Press, [2022]
Identifiers: LCCN 2022045424 | ISBN 9781736189344 (trade paperback ; alk. paper)
Subjects: LCGFT: Novels.
Classification: LCC PQ6657.A6965 A65613 2022 | DDC 863/.64--dc23/eng/20220919
LC record available at https://lccn.loc.gov/2022045424

Swan Isle Press also gratefully acknowledges that this book has been made possible, in part, with the support of grants from:
Literary Arts Emergency Fund: Administered by the American Academy of American Poets, Community of Literary Magazines & Presses, National Book Foundation, supported by the Mellon Foundation
Illinois Arts Council Agency
Europe Bay Giving Trust
And Other Kind Donors

This paper meets the requirements of ANSI/NISO Z.39.48.-1992 (Permanence of Paper).

For Almudena,
because I follow her, and she leads me to myself.

For Paco Portillo and Pepe Cid de la Rosa,
with loyalty to your dream.

Ahora voy a contaros
cómo también yo estuve en París, y fui dichoso.
Era en los buenos años de mi juventud,
los años de abundancia
del corazón, cuando dejar atrás padres y patria
es sentirse más libre para siempre, y fue
en verano, aquel verano
de la huelga y las primeras canciones de Brassens,
y de la hermosa historia
de casi amor.

—JAIME GIL DE BIEDMA

—Te quiero, Tina. Y te necesito. Nunca he sabido querer a nadie ni a nada...
—Creo que yo tampoco. Ayúdame, amor, ayúdame. ¡Por Dios, ayúdame!
—aplastó el rostro en el pecho de él—. Quédate conmigo, por favor...
¡Quédate a mi lado, no puedes dejarme ahora!

—JUAN MARSÉ

SOMEONE SPEAKS YOUR NAME

The calendar in this café is suspended in time and space. Nothing changes, no one escapes from here. It's stuck on a single day, April nineteenth. Not the last eleven days of April or any days in May or June. Nor, as Vicente Fernández would point out later, the last two hundred and fifty-six days of nineteen sixty, nineteen sixty-one and nineteen sixty-two, or the first one hundred and eighty-one days of nineteen sixty-three. I like literature better than math, so I use letters and words to express numbers—although, it's true that when I write poetry, I do use numbers to count the syllables… *Together we live in a suspended time*, eleven syllables, that's a hendecasyllable. *An angel with its enormous wings of chains* is another. Eleven syllables.

Today is July first, nineteen sixty-three. The ancient, practically prehistoric calendar is a metaphor for our paralyzed nation. I assume the Café Lepanto will be my regular hangout for the next three months since it's right next door to Editorial Universo, the publishing house on Calle Lepanto. My literature professor told me that learning to write is like learning to see, you have to focus on details that help you make sense of the world. Right now, I'm focusing on a calendar that's stuck on a single day, and thinking about this parched nation, this sweltering, torpid city, this existence with no future. In a way, I'm grateful for the old-fashioned wooden calendar, with its slots where you insert the days and the months that are painted on small wooden slats. The photos on the calendars in the other bars and shops around the neighborhood are stale. At least here in the Café Lepanto there aren't any photos of holy week processions, no virgins, no saints, no starlets, no tacky women posing with bottles of Soberano cognac which is being promoted as a man's drink. I love depriving the church of its capital letters. My literature professor says that to become a writer you need to cultivate a few obsessions. It gives you personality, worldliness. Artists are obsessives. The poet Juan Ramón Jiménez used to write the letter *j* in words that everyone else spells with a *g*: antholojy, jeneration, relijion. It's painful to read, but that's the point, to write and cause discomfort. I am the master of the premeditated spelling error. Some of my professors condemn my use of the lower case to write god. But that's my obsession, my insolence. In my village, I'm famous for being insolent. I want my writing to be famous for insolence, too.

3

Beneath the battered old wooden calendar with an air of dignity but suspended in time, the Café Lepanto fills up with seekers of water and coffee. Vicente Fernández greets them, people come and go but there, inside, time stands still. We're suffering the heat and the drought of a summer that is prehistoric, dense, and distracted. My literature professor likes Ramón del Valle-Inclán because he was a novelist who wrote unforgettable descriptions using three adjectives. Madrid was *absurd, brilliant, and starving.* El Marqués de Bradomín, Valle-Inclán's most famous fictional character, was *ugly, catholic, and sentimental.* Summertime in Granada is like his life: *withered, dense, and distracted.* Time will not march on, no one will update the calendar, and we will continue stuck in the same day, the same month, the same year, even though a new school year will start, the cold will come, the mountains will wake up white with snow, my parents will get older, and I will take more Latin and language history classes at the University. Time will not pass, and we will continue to inhabit a city that's *prehistoric, dense, and distracted,* a city with no future, nailed to a calendar that can't move.

Not a bad metaphor to kick off my writing about this summer. Today, Monday, July first, nineteen sixty-three, I climbed the stairs to the Universo offices. Shadowy, shabby, and asthmatic, that describes the stairs at number seven Calle Lepanto. I had a noon appointment with Vicente Fernández. The secretary, who seemed nice enough, paused her phone call to tell me that Don Vicente had gone out for coffee. She said I could wait in his office or go look for him in the Café Lepanto. I decided the café was better. As the secretary turned back to her call, the swoosh of the electric fan stirred up only sadness.

"Yes, you're in Motril, right? Your name? Yes, please. Your phone number? As soon as someone from sales is available, he'll contact you. Pardon? No, I don't have that information, but …. In half an hour. Of course. Thank you, sir."

The state of the office was enough of an excuse to choose the café: a metal bookshelf, paint peeling off the walls, the smell of aging and yellowing wallpaper, two closed doors, a secretary on the phone and a couple of armchairs too scary to sit in. All that, and the fact that I hadn't had breakfast yet. My literature professor is partial to the intelligent use of humor when writing about pretty much anything. Go for the smile, even at the saddest moments. To write is to seduce. Humor with tears, humor with hunger, café con leche.

I got to the bar to find the calendar waiting for me, suspended on April nineteenth, nineteen sixty. What did I do on that day three years ago? My literature professor insists that to write is to negotiate with memory. I have a good memory, it's the forgetting I'm no good at. I remember those who've helped me, and I never forget those who've done me wrong. My mother thinks that only spiteful people hold a grudge. I'm not spiteful. I do forgive, but I don't forget. I don't like Don Mateo, for example, the high school teacher who threw me out of his class on April nineteenth, nineteen sixty, just because he didn't like me. He expelled me five and a half times during the two classes I suffered through with him. The half was because one day he threw me out, then changed his mind and followed me out into the hallway to ask me to come back.

"Come on back, León, I don't want to throw you out today. It's your onomastic."

I'm not sure if it was April nineteenth, nineteen fifty-nine, or April nineteenth, nineteen- sixty. But he threw me out of class and then forgave me, because April nineteenth is my saint's day, the feast of pope León IX, saint León, the same date that's suspended forever on the wall of the Café Lepanto. Every day is my saint's day, or my onomastic, as that pedant Don Mateo would say. I promise I won't write the word *onomastic* again, ever. Farewell, onomastic, farewell. My saint's day! Even if you don't believe in miracles you have to admit that luck plays a mysterious part in our lives. Farewell, Don Mateo, may you remain, sir, forever entombed in your classroom, and you can keep your onomastic and your expulsions, because now I've successfully completed my first year at the University of Granada.

The barman said he became a widower on April nineteenth, nineteen sixty, the day his life lost all meaning. His wife died on my saint's day. Strange coincidence. I prefer to think of death not as stillness but as absence of life. They're not the same thing. The dead are in cemeteries, surrounded by flowers and forgetting. The absence of life walks the streets every day, it goes to work, to school, it has coffee in the bars, and it seeps into our bodies when we try to think or dream. I'm not a resentful person, I just don't want anyone to force me to keep quiet. Sometimes no one can shut me up. I'm not domesticated like a mule, or like my father. I refuse to follow orders. My father curses the day he decided to call me León. He's convinced that naming me for a wild animal shaped my character.

"So, you're León Egea Extremera."

"Yes, Don Vicente."

"You can drop the 'Don.' I'm your colleague, not your boss. The boss is Don Alfonso, but you won't see much of him in the office this summer. Would you like a coffee?"

Yes, and some toast. Vicente seems like a good person… too good. One of those guys who never gets into trouble.

Vicente knows my literature professor. They met when Universo published my professor's book. That's the connection that got me this summer job. It's a great opportunity that I'm really excited about, and really need, and something else I owe to my professor's classes and his way of thinking. I don't think he and Vicente are actual friends, though, because their personalities are so different. Vicente's got that respectful, solicitous manner of a salesman: he talks, he smiles, he clams up. He's pleasant, he listens, he's attentive, he tries to be friendly, but as soon as you start talking about your own life, tell some story or start to describe some event, he withdraws, and says he doesn't need to know about that. Sharing confidences with someone he just met must make him uncomfortable, I guess.

I'm jotting down these memories of that meeting and my first conversation with him so I can develop a profile of my impressions. We sat at a table instead of standing at the bar so I could eat my breakfast comfortably. The widowed barman served me, on Vicente's tab, a café con leche, toast with butter, and a glass of Lanjarón mineral water from our very own Sierra Nevada. Today the city drought managers turned off the tap water at eleven-thirty in the morning. A drought. Just what a city suspended in time needs. But I'm not complaining. I ate a good breakfast. Vicente is generous if a bit lacking in spirit. I started babbling out of sheer gratitude, content with the breakfast and my new job. When I shared some details about my life, my friendship with my literature professor, my run-ins with the priest who teaches Latin in my village, my father's fears, the advantages of not going home to my village this summer and avoiding another argument with the mayor, Vicente said:

"I don't need to know about that."

His indifference put me off a bit, but then he smiled and began to tell me about my new job. Universo just published a three-volume encyclopedia set. The ad campaign they're running in the newspapers around Granada province promotes the Universo Encyclopedia as "an essential learning tool for schoolchildren and a source of wisdom for all." Well, I declared, in this country we're all still children, even people over fifty. Nobody knows anything. Ignorance rules. Ok, Vicente said, I guess that's one approach to pitching an encyclopedia sale. But you should be careful how you talk about these things. It doesn't help to complain and to look down on others, insult them, criticize their illiteracy, as if you were the only wise man in a village of idiots. You'll get better results displaying optimism, advocating for your passion to help our nation improve and advance, to help our children progress and to get all our families to contribute. You have to open a window to the world for them, to dazzle them with illuminating rays of knowledge. Ok, ok, I told him, I get it.

Then we went up to the office to continue the orientation. Vicente introduced me to Consuelo Astorga, the secretary, and we all went into the space we're going to share. The calendar on Consuelo's desk and the almanac on the wall are up to date. The office is not as lively as the bar, but at least up here no one has barricaded himself behind a suspended date. July welcomes me with open arms, as one who aspires to fill the towns and villages of this province with encyclopedias. Consuelo works in the small reception area, just big enough for the two armchairs, a shelf with Universo books on it, and a desk where she receives visitors and screens phone calls. The door to Don Alfonso's office looks like it'll be closed all summer. That's better for me because I don't do well with authority figures. The office I'm going to share with Vicente has a window that overlooks the interior patio. In winter, the aroma of simmering stew will seep through the windows, just like in the interior patio of my apartment building. But I'll be gone by October, so that aroma won't be making me hungry here.

Today, the only thing seeping through the windows is the sound of a radio. Our office has a meeting table, five chairs, another shelf full of books and three huge filing cabinets that organize this vast, parched, downcast world of Granada into three sections: A to G, H to O, P to Z. There's a door to a bathroom with a mirror, a wash basin, and a toilet. Everything is clean but shabby. The mirror shows little interest in reflecting the image of any hand washer who stands before it. The obstinate stink of disinfectant competes with the murky odors drifting in from the building's interior. Powers of observation: another essential quality in a writer and a must for someone who's studying how he's going to spend the next three months. This will be my kingdom until fall term.

The work is easy. It consists of answering the phone when some sap falls for our newspaper ads and calls in. We try to sell them encyclopedias. Once we set the hook, all we need to do is fill out the forms and thank you very much. If they hesitate, you have to pitch a personal visit to their homes to demonstrate the books. Arrive, observe, convince. Access to this compilation of knowledge about the universe benefits any home, school, library, office, or city hall. I have a hunch that travel will be the most interesting part of this job. According to my literature professor, anyone who aspires to be a writer must acquire knowledge of the human condition and of life in Spain's villages. Experience feeds the ability to see. Learning to write is learning to see.

Everything's in order. Everyone's happy. I didn't want to go home to my village during summer vacation and now, luckily, I have a job that lets me stay in the city instead. My father wanted to avoid any more problems with the mayor, and he was relieved to keep the danger, meaning me, far away. My landlady was happy to charge me half the normal rent during these months when students abandon the city and the apartment rental business collapses. With my salary, I'll be able to save enough money for next semester's books. And I'm going to take full advantage of this real-life experience to develop my skills as a writer. I'm going to learn how to see, develop my memory, cultivate my powers of observation, elaborate series of three adjectives and cultivate my use of humor. I think the intelligent humor bit is going to be easy for me, from what I've observed in the office and knowing that we have some trips to the provinces coming up. That's where I'll find interesting characters and their humble affairs suspended in time, calendars with no days and faucets with no water. I won't need to be super smart to seem super smart and fill the pages of this journal with good humor. I'll recount the adventures and adversities of a future writer during this hot, dry, prehistoric, and bewildering summer of nineteen sixty-three.

Vicente Fernández Fernández isn't tall or short, skinny or fat, smart or stupid, agreeable or disagreeable, friend or enemy, young or old. I've been working with him a week now, but it's hard to form an opinion. But then, is it really necessary to have an opinion about someone? Well, it's never a bad thing to know who you're working with, who's giving you advice, who's inviting you for a cup of coffee. Also, if you want to be a writer you have to delve into the human condition. My literature professor, Ignacio Rubio, constantly repeated that advice when he was talking to us about Benito Pérez Galdós' novel *Misericordia*. Capturing the human condition is always your objective, the prize for words woven as finely as a spider's web.

I've met a lot of people in my life, each with a unique name and unique personality. I know more dark-haired people than blondes, more thin people than fat, more short people than tall. But those aren't the important things. My mother organizes people into the good and the bad, those who have a righteous heart and those who live with bitterness. But reality is organized differently. What counts is hierarchy and power, not whether you're a good egg or a bad egg. In the end, there are those who give orders and those follow them. Of course, there are always exceptions, and I like the kind of people who, whatever their luck of birth, don't feel compelled to give orders but don't necessarily obey them either. I get along with people who seem in command without barking out orders, and who refuse to obey, even though they may have to bite their tongues in the process. And there you have an example of introspection, something else I'm going to practice now and then in this journal.

I know I'll get to like Vicente because he never tries to humiliate anyone, or to order anyone around. When it comes to the people I love, especially my family, I've learned to respect them even if they were born to obey. I acknowledge this and I accept it, it's understandable being from the village I'm from and having the father I have. But affection aside, I confess that I only truly admire those people who refuse to take orders. Pedro el Pastor refused and broke his walking stick over the back of the mayor's son instead. I can't obey either, it's very hard for me to shut up and stay still. I bury myself in my books as a way to avenge injustices without causing trouble. My father knows the score. He feels sorry for Pedro el Pastor. But he's afraid to say what he thinks because it might lead to conflict. He just looks away, smiles, and murmurs good afternoon. He always says that he may not know how to read, but life is not a novel, and in this country the beatings, the detentions and the deaths are very real.

I suspect Vicente is one of those people who just quietly does his job without getting into any trouble. But I don't really know. It seems hard for him to converse, comment on stories in the newspaper, talk about his life. He's polite and pleasant enough, but his silences impose a distance, a lack of spontaneity. Silences without secrets suggest fear, not sincerity. It's a safety measure. Like he's afraid of something unexpected. It seems odd for a man of the world, who's travelled, who's been to Paris. Sometimes you'd think he's never even really left the office. He's nothing more than a good man who's willing to put up with tedious hours at a desk, glasses of water at the Café Lepanto and the rumbling engines of the provincial buses.

Consuelo's told me just about everything I know about Vicente, which isn't much. He was born in Moraleda de Zafayona, a village west of Granada; he just turned forty-five, he's married, he's always tidily dressed in a dark blue jacket during the winter and a beige jacket during the summer. I've only seen the beige jacket, but Consuelo says that he's just as faithful to the blue one. He arrives at the office, says hello, scans the list of calls, wipes the sweat from his brow with a white handkerchief, rolls his shirts sleeves back down, arranges his paper and his pen and gets to work, responding patiently to clients' questions with submissive, repetitive, and claustrophobic amicability.

"Yes, there's a lot of information about raising rabbits and hens, yes sir. It's like having a veterinarian right in your home. Yes, that's correct, that's what encyclopedias are for. These days there are unprecedented illnesses, plagues that can wipe out your livestock in just a couple of days. Children? They'll be able to learn about santa teresa de jesús or Don Juan of Austria ...."

The Universo Encyclopedia, promoted in the papers as an alphabetized collection of world knowledge both ancient and modern, is filled with facts about Juan of Austria, the capital of Norway, diseases affecting beet crops, hunting techniques, the care and feeding of pet goldfinches, and even proper sexual practices for married couples. Vicente Fernández mops his brow with the white kerchief, he continues explaining, he lists all the advantages of erudition, he offers up facts, he points out important names, he urges as far as amiability allows, he closes deals with delight, absorbs failure with patience, and notes the addresses and possible dates for follow-up visits.

"Tuesday or Wednesday next week. That's fine. Of course. I'll leave you a message at the telephone exchange. Thank you very much, Don Pablo. All right."

Vicente isn't fat or skinny, tall or short, young or old. When he's in the bar, talking to the widowed barman or ordering a beer to toast the end of a workday, he seems like a normal person; stocky, about my height, still youthful. But when he speaks to a client, or when he shuts down in the face of an unfriendly comment, or when he murmurs from a cautious distance that stupid phrase, "I don't need to know about that," Vicente becomes smaller, fatter, older. It's pathetic to watch him say goodbye at the end of the day and head home, withdrawn into himself, with his clumsy stride, his black briefcase in his hand and the full weight of the city's heat across his shoulders. He's the kind of guy whose shoes always pinch his feet.

I can't believe he spent five years in Paris, the city of philosophers, cabarets, and liberty. Consuelo says he was there until nineteen sixty. Then he returned to Spain, married a woman from Madrid, and found a job with Editorial Universo. It didn't take me long to figure out that this office isn't Universo's headquarters. Too poor, too dead, too insignificant. This job that Ignacio Rubio, my literature professor, helped me find is in a simple provincial office. You have to start somewhere. Maybe one day I'll get to visit the main office in the Puerta del Sol, the heart of Madrid. That's where the writers go to sign contracts and to plot grand projects. All we do here is put ads in the local papers, talk on the phone, and plan bus trips along torturous mountain highways.

In our provincial office, we don't even get to collect subscriptions. The head office already signed an agreement with the local association of retired non-commissioned military officers, Guardia Civil members, and national police officers. The association's members are the ones who collect the monthly payments in exchange for a modest stipend that helps them top up their measly retirement incomes. It's sort of funny how all that authority just disappears with retirement, all the "I order this," and "I command you to do that," turns into nothing more than friendly visits to collect monthly encyclopedia payments. It makes me feel a little bit sorry for Sergeant Palomares, who always jumps when the mayor of my village calls and always jumps at the chance to smack me around in their little station house. Let's just see how many encyclopedia payments he'll need to collect to get by after he retires. Pedro el Pastor treated his dog better than the mayor treats his sergeant.

My literature professor says it's important to distance yourself from your subject matter, use your intelligence to make sure your writing doesn't turn into emotional venting. To practice the art of introspection, you must first achieve detachment. Without a profound diagnosis of the human condition, you can produce nothing of value. Vicente went to Paris as an emigrant, which meant he was condemned to feeling like an outsider, seeing everything with resentment. He embraced the city, but then withdrew, preferring to move to Madrid. There he continued withdrawing into himself, getting fatter, older, and finally ending up in a provincial office of Universo, very close to his home village of Moraleda de Zafayona, with the only remaining ambition of knowing as little as possible, just the essentials. And saying as little as possible, just the essentials. Vicente Fernández has the soul of a clerk. He'd be happy if he never had to get up from his desk, if he could limit his work life to patient telephone conversations about the glories of universal knowledge. I suspect he views as tragic our upcoming trip on the Corto de Loja regional train. There is only one mystery in Vicente Fernández Fernández's (even his names are repetitive) methodical existence. It's also the big mystery of our office. Consuelo doesn't know where Vicente lives. When he steps out of the office, or the Café Lepanto, with his shuffling pace and his black briefcase, he heads off into the unknown.

Consuelo Astorga also has an uncertain air about her. It's important to use words precisely. Many people use the word uncertain to express something that's false... and they are wrong. I'm not saying Consuelo is false, just that it's difficult to read her because her looks are deceiving. She's sort of nondescript. The first day she seemed like a conventional secretary with a hairdo like a woman of almost fifty. Neither pretty nor ugly, her air of professionalism dominates her looks, the exemplary secretary with her smile and her glasses, a caricature of correctness. She reminds me of my Aunt Rosario.

However, she gets better the more you talk to her, and you start to see her in a different way. Yes, each day she gets a bit better. I haven't asked how old she is but now I think she's closer to forty than to fifty. The sadness in her eyes wasn't born there. She's been contaminated by the plastic flowers, the useless ceiling fan, the scruffy armchairs, the papers on her desk, the noisy telephones, the rickety filing cabinets, the office. Vicente is a man with the soul of a pencil-pusher. I don't think Consuelo has the soul of an old maid. But she is overwhelmed by her circumstances. She looks a lot like my Aunt Rosario, who didn't have a suitor by the time she was twenty-five, so she had to resign herself to life on the shelf. Consuelo isn't on the shelf, but she does organize files, take messages, sharpen pencils, persist with the disinfectant in the bathroom each day, put up with Vicente's silences. She's demure in her remarks, never jokes, never goes into the Café Lepanto, is always the first one in the office in the morning and the last one to leave in the evening, locking the door behind her. My Aunt Rosario has dark hair and Consuelo is blonde, but they have the same face, they look a lot alike. Consuelo is blonde, perfect, and overlooked.

When she told me she had never married, right away I thought of my Aunt Rosario. My mother's sister behaves like a proper young lady, the daughter of a pharmacist, brought up in a house in the center of town, right next to the church. My father says he's had to swallow more morning church bells than toast for breakfast over the years. My grandparents were not happy that their eldest daughter ended up having to marry a farm worker; they'd hoped for a different future for their first born. The union was a millstone around their necks, but they were stoic in the face of the scandal of my mother's pregnancy. They felt themselves above the sniping of boorish and sanctimonious villagers who always looked down on my father. And then came more bad luck with their second daughter not marrying at all. In the end they weren't sure which was worse. Not that poor Rosario ever lacked for work. She took care of my grandfather when he had pneumonia, then my grandmother when she had a stroke, and finally, when my mother opened a small grocery store with her inheritance, Rosario once again devoted herself to taking care of family. She wasn't asked to stack cans of tuna or tomatoes. She never even learned to sell aspirin in her father's pharmacy; selling didn't suit her character. Instead, she started taking care of me, preparing my snacks, helping me with my homework, cleaning and caring for my clothes. She became my second mother, with my father working in the fields and my first mother in the store. Having to play the part of mother because you have no other role is even sadder than that old ceiling fan in the office.

Discreet, perfect, kind, Aunt Rosario is at the core of our lives but somehow always out of place, like a boy who has to peddle through the streets on a borrowed bike. Resignation defines her kindness, she's internalized her spinsterhood, her eyes reveal an intimate solitude, the stinging brand of a creature not needed in this world. But Rosario is not one of the bitter ones. Her bad luck did not spur her to hate. Instead, she cultivated resignation. Ever since I've known her, she's been impervious to happiness and misfortune. When I started getting good grades and excelling in school, she didn't show any pride. When I punched the mayor's son in the face, she didn't get angry. That's just life, a combination of good and bad moments that she accepts into her home, but accepts as if she herself didn't belong there, and had no right to speak either the first or the last word. It's enough for her to simply carry on with the tasks of her modest routine.

Consuelo has not internalized her spinsterhood. She's younger than she seems, and her eyes often widen with interest in life, with an appetite to have her say. She even shoots me the occasional look of solidarity when Vicente says something strange or retreats into one of his silences. At those moments, our eyes meet, and sparks start to fly. Being single in the city is different. Here they say everyone knows each other, that Granada is like a village. But those of us who were born in a real village know that's an exaggeration. Nobody recognizes me in the streets here, no one knows who my father is, what I study, where I work. No, Granada is not a village, and Rosario's spinsterhood is not like Consuelo's, even though they look alike, are both equally perfect, and both conform to the demands of their roles.

Of Consuelo, I only know that she's single, she doesn't have any nieces or nephews and she studied typing. She hasn't told me how she came to work as a secretary in the Granada office of Editorial Universo. Just the way things happened, she murmured, with a thinly disguised effort to change the subject. I've hit a nerve without meaning to, I think. The closed door of the boss Don Alfonso's office could conceal many stories. Perhaps a love story. Imagination is another essential virtue for a future novelist, and I have no trouble imagining things. I can see Consuelo getting up each morning, selecting with calculated neutrality her perfect secretary outfit—a print blouse, a knee-length skirt—all the while nurturing a secret passion for the boss who entertains her and occasionally treats her to some quick lovemaking in the office during the afternoon break, or to a clandestine trip to the vacant hotels and beaches of the wintertime in the Costa del Sol. It could be…why not?

Then summer comes, and Don Alfonso is a married man, so he does his duty by his family and disappears to spend his vacation with them on a crowded seashore, with beach umbrellas and decency, with children, buckets, spades and strolls by the sea, greetings, a lot of "yes, yes, my dear," "yes, my darling," "of course, my love," "Look how Alfonsito has grown." Consuelo Astorga masks beneath her blouse and skirt a body that is still young, capable of carrying on an adulterous affair with the boss. Good breasts, good hips, good legs. I bet Don Alfonso has one of those mustaches that married men have. In the summer he disappears, and the secretary stays back at the office because there is no question of bringing her along with the family and because encyclopedia sales in July and August are crucial to meet revenue targets. There are lots of reasons someone might notice a newspaper ad about encyclopedias during the summer: a child's failing grade at the end of the school year, kids needing help with homework, the irritation of having them around the house or the danger of letting them loose in the streets, teachers taking stock of their needs, and planning ahead for the school year are all magnificent incentives. You get a discount if you pay the full price up front or you can pay in low monthly installments with a slight surcharge. Love in installments also has a surcharge: secrecy, waiting, a life filled with sharp curves and potholes, like the buses that bump along poorly paved highways.

That could be Consuelo's backstory and explain her presence in the office. Or maybe Don Alfonso was doing a favor for a friend who was trying to end a bothersome affair and was looking for somewhere to dump a woman fallen into disgrace. It's hard to imagine that's the case with Consuelo but what's certain is that there's no resignation in her eyes, no private loneliness or internalized spinsterhood. Instead, her eyes convey a carefully disguised carnality. Examining each detail of her body adds to the overall impression. If she didn't look so much like Rosario, I might dare to write that Consuelo Astorga is a desirable woman.

The Corto de Loja is a provincial train line that runs west from Granada through the villages of Atarfe, Pinos Puente, Íllora, Tocón, Monte Frío, Villanueva y Huétor Tájar. It's an interesting journey but a slow, chaotic, gossipy train. Travelers get on and get off, but they never stop talking; they invade each coach with their chatter, shamelessly sharing personal details of their family lives, fits and starts of employment, debts, the son who lives in Germany, the daughter who's getting married in the fall, the daughter-in-law who's due any moment, how good this season's chorizo is, the saintly hands of the doctor, or the healer, or the veterinarian. I try to focus on the scenery, concentrate on the withered river, the bridges, the poplars, the clusters of houses around small station stops. The truth is there are more goats, rabbits, hares, sparrows, and doves in the conversations on the train than in the countryside passing by the framed window. The arid landscape has none of the lushness of the gossip inside the train where, suddenly, a wedding makes its escape and dashes down the aisle, or a bitter property line dispute takes flight between the seats.

I'm so grateful for the fresh breeze blowing in from the countryside. The air is still cool from the nighttime, and as it lifts a vivid evocation of plant life through the window, it seems to have forgotten that more than a year has passed since the last rainfall. The fresh air gives me a fleeting sense of wellbeing. I can't open the novel I brought with me because I find it impossible to look away from the scene inside the train. I'm immersed in the locomotive's wails, the rail car's laments, and the lives of the chatty travelers. No one's reading, not even a newspaper, so there's no chance of anyone taking the bait of our ads about Universo encyclopedias. I mention this to Vicente, but all I get in return is a murmured corrective, delivered with a smile:

"Don't look down on people."

"I'm not looking down on anyone," I protest. "But if they don't read the newspaper, they'll never know we're selling encyclopedias."

"Maybe they listen to the radio."

"We have radio ads?"

"Of course! 'Universo Encyclopedias: The Tree of Knowledge is rooted in its pages.'" Vicente has put on his radio voice. "Anyway, today we've got a sure thing. Two clients."

And then he goes silent again. My traveling companion is the only silent one in the entire carriage of chatterers. His restraint is so extreme it seems inhuman. When the train gets to Loja, a woman in the next carriage suddenly goes into labor. I'm not surprised. This journey is so long and slow and has so many station stops and delays along way that anything could happen: engagements, weddings, births, baptisms, funerals. Childbirth! Now that's an impactful human event, the kind that becomes news and fodder for those year-in-review reports they put out around Christmas time. For sure, tomorrow, everyone will be talking about this story. No doubt this unexpected delivery—that's how the headlines will describe it in the newspapers and on the radio—will attract more attention than any encyclopedia ad.

Travel turns life into a box of surprises. Naturally, pandemonium erupted at the station when we arrived. Somebody called the Guardia Civil, someone else started offering advice, others improvised a stretcher. Everyone jumped into the hubbub. Everyone except Vicente, that is.

"Let's go, we'll be late."

"But a woman there is about to give birth...."

"The Guardia Civil will call the doctor."

"She might need help." I protested. "Maybe we should ...."

"Women know more about these things than we do."

When we got to Loja City Hall, the mayor was waiting for us nervously. He's in a hurry to close the deal because he's just been told that a woman went into labor at the train station. It seems that all went well, and now the mayor wants to have his picture taken with the mother and her newborn. It's a big event for this village. The mayor asks if we've just come from there, and Vicente tells him that yes, we were in the same rail car as the pregnant woman and that the reaction of the people of Loja was spectacular as was the efficiency of the Guardia Civil and their swiftness in calling the doctor. I think it'll be the human-interest story of the month. But Vicente's interpretation of events leaves me dumbfounded.

"This encyclopedia is a luxury," Vicente says, with a tone of absolute conviction. "It unites the head and the hand, ideas and action, knowledge and experience. Let's see what it tells us about birth." He asks me to give him the volume I'm carrying in my bag, and when I hand it to him, he opens it to *B, Bi, Bir* ... and he pursues the word with his finger. "Here it is. Birth: A person's origin or ancestry. No no, that's not it. Let's see: genesis or dawn of something. No, that's not it either. Ok, this is it. Birth: The act of giving birth. Look at this Don José. It's a miracle come true. Advice for emergency childbirth if a woman is not able to reach the hospital or if there is no doctor present. First: controlled breathing will help delay the impulse to push along with the contractions, buying time for a doctor or midwife to arrive. Second: the Good Samaritan who arrives to help should be sure to wash his hands and then wash the vaginal area with soap and water. Third: place clean towels or clothes on the ground underneath the buttocks to keep them elevated and protected from unclean surfaces. The woman should place her hands under her thighs to keep them elevated." The mayor is listening, slack-jawed, as if he were seeing a ghost. Knowledge that can resolve all of life's surprises. "How about that, Don José? What do you think? Fourth: when the baby starts to crown, you should never pull on the emerging head. All movements must be gentle. Fifth: nudge the head downward to help the shoulder emerge. The other shoulder will follow naturally. Sixth: wrap the baby in a clean towel. Seventh: do not pull on the umbilical cord or the placenta until medical help arrives. How about that Don José? This is an essential book."

"Yes, of course. I'm feeling a little dizzy. It's quite warm in here."

I don't say a word. The portraits of government officials on the mayor's wall dampen any interest I might have to intervene. Acquiescence permeates the room. Don José quickly and generously agrees to the purchase. One encyclopedia set for the recently opened Loja City Girls' School. It will be a gift from City Hall to Doña Hortensia and Doña Olga, the teachers who saw the ad in the paper. Another encyclopedia will go to the Natalio Rivas National School, a thank you gift for their consistent collaboration in organizing cultural events. And another encyclopedia set for the Academia virgen de la caridad. The director wants it as a gift for the teachers who come from Antequera for testing. Another encyclopedia for City Hall because facts at your fingertips always come in handy. And another set for the mayor, a father of three school-age children and husband to a woman young enough to have even more children who need encyclopedias. All in all, a brilliant bit of business.

"We have a little extra money floating around." Don José is an affable man. Despite his hurry, he proudly cites his successes. "This year we've had many illustrious visitors. In February, Don Jorge Vigón, Minister of Public Works was here. The Caudillo himself honored us with a visit in April. In June, it was cardinal Larraona. A lot of VIPs. The regional governor helped us fund our official receptions budget. There's a bit of cash left over. What better investment than in education? And please, give my best regards to Don Alfonso."

Twice. That's twice that El Caudillo has visited Granada this year. I saw both visits covered in the NO-DO newsreels, which they show just before the movies and seem like movies themselves, filled with applause, flag waving, shouts of *Franco, Franco, Franco*, fervor among the throngs of followers, fishing boats tooting their horns, naval destroyers saluting with gunfire the arrival of the *Azor*, his Excellency's yacht, its masts festooned, people crowded onto the dock, in the streets and on the highways. The newsreel announcer proclaims that a visit from El Caudillo is a promise of efficient relief from misfortune, and of reliable and peaceful progress. Franco in civilian dress, Franco visiting in person to sympathize with the pain and suffering of citizens affected by a drought or a flood, Franco on hand to inaugurate a new building, or a futuristic construction project, all signs of our unquestionable advance toward the future.

"Now that I think of it...." The mayor pauses in the doorway. He's just had an idea. "Can you get any more encyclopedias here by Thursday? We've organized a reception for the Alzamiento Nacional commemoration on July eighteenth."

"I'm so sorry, we need at least a week. I am truly very sorry." Vicente would've liked to be more obliging. His face becomes a mask of infinite sadness. "It's just that ...."

"No matter, no matter. It's just that we could have included them as gifts during the celebration. The twenty-seventh anniversary of the Glorious National Uprising! How time flies!" He glances at his watch. Suddenly he's in a hurry again. "But don't worry, it doesn't matter."

I'm going to look up "courtesy visit" and "inauguration" in the encyclopedia. Talking nonsense is another way of trying to seem intelligent like my professor. The courtesy visit: an obligation of caudillos, ministers, governors, and mayors; an immense lie, a theatrical event performed in a troubled city in which they've closed the schools and the University so that students can demonstrate their enthusiasm for officialdom, wave flags and cheer enthusiastically, grateful for the generous benevolence of the authorities, their sole comfort after earthquakes, accidents, droughts, and floods, in sickness and in health. Inauguration: to begin or introduce something to a nation, for example, to give morals and commandments to a nation, or to something that's called a nation, but is really a flock of sheep accustomed to cheering and celebrating on command. Any future customers whose names start with *V* or with *I* will be assigned the words visit and inauguration.

The advice on what to do in an emergency childbirth situation is a variation on Vicente's usual technique. He adapted his pitch to the circumstances with a speed I didn't expect in someone so quiet. His usual strategy is to play with names. In the office he explained to me that buyers feel more committed when they hear a visitor speak their names. It creates an intimate bond that's hard to break. A successful salesman must understand his clients but also help them understand themselves, their own shortcomings, the things that they truly need.

Vicente thinks that names and surnames seep into our souls. Our personalities establish a secret relationship with our names. The subconscious, he says, is a deep well of words. And, of course, names and surnames occupy a very important place down there. We're called by our names every day of our lives, going to school, checking into a hostel, or applying for a job. Falling in love is as simple as drawing a heart around two names. The names are never missing. Even those of us who are loners, we hear our names spoken thousands, millions of times. The first thing we do when we want to hide is conceal our names. The first thing we do when we meet someone is speak our name. That's why you should repeat names over and over. It triggers sympathy or fear, an unconscious relationship of dependency.

The use of names, Vicente explained during my first training session, can be a great sales tool. If you call on someone named Baltasar, flip through the encyclopedia to the letter *B*. Ok Señor Baltasar, let's find the meaning and the history of your name. And then you find a country that begins with the letter *B*. Let's see now, how about Brazil? What a huge country, so vast. And then an animal, a buzzard, no, better a buffalo because no one likes to be compared to a buzzard. A buffalo will inspire positive images, adventures, Western movies. And then you move on to anatomy, and you talk about the importance of the brain, which starts with a *B*, like Benedict XV, or Bécquer, or Belmonte, the legendary bullfighter (to cover all the cultural bases). See what I mean? It's the power of the letter. And if you really want to close the deal, find out your esteemed client's profession ahead of time. Because if he's in the military, you'll get a lot of mileage out of the word battle and if he's a doctor, look up blood pressure and if he's a priest impress him with the article on the basilica or on the starving children of Biafra, depending on his personality. See? Everything starts with the name.

Vicente never forgets the importance of the surnames either. He has an obstinate and insistent personality because his own surnames make him favor repetition: Fernández Fernández. The double *F*. I don't escape the tyranny of the surname either. My two surnames begin with *E*. Egea Extremera. Although to be honest, the biggest impact on my personality is my first name: León. It's odd, but Vicente's sales technique is completely in line with my father's perspective on names. My father curses the day he named me León. It's instilled too much ferocity in me to live a peaceful life. The mayor's son, my classmate in grade school and in high school, was constantly saying how one of these days he was going to declaw a "lion" he knew. I didn't bite him, and I didn't scratch him. But one day I did land a good punch on his nose and put him in his place. I told Vicente about it, but he didn't ask for any details. He never asked what happened or what the mayor's son had done to me. Nothing. His only comment was to observe that the human subconscious is a deep well full of highly reactive elements.

Vicente asked me if I knew the name of the Minister of Education. Yes, I said: Humberto Vaca. Vicente thinks that Humberto's taste for honors and homage, partly inspired by the *H* in his name, is really because of his anxiety over his family's surname, Vaca. You know, León, Vicente said, it's just not the same to have the name "lion" as "cow." But that's just the way life is, and sometimes traumas are like swarms of wasps which might give cows a set of claws and lions a feeling of benevolence. That's why a good encyclopedia salesman has to study psychology and know all his saints.

Vicente's ideas are ridiculous. Armchair psychoanalysis. That was my reaction, anyway, when he explained his hollow, awkward, and distressing sales strategy. A university student can't take this kind of low-rent reasoning seriously. But the truth is that in practice this stuff helps; it can be a good icebreaker and build a bridge during those first moments of conversation. I understood this when I saw it in action. I'm thinking specifically of our second visit to Loja. In Don Juan's case, it was easy. He had clear educational reasons to make a purchase, he had the money, and I'm pretty sure that Don Alfonso had contacted him before we even got there. But selling an encyclopedia set to Pablo Aguayo was a different story; you could almost call it unfair.

"Why does that man need an encyclopedia?" I asked Vicente, uncomfortable, when we had returned to the train station.

"Because we are encyclopedia salesmen, and he can buy one from us. Isn't that a good enough reason?"

Pablo Aguayo lives in the outskirts of Loja. After making our way through a miserable slum and up a dirt road into the hills, we arrived at a farmer's modest home. His wife heard us and came in from the farmyard. She told us Pablo would be back shortly and said we could wait for him in the dining room. With curt politeness, she offered us wine. I couldn't tell if it was the brevity of shyness or the chill of a bad mood. Her husband returned about ten minutes later, greeted us with a frank smile, requested a moment to wash his hands and then took a seat with us. Pablo Aguayo is a man of about forty years, bald, with leathery skin. The age of his body multiplies in the reflection of his eyes. He looks good, with a rustic and hospitable innocence that matches the atmosphere of the room. I was impressed by the size and strength of his hand as he shook mine when he arrived. He works the land he inherited from his parents. Two friends from the village work with him because he has no sons. The land doesn't produce much, barely enough to live. They make ends meet with the farm animals tended by his wife. In years of drought, they bring in more from the hens than from the crops.

Vicente unveiled his strategy, calling him by his first name Pablo and hailing its importance, alluding to the fall on the road to Damascus and to the voice of truth. Then he moved on to Paris, the City of Light whose name is written with a capital *P* as tall as the Eiffel Tower. From there he exalted pacifism, the party of prudent men, the wisdom of the Greek philosopher Parmenides and the importance of global fauna such as penguins, pelicans, pheasants, pigeons, and parrots. *P* for Pablo and *P* for plenty of birds. Look, Pablo, it says here that passerine is a generic name for perch-

23

ing birds. A man who is astute, wise, and prudent is also a man who can distinguish between, for example, Pakistan and Peru; between the Pantocrator and the Pentecost. You follow me, Pablo?

It's a good strategy. What can you talk about when you sell encyclopedias if not words, letters, the world offered up in alphabetical order to pique the curiosity of a man whose name, the one he's carried around for a lifetime, ends up in ink on the Universo receipt, thanks to the clear looping handwriting of the salesman? Vicente asked me to run ahead to the station to buy our return tickets to Granada while he finalized the contract with Señor Pablo Aguayo. Back at the station they were still talking about the unexpected birth of the baby. Everything turned out fine; the doctor arrived in time to take care of the umbilical cord and the placenta. The mother was now recovering in the home of the mayor, who'd offered her a room until her husband could come and get her. It was a girl. Perfect, a successful visit. But I was still feeling a little down. Selling an encyclopedia set to someone who didn't need it left a bad taste in my mouth. I said as much to Vicente when we went to buy a sandwich in the cantina, but his only response was to remind me again that we're just encyclopedia salesmen.

With Vicente Fernández, it's hard to stay mad for long—or irritated or friendly or admiring, for that matter. His neutrality toward everything in life snuffs out any spark of goodwill or ill will. After lunch, on the way back to the train station, I succumbed to the temptation of playing the hot shot encyclopedia salesman and told Vicente we should try to get in on the photograph of the mayor and the new mother. We could talk to the mayor, maybe even the governor, and explain to them that we were right there on the same train with the woman as she went into labor. We could donate an encyclopedia to the city government to give as a gift to the newborn girl. What a lucky break, a publicity coup. The baby girl who came into the world with an encyclopedia under her arm.

"I find it's always best to ignore governors," was his response. I was shocked at his lack of enthusiasm for my idea to do exactly what he had done so successfully earlier in Don José's office. The coldness of his response also suggested his own disdain for authority and disrespect for the office of the governor. And actually, that's my role. I'm the impertinent uni-

24

versity student, the son who worries his father and has problems with the village mayor and his son, the one who's rebellious and vexed by life in a futureless city where calendars are stuck on a single day, outside of time. But I stuck my nose in where it didn't belong, and Vicente put me in my place.

Irritated, I decided to launch an angry commentary about an article in the newspaper I'd grabbed from the cantina so I could read between looking out the window and eavesdropping on other conversations. On the return trip, the passengers were more subdued in the heat of the afternoon and the fatigue of the day's work. As we arrived in Montefrío, I was reading a political story that had nothing to do with inaugurations or ministerial visits to the province. Authorities had finally sentenced the Communist Party leaders they had arrested three years ago. The story was written up as a big police success, a flawless operation that brought down the entire clandestine leadership.

"This is barbarous. One of them is getting twenty years, the other one is getting fifteen, and four more are getting ten years each. Those are incredibly harsh sentences."

"Yes."

"This is intolerable." I was starting to raise my voice, pleased to see I was finally getting a reaction from Vicente. He cast a furtive glance around the rest of the rail car. Now I was the one scaring him, the one who was the most disdainful of the government. "What a country we live in!"

"That's just the way it is."

"They arrest them, beat them in the police station, subject them to a farce of a trial and now they're going to rot in jail. At the University, we hear about these things. Some of my classmates are very well-informed. Did you know that they torture people in Spain?"

"I don't need to know about that."

I shut up. I could see fear in Vicente's eyes. It was that same fear that I often saw in my father's eyes. The same fear I saw in the eyes of my high school principal when he brought me to his office for a talk after the mayor had spoken to him. The same fear in Pedro el Pastor's eyes when he ran into the mayor's son the day after he was released by the Guardia Civil. Pedro had no choice but to endure the boy's insults and cowardly threats.

25

"I bet you're shitting yourself, aren't you Pastor? Smartasses get their nuts chopped off real fast around here you piece of shit, and I am going to beat the crap out of you if you even dare to come near me in a bar or anywhere else in this town. Do you understand me?"

I can't stand seeing other people's fear, their impotence, their bowed heads, gazes fixed on the floor. Watching humiliation drives me crazy. But what else could Pedro el Pastor do? Or my father? What else could Vicente say? We live where we live and here everyone's feet hurt when we walk. Our shoes pinch.

"Madrid is a city of more than a million cadavers, according to the latest statistics." I'm spending this long Sunday morning repeating that line by Dámaso Alonso that impressed me so much. My literature professor read the poem out loud in class and ever since then whenever I have a bad day it pops into my head. Everyone has bad days. They're like a black hole you peer into, contemplating yourself as just another dead man buried amid the statistics on hundreds, thousands, millions of cadavers.

The morning started out ok. My roommates had gone off to their villages, their parents, their vacations. I hadn't seen the landlady in a fortnight. The discount on my summer rent means I have to take care of the place on my own. But that's fine, this way I have it all to myself. I can sleep peacefully, have breakfast, go back to bed, read *Anna Karenina*, masturbate to the words of Tolstoy, get up again dreaming of a shower that is not to be because city drought managers have turned the water off again, straighten up my room, mend my shirt, inspect the furniture in the apartment, so fragile and so inhospitable, and then ... fall into a funk. There are few things as shabby as a student rental apartment. So, I spent the rest of the morning feeling depressed; that and giving into the temptation to rehearse my own salesman script. I don't want to be unprepared if I get the chance to take the lead during an encyclopedia sale. I'm sure one day next week, before the end of July, Vicente will suddenly hand things over, ask me to be the one to speak. And he'll do it without warning, without smiling, as if it were just part of the normal process. "Go ahead, you explain to the gentleman the advantages of the encyclopedia."

Greetings to you Lev Nikolayevich, Count Tolstoy, I am Señor León. My name means lion, a carnivorous mammal belonging to the feline family. It's important to know that there are many other animals whose names begin with the letter *L*, leopard for example, which is also a very fierce animal, but without a mane. The *L* is present in our bodies through the lungs, and in the sky thanks to light, and in our literature thanks to poets such as Luis de Góngora and Fray Luis de León, who, in the tranquility of his religious retreat, luxuriates in his two *L*'s, as you yourself do Leo Tolstoy. The *L* shines in history as well as in literature. There are many popes named Leo and many queens baptized with the name Leonora, and a revolutionary from your very own country named Lenin, not to mention the many interesting legends that any man of letters will know because his library will be full of books about the African landscapes of Lesotho and the palaces of Latvia and the droughts of Lebanon. If your eyes are bad, use lenses. For nighttime reading use a lamp. And for drought, lots and lots of liquid.

What more can I say, Leo? How about this whole exercise is really for losers? A loser is an idiot written with an *L*. The *L* is a marvelous letter, useful for thinking about lice or leprosy or a hand sticky with seminal liquid or lies that everyone here tells about the word liberty, or life without water, or about the eighteenth-century French military officer Santiago de Liniers' bad luck when he decided to become a Spaniard only to be executed later by his new countrymen in Río de la Plata. What more can I say, Leo, sir? I can say that I'm going crazy in this empty apartment and I'm getting out of here right now.

I head out of Realejo turning north toward Calle Pavaneras. I keep walking until I hit the intersection with Calle Reyes Católicos. I look at my watch. One thirty. I look up at the sky, blue, taut, and raw despite the heat. I look in the display window at the Pastelería Bernina. I cross the street. I enter the Plaza Bibarrambla. I observe the flower kiosks and edge away from the couples heading home arm in arm with their little packages of pastries. "Madrid is a city of more than a million cadavers, according to the latest statistics." That's what Dámaso Alonso wrote, that's what Ignacio

Rubio read to us in class, and that's what I'm thinking right now, surrounded by flowers, pastries, couples, fine things, and good people all of which today seem unbearable. My literature professor never talks about politics in class. He reads poems, discusses novels, profiles the lives of writers and explains that we must, without fail, learn to see. I see, I observe, I write. I've seen myself today in the mirror, and I have to say I can't stand myself, Señor Tolstoy. I hit the streets to work up a fury about whatever I see out here. Good but unbearable people, protagonists of the great indifference, of the look-the-other-way-because-I-don't-want-to-see, of the I-don't-need-to-know-about-this-or-that. The great indifference of those who look away or turn up their noses like they had a stick up their ass, happy to settle for a life that offers nothing more than pastries on Sunday mornings. They don't exist. They are dead, more than a million of them according to the latest statistics and a bad mood on a bad morning.

I prefer bad guys. It makes sense to me that evil people become the leaders. Authority wants to hold on to its power, its rules, its threats. Fear is its humble servant. I admire a mayor who doesn't forget he's mayor, and a mayor's son who gets good grades precisely because he's the mayor's son, who is cruel because he is the mayor's son and who enjoys his revenge because it's good to keep the memory of fear and punishment alive. It makes sense that the mayor's son wants to enjoy himself, that he doesn't accept any limits. It's completely logical that one fine day he and his friends decide to steal a sheep from Pedro el Pastor and kill it. He's used to shooting at the priest's doves after all. A frog, a dove, a sheep—what difference does it make? So, you chase the frightened sheep around, you pretend you're a bullfighter and the sheep is the bull, and then you slaughter the sheep, and you make a nice mutton stew. And if Pedro el Pastor finds you and humiliates you in front of your friends, what could be more logical than to seek revenge? You call Pedro el Pastor's dog, you pet it, you take it to a nearby tree, you put a rope around its neck, and you hang it. The hanged dog is a warning that trembles on the olive branch. The dog no longer bites. Its cadaver does.

After the loss of his sheep, Pedro el Pastor presented himself at the mayor's house to demand compensation for the damages caused by the son's vandalism. Pay up and that's that. But the dirty trick with the dog, that's a whole different thing. That violence shattered custom, patience and logic, and inspired fear. The response had to be definitive. So, if Pedro el Pastor decides to go looking for the imbecile son and breaks his staff over the boy's back, knocking the wind out of him—along with his pride and his consciousness for a few seconds—it's completely logical that the mayor would call the Guardia Civil. Also logical are the two brutal beatings Pedro el Pastor received in police headquarters in front of the mayor, the fine he had to pay and the week in jail while everyone waited, including the Guardia Civil, for the mayor to get over his fury and his attack of hubris. Mission accomplished, Sergeant Palomares.

All of this is completely logical. It's the mayor's world, his upbringing, his creed, his privilege. Evil in those who command is understandable. Less so the indifference in those who obey. Pedro el Pastor's fear is understandable. So is my literature professor's prudence in cutting off any controversial discussion by saying the classroom is not for politics, and that his syllabus does not include arrests or police stations. My professor, the most famous rebel in the University, takes a step back. Literature is about how you look at things, with imagination, with series of three adjectives, with intelligent humor, with objective distance ... and with the threat of an undercover cop infiltrating the student body, two ears and two eyes ready to collect any and all information. You can understand Ignacio Rubio's reserve. When students criticize his political timidity, the weakness of his social commitment, I defend him. He's got a lot at stake. But the indifference of those who have nothing at stake is a lot harder to accept. I don't need to know about that, murmurs Vicente Fernández. I could run into him at any moment in the Plaza Bibarrambla, on Calle Reyes, with his mysterious wife and a little package of pastries. If only those statistical million or so cadavers would dare to breathe, to say no, they would bring an end to Pedro el Pastor's fear and to the mayor's hubris. I'm starting to admire the mayor and hate the indifferent. Evil is better than little packages of pastries.

As a result of the Pedro el Pastor situation, there came a moment when I erupted into a fit of rage, which is sort of like succumbing to an attack of evilness. One day, when the mayor's son went into a bar and saw Pedro el Pastor sitting at a table, he went after him with a cockiness that was as inherited as any piece of prime farmland. Have you learned your lesson you sonofabitch? Around here, assholes get their balls chopped off quick, he said. And suddenly I remembered how many times this same imbecile had threatened to "clip my claws." I couldn't bear the humiliation in Pedro el Pastor's eyes. I couldn't bear the police file filled with lies about Pedro and concessions for the mayor's imbecile son. I went for him and delivered the punch that Pedro el Pastor couldn't.

That punch was my big heroic moment, Señor Tolstoy. Occasionally, I win the battle against my own indolence, and I find the time and energy to sit down and write. This is a victory, a way to learn and to make sense of this summer. That punch is my big heroic moment, but a scandal in a village where kids are constantly fighting with sticks and stones. I've fought a thousand times with all sorts of different friends: the good students, the average students, and the poor students. Play comes to a halt, a fight breaks out, then just as suddenly that's it, it's all over and back to play. But some punches can be dangerous, an older man smacking the mayor's son in the face, for example. A dirty business. A dog's life. Dog, a carnivorous mammal that belongs to the canine family. Man's best friend. Great strategic tool to sell encyclopedias to clients named David, Diego, Daniel, Dylan, Darío, Demetrio, names written with a *D* for dog, as in lap dog, police dog, hunting dog and sheep dog, which cares for and guides the livestock. It's a dog-eat-dog world and all because of the indifferent. And here I am in the city, partly because I want to be, and partly because I'm in exile for my own good because dead dogs—or exiled dogs—don't bite. I'm an encyclopedia salesman. Blessed be those who feel hate, rancor, fear, the impulse for vengeance, arrogance, cruelty, and rage. The indifferent be damned!

Anyone can have a bad day. I'm having a bad Sunday, a bad July twenty-first, nineteen hundred and sixty-three. I can't stand myself, I can't stand my apartment, I can't stand this street, I can't stand these people. The married couples pass by with their little packages of pastries, very dignified but very stinky because, unless they got up before nine in the morning, they won't have had a shower since the water was turned off. Rain falls

30

on Paris and on hearts. Here, we've internalized the drought in our atmosphere. Earth, dust, smoke, shade, nothing. An epidemic of dry farmland, dry taps, dry showers, dry calendars. People are passing by, very dignified, coming from mass; they buy flowers, they go in and out of the Pastelería Bernina and they hide behind their indifference to avoid contagion. Where is the doctor who can cure indifference? Medicine: science that deals with human illness. Doctor: someone legally authorized to practice medicine. Pills for indifference. Injections for indifference. Syrups for indifference. Pharmacists willing to fill prescriptions for indifference. Again: the mediocre are more dangerous than the evil. I'm going to write a thousand times in my journal that I must flee from mediocrity, flee from mediocrity, flee from mediocrity. In this country, you emerge from adolescence through the portal of the indifferent. Adolescence: the age following childhood. A period of profound physical and psychological changes that for women occurs between the ages of twelve and eighteen years and for men between fourteen and twenty.

I go back to my apartment. I make something to eat. With the cash advance from Universo and my share of the commission from the first sale, I've got a full pantry, two cans of tuna, yesterday's bread, and a beer. There are ten days left in July. Two months before school starts. Six months before I leave adolescence behind. One hundred and forty pages before a train runs over Anna Karenina.

I'm going to tell the whole story in chronological order for the pleasure of surprising myself again with events as they unfold. Tuesday, July twenty-third ....

I arrive at the office at five minutes after nine. Consuelo Astorga is already at her desk. She reads the newspaper and waits for the phone to ring. She's exchanged her brown glasses for some more modern ones with white rims. A little bit later, Vicente arrives looking like he hasn't slept well. He complains about the heat even before saying good morning. Some nights the cold drifts down from the mountains and seeps into the asphalt and the bricks. On those nights, you can sleep well with the window open, and you might even be grateful for the nearby sheet tangled up in your dreams. But other nights, the darkness is immobile, and the heat becomes an oppressive mass that keeps you from breathing so that to suffocate, you don't need another nightmare about prison sentences and forced labor. Insomnia will do it for you. Vicente Fernández arrives at the office with a face full of defeat. He must have had a rough night.

At nine thirty, we divide up the calls. Vicente gets A to O. I get P to Z. Give them the basic information, explain the conditions of sale, seal the deal or, if the circumstances warrant, rope the client into a face to face meeting. The personalized approach adds a more human touch to cultural and financial discussions. I go slowly, taking it easy, hesitating before dialing each new number, and it takes me a while to work through my list of calls. Vicente is faster. He runs one call into the next, he doesn't stop talking or racing through flora, fauna, and world geography. He takes out his handkerchief, wipes the sweat from his face, tips his nose toward the ceiling, stretches his neck muscles as he listens to the client, takes notes with his pen, and then closes the deal. In-person visits are only needed when there's a bigger deal in sight, like the one the mayor facilitated in Loja. It's also good if the client's able to influence others around him to buy. He who plucks one grape may get a cluster. Now and then when he finishes a call, Vicente looks over at me. He decides to indoctrinate me.

"What's up? You aren't doing anything."

"I'm listening to you. I'm learning."

"Well, if you really want to learn, start by convincing yourself that it's just as dangerous to be too timid as too aggressive. Apathy is just as bad as being caught with your pants down. You need a clear vision for where you are going, choose a path and stick to it. You're an encyclopedia salesman. Tomorrow you'll be something else, you'll have another goal. But you have to live each day according to the goal of the moment. For now, an encyclopedia salesman. The mission is to accomplish your goal. Strategy is based on discipline. Not on shyness and not on recklessness. Go ahead. Call someone now. Don't think about it. Dial. I want to hear you."

Two-bit philosophy from a mediocre man. Cautious men don't get ahead in life. They're office fodder, obedient pencil pushers. They snuff out all sparks. But there's more to life than dousing flames. Me, I want to change things, burn things, erase, delete, scream. And I'm not shy, I just don't buy into what I'm doing here.

At eleven, Consuelo approaches Vicente's desk with a message from Don Alfonso. Call him as soon as you get off the phone with your client. Universo Publishing is about to close a deal with the Department of Education and Recreation. They're going to buy and distribute encyclopedias to all the hotels, cinema clubs, business groups and even to the many caving associations around the country. The smell of a hot business deal floats through the office like the scent of a birthday cake just out of the neighbor's oven. We may have picked the winning lottery ticket. Don Alfonso's contact list is worth its weight in gold, Consuelo says, and I perceive a trembling tone of pride in her voice. Unlike Vicente, she looks like she's had a good night. She's gorgeous in a white dress, white shoes, and a white smile. All of which matches her new white-rimmed glasses and the big white handbag dangling from the back of her chair. She doesn't look like a little girl dressed for first communion, nor does she look like a bride, but she is radiant. I sense, or I imagine, the reason why. It could be that this deal between Don Alfonso and Education and Recreation has led to a pause in the boss's family vacation, and to an unexpected bit of office business that might include the secretary. I'm mortified when Consuelo looks up from her paperwork and catches me watching her. The same thing happened yesterday. And the day before. And this is already the third time today.

What's changed is that now I don't just look at Consuelo, I see her. I spy on her, I check out her hair, her lips, her gestures, and I'm looking for that Bohemian from Paris. It's all Vicente's fault because yesterday afternoon he unexpectedly erupted with joy when he heard on the radio that Fernando Manzaneque had won the Grenoble-to-Val d'Isère stage of the Tour de France and that Federico Bahamontes was wearing the leader's yellow jersey and screw those French anyway and viva España, and miracles are still possible. Consuelo got mad and said France wasn't to blame for anything and that's when I learned that she too had lived in Paris.

"It's obvious that you've never worked in a factory." Vicente's tone thickened into a kind of pride that I didn't understand. "Of course, that's because you were living with artists, enjoying the Bohemian life."

Now I find it impossible not to watch Consuelo, impossible not to imagine what her glasses have seen, what her hands have touched, the people she's met, that world that's even better than a Tour de France victory. My eyes cannot keep still.

At eleven thirty, after talking to the Department of Education and Recreation and to whomever from the Spanish Trade Union Organization, Vicente invites me for a coffee. Before heading down to the Café Lepanto, he stops at Consuelo's desk to gossip about the day's big surprise and the mystery of Don Alfonso. How is it possible that such a succulent piece of business from a national organization landed in a small provincial office? Only god and Don Alfonso know the answer.

"Ok, we're heading out," he says to Consuelo with an expression of delight rarely seen on his placid salesman's face. "I don't think they're going to add this particular sale to our local office win list. But what an amazing commission we'd have gotten, don't you think? León and I are going to get a coffee. Can you call this number in Motril, please? We need to set up a meeting."

At a quarter to twelve, the Café Lepanto serves its last coffees and its first beers. The coffee isn't sitting well with me today. April nineteenth, nineteen-sixty, that suspended date in the Lepanto, bothers me more than ever after a hot night that was as hard on me as it was on Vicente. A hot night is like a paralyzed calendar. The widowed barman was arguing about Granada's soccer team with a group of medics from the Casa de Socorro. He's pessimistic, it's hopeless, everything's a mess. Last year they overhauled the whole team, they booted the president, they turned the club over to a management committee, they fired twelve players, they signed a bunch of new ones, and then? Well, nothing and more nothing, Granada hasn't come close to making topflight. The best they could do was sixth place in the Second Division. I'm not sure why I bought a season ticket, he complains. I've jinxed the team.

One of the medics thinks that signing José Millán as the new coach will change the course of the team's history. The widowed barman admits that he admires Millán a lot, he's an example of someone who's loyal to the team. These days, he says, no one bothers to stand up for the team jersey, no one sacrifices himself for the team colors. As we're about to leave, I get up the courage to ask him more about Millán.

He looks at me with a smile of superiority. If Granada were to win promotion this year, the widowed barman might even revive his suspended calendar. "You're so young, so very young. Millán's a superstar, one of the very best along with Candi, Vicente, and González."

"Hey Vicente! Have you played for Granada? Honestly, you are full of surprises." I feel like I can joke with him because we're both so elated by the Education and Recreation deal. If Universo does decide to pay us commissions, I'd be able to support myself in Granada for a long time. I'd love to surprise my father, to leave him speechless, but I don't think that's in the cards, at least not for me since I just joined the company.

"There are many Vicentes in the world, my dear León. I have never in my life kicked a soccer ball."

At two o'clock sharp we close the office. Everyone has lunch at home. At five o'clock we're all back in the office to continue answering the phone now with the whir of the electric fan in the background. At five-thirty, a delivery man from La Estrella Department Store arrives with two long wooden poles. Consuelo wants to install new curtain rods in her apartment. The one in the living room broke, so she's replacing it and decided to install a new one in the bedroom while she's at it. At seven, Vicente says goodnight. I watch him leave with his aching feet, a handkerchief in one hand and the black briefcase in the other. At five minutes after seven, Consuelo says it's closing time. Time to go. She won't be able to take the tram with those curtain rods. It would be too hard to get on, get off, find a seat, avoid hitting other passengers on the head, breaking any windows. Since I don't have anything to do, I offer to help her carry the curtain rods home. It's a nice walk. I want to behave like a gentleman.

The curtain rods are heavy. The main difference between a student residence and a proper home is the weight of the objects you find inside. The furniture in my apartment isn't built to last. It seems like it could disintegrate at any moment. In the old-fashioned guest houses the furniture was as weighty as the history of its residents, with memories of families fallen on hard times who make ends meet by renting out rooms. But the student flats that have been opening across the city are filled with junk rather than memories. They all feel provisional. It's the dynamic of quick investment. Wardrobes built just to get by, beds to use and throw away, tables and chairs no one expects to last more than a year or two. Maybe that's the crack where time sneaks in and the calendar starts to drop its pages. Consuelo's curtain rods are as weighty as a lifetime.

At seven twenty, we pass the Fuente de las Batallas. No water in the fountain. At a little after seven-thirty, we get to the Fuente del Salón. No water there either. The smell of roasted potatoes and beer drifts out from the Kiosko Las Titas, but I'm afraid to suggest we stop. I don't want Consuelo to think that the poles are too heavy for me. I dare to shift them to my other shoulder, so I don't wear out just one side of my body.

"Are they heavy?"

"No, not at all."

At eight o'clock we arrive at number four Calle Transversal de la Bomba and climb up to the fourth floor. A home tastefully decorated with real furniture. Shadows, order, and memories. Most of the furniture is my parents', she says, thanking me for the compliments. She's hung the white handbag on the coat rack in the hall and kicked off her shoes by the bedroom door. For my gallantry she offers me a beer. Walking around the house barefoot, she goes to the kitchen and returns with a tray. Two glasses, a large bottle of Alhambra, two-thirds full, a pack of cigarettes and some matches. She asks if I smoke and when I say no, she says she hopes I don't mind if she has a cigarette. I've never seen her smoke in the office. There are things, Consuelo says, that I only do at home. It's eight fifteen.

She wants to know about me, asks about my family and my studies in Granada. I tell her about my mother's grocery store, my father's farm work, life in the village. Then I recount my adventures as an itinerant student who has just finished his first year studying romance languages with very good grades. I offer her some details about my friendship with my literature professor Ignacio Rubio, openly declaring my admiration for him and my intention of becoming a writer. Ignacio helped me endure a department with too many dried-up leaves in the fall and too much cold in the winter. I'm not very interested in Latin, Greek, or Spanish grammar, and I confess that I'm in romance languages only because I want to write. I figure it's the best fit for a solitary soul like myself. I also confess to her, in a display of my profound self-awareness, that my reclusiveness isn't because I'm alone in Granada during the summer, with the university closed and no family or roommates around. For me, I say, solitude is like the underwear of my consciousness, the inner lining of my most intimate state of being, my form of existence. And then I start to feel a bit ridiculous. I sound like a student trying to write a paper on his own personality, as if I'd gotten complete-ly carried away writing in my private journal. I'm furious at falling into such an infantile trap. The underwear of my consciousness!? But Consuelo interrupts both my confession and my raging shame with a recitation of Pablo Neruda. It's a quarter to nine. "I like you when you are still because it's as if you were absent, and you hear me from afar and my voice doesn't touch you," she recites. Pablo Neruda, I say stupidly, as if I were answering a riddle. She continues: "It seems as though your eyes have flown away, and it seems as though a kiss has closed your mouth." That's right, she said, *Twenty Poems of Love*. Consuelo confesses that when she was young, she wanted to be a poet, she read a lot of poetry and wrote some kisses, oops, I mean verses, herself. But then you never know where life will lead you, always toward the unexpected. Instead of a publisher for her own writ-ing, destiny offered her a position as a secretary working for a publisher of manuals, guidebooks, dictionaries, and encyclopedias. She doesn't want to complain and she's not going to complain, but underneath her modest appearance and her retreat from literature, she still carries a torch for po-etry and still remembers Pablo Neruda and Federico García Lorca and the great timeless love poems. As for me, she says, I'm definitely not timeless. I know I'm starting to get old.

At nine o'clock I tell her that's not true at all, that since I've met her, she's gotten a lot younger. I can't exactly interpret the odd expression on her face when I say this. As I try to explain that I was fooled by my first impression of her at the office and that I learned to look at her in a different way, the sound of rumbling water pipes seizes the apartment. It's an unmistakable announcement, one that we've become accustomed to over the last months. Water, says Consuelo happily. Time to shower. She rises, enters the bathroom, and leaves the door partly open.

At ten minutes after nine, I hear the tap running. At twelve after, I hear the shower running, water beating on the bottom of the bathtub. It's twelve minutes after nine, the door is ajar, I'm a gentleman, I don't dare get up, I have a sip of what's left of my beer, I look at the broken curtain rod lying in the living room, the two new ones propped up against the wall, I think I should just go ahead and put them up, Consuelo would be grateful. From behind the tempting, half-open door emerges the impatient thrum of falling water. I imagine Consuelo's naked body, her damp blonde hair, the rain drops trickling down her body, a summer storm falling across her shoulders, her breasts, her belly, her sex, her thighs, finally arriving at her painted toes, those same toes that walked barefoot from the dining room to the kitchen, from the kitchen to the sofa, and from the sofa to the bathroom. Beneath her disguise as a demure secretary, there is a passionate world, a world that needs water, earth, fire, and air. A long shower, almost a quarter of an hour, as if the water and Consuelo's body were waiting for something.

"You don't want to take a shower?" she asks me at nine-thirty, completely naturally.

I get up, I walk to the bathroom door. I see her naked for just a moment, the time it takes her to cover herself awkwardly with a towel. I saw my mother naked once when I was ten years old. That's about it for my experience. I'm unsettled by her damp hair, the blue towel draped around her wet body like a flag on a windless day. Her shoulders exposed, her hands across her chest, her hips and thighs barely covered.

"Sorry. No, no thanks. I'll shower when I get home."

I'm acting like I'm some timid kid trying not to be a bother. Dirt should be removed in one's own home. I return to the sofa and watch Consuelo walk from the bathroom to her bedroom wrapped in her towel. She leaves little steamy footprints, as if she were walking along the shore of a movie or a novel. Did I do the right thing not taking a shower? I ask myself over and over. What would a worldly, modern, open-minded man do? Swoop down onto the naked body before him, or wait until the situation became clearer? A woman has a right to a shower when water appears in the middle of a drought. She can take a shower in her own house without this implying a blatant proposition. And what would a boy do, a dumb-shit adolescent afraid of the age difference, of his own ignorance and of his paralyzing anguish at the thought of making a fool of himself?

Consuelo emerges from the bedroom wearing pajama bottoms and a plaid shirt. I struggle to make conversation. We tip-toe around neutral topics, work issues, the itinerary she had worked out for us. Tomorrow I'm going to Motril with Vicente. We've arranged a visit to the Guardia Civil station there. We also have appointments with two doctors, a pharmacist and a lottery ticket vendor who lives in the port.

"The two of you are spending the night in Motril. I reserved a hotel room. You'll share a double room. We save money that way. But be careful."

"Why?"

"I've heard rumors that Vicente is gay."

"But he's married."

"I've never seen his wife. Anyway, you never know. You can't trust anybody. It doesn't matter if he's married."

At ten fifteen I leave Consuelo's apartment. I head toward the river that's almost run dry. As I walk along the balustrade, I pass young lovers seeking refuge from another hot night in the cool air of the Jardinillos de Genil. At eleven o'clock I open the door to my apartment. On the way home, I walked past City Hall and the virgen de las angustias basilica. Everything's clear to me now. When I got to virgen de las angustias, I decided that Vicente wasn't gay. I would have noticed by now after working and traveling with him for the better part of July. By the time I reached City Hall, I convinced myself that Consuelo was actually suggesting that I was gay, not Vicente. How about that, the homosexual turns out to be me. I made a fool of myself. Solitude is the underwear of my consciousness, my most intimate state of being. What a child I am ... what an opportunity I missed.

⌒

Resist. This is Vicente's advice when he sees my face blanch as we round the third curve. Anyone can make it through one hairpin turn, maybe two. The biggest problem is my awareness of time. When you're on a torturous road trip, the question of are-we-there-yet gets brutal. Our destination becomes blurry. The threat of a bleak future makes the present even more bleak, and I'm afraid of how nauseous I'm getting. I'm starting to feel hopeless. Noticing my pallor, Vicente tries to encourage me.

"Here's the trick. Don't think about anything but the next curve in the road, just the next one, and when you get past that, the next one. Try to forget that we still have three hours to go. That'll lift your spirits and you'll be able to resist until you finally get used to it."

Only the next curve. The next bump. That's the upside of forcing yourself into a routine. But you have to consider both sides. The same strategy you deploy to avoid an embarrassing bout of motion sickness can also be used to quash the imagination and turn you into an indifferent soul. Routine is a rut, bracing yourself for a curve, and then another, and another and another without thinking about the long journey, the hot bus, the uncomfortable seats, and Vicente's body which the inertia of each turn keeps pushing toward me, invading what little space I have in seat number twenty-two. A couple of seats back, a boy is vomiting in between wails, a mother offers a sick bag, a man points to the land scorched by the sun and complains about the drought, the driver shifts gears, turns the immense steering wheel, leaves a pungent smell of gasoline every time he goes up or down a hill. Focus on the next curve. Only the next curve. Vicente's right. At some point distress, fatigue and suffering become routine.

The bus to Motril is full. As it weaves through the mountains, it stops in every village. Advancing a few miles without stopping counts as a huge achievement for this infinite journey along a very short route. The vacationers on their way to the beaches of Motril, Salobreña and Almuñécar stuff the belly of the bus with suitcases. The villagers occupy the center aisle and pack their huge bags into the overhead shelves. As we approach Vélez de Benaudalla the curves in the road buck and weave like a roller coaster. But by now I'm numb. I try to forget about the next curve, think about something else, focus on the people. But conversations on the bus are more secretive than on the train. Passengers speak to each other in pairs. Suddenly there's an outburst, a shout, a guffaw, someone calls to a friend in another row, someone sings the praises of Vélez's pestiño donuts. But on the bus, it's impossible to follow the details of stories about baptisms and weddings with all their joy, sadness, resentment, surrender, kindness, and evil of the kind that seize the mornings on the Corto de Loja train. Vicente stays silent. You have to resist, he says, and stay silent.

It must be a bad joke. Consuelo was giving me a hard time. That's got to be the reason she reproached me so mysteriously for acting like a gentleman at her apartment. Why else would she mock my awkward shyness since Vicente doesn't seem at all effeminate. People leave you alone if you are a rule-breaker in life. They don't want to get caught up in someone else's problems. On the other hand, if you try to be respectful, polite, and cautious, you end up looking ridiculous and acting like an idiot. That's how I've felt ever since I left Consuelo's apartment. A stupid, wretched, humiliated, pusillanimous child, more bumpkin than gentleman, more cretinous than courteous, more prudish than prudent. To punish myself, I'm going to search the encyclopedia for all the words related to idiot.

When we step on to solid ground at Motril, I feel like I've just disembarked from a transatlantic voyage. I feel seasick all through our first sales visit, as Vicente plays with the letters A and H in the home of Alberto Hidalgo, a prestigious local physician. The nausea continues through the second visit, although I start to feel better watching how skillfully Vicente pitches to a more difficult target: Doctor Rafael Yanguas. In a display of pure passion for his craft, Vicente skips past the easy R and leaps directly to the Y of the surname, trekking across Yemen and evoking the powerful ruminant mammal known as the yak. Leveraging the doctor's love of things naval, Vicente revives the tale of Vicente Yáñez Pinzón, brother of Martín Alonso Piñon and captain of the glorious caravel La Niña, which sailed thousands of nautical miles with Cristobal Colón on his first journey to America. A fantastic finale.

By the time we get to the Guardia Civil station, I've regained control over my roiling stomach and brain. As I say hello, I think of Sergeant Palomares back in my village, and in a maximum state of alert, state my name and take a seat. A collection system that relies on the productive leisure time of Guardia Civil retirees opens many doors in today's orderly and uniform Spain. In my village, when someone runs into trouble or needs something, he goes to the big landowner, Don Diego, and asks for a loan. Two hundred, three hundred, five hundred pesetas. Later, Don Diego sends Paco Weekly, as everyone called him, to collect the payments once a week. Except that these days Paco collects only once a month instead of weekly like the old days, though they still call him Paco Weekly. Universo's easy monthly installment plan is the modern version of the same thing. And the Guardia Civil are the new version of Paco Weekly. León! Come here! Yes, sir, Sergeant Weekly, sir, sorry, I mean Sergeant Palomares, sir.

In honor of our visit and in recognition of the warm relationship between the Guardia Civil and Editorial Universo, Lieutenant Casares has called together Sergeant Castillo, Private Pérez, Private Martínez and three other men called Valenzuela, García and Cospedal. Vicente's reluctant to do the surname dance with so many different options, so instead he goes directly to the first volume of the encyclopedia and opens it to *B* for the battles, starting with the Battle of Bailén, to exalt the heroism of Spanish troops who, in July of eighteen hundred and eight, gave Napoleon's invaders what was coming to them. Too bad for General Dupont. And what a hot day for a battle out in the middle of an open field, I'm thinking, but I don't linger on my ruminations because the conversation is racing ahead through history. If we speak of Bailén, then we also speak of the Battles of Las Navas de Tolosa, or san quintín, or Lepanto, a great victory that lent its name to the street where Editorial Universo has its provincial branch office. Or the Battle of Ebro, adds Lieutenant Casares, paying homage to his own youth fighting in the Civil War. Or the Battle of Ebro, confirms Vicente.

"What about Lieutenant Carrasco?" Lieutenant Casares asks. He's pleased that his team is buying into the encyclopedia idea. He wants to expand his success with another player. "He's also a father. Today he's on duty in Torrenueva, but when he gets back, I'll explain the deal to him. If you give me your home phone number, we'll call you tonight to get the details."

"We're not going back until tomorrow," Vicente says.

"Tomorrow then."

"It's el día de Santiago, so I won't be in the office. I don't have a phone at home." Vicente's voice is tinged with shame and reluctance to continue this line of conversation. "But I can give you my card with our office number on it."

"Ask for Consuelo," I interject, trying to be helpful.

"That doesn't matter. Any one of our secretaries can help you," Vicente responds deploying his powerfully augmentative imagination. I don't quite see how that's necessary here. "We'll pass along the information this very day. We are very grateful, Lieutenant, sir."

"You're welcome. At your service. Knowledge is a benefit for all."

Lieutenant Casares' spirit of collaboration is solemnly reflected in the bright whitewash on the walls of the Guardia Civil station, in their tricorn hats, in the proudly displayed national flag. A group of children defy the midday heat in the patio. They play soccer in a corner cooled by a bit of shade. "Stop that racket," a terse maternal voice warns through one of the open windows. The Guardia Civil of Motril are different from the officers in my village. A little less scary. They don't seem to be following orders from a petty local tyrant.

"At your service, Lieutenant, sir," I say as we leave.

"Do you have many more meetings?" He seems interested in our work-load.

"No, we're almost done. This morning we saw the doctors Don Alberto Hidalgo and Don Rafael Yanguas." Vicente pronounces solemnly the names of these two clients he considers very distinguished, a source of pride for our company.

"They are good men. Top notch. Don Rafael's a saint. He's treated my stomach trouble."

"We still have to meet with the lottery vendor down at the port. Don Juan Benavides," I add to complete the explanation.

"You're selling an encyclopedia to him? Not a chance. He's an animal. He's against us. Whenever there's trouble you can be sure he's in the middle of it. If I were you, I wouldn't even bother going to see him. He'll try to con you. He's a piece of work. Trust me, if you want to avoid problems stay away from that lotero."

"Thank you for that warning," Vicente murmurs diligently. "In this line of work, we often run the risk of falling into disreputable hands."

We head for the bus station. Vicente buys two tickets to the Port of Motril. I'm surprised. I thought after the warning from a Guardia Civil lieutenant we'd cancel the visit to the lotero. Vicente looked very serious after hearing about the dangerous tendencies of our potential client. And the lieutenant's comments sounded a lot like an order.

"León, you talk too much. You say things that people don't need to know about."

"But he asked us and how was I supposed to know? I was just trying to keep the client happy. Plus, it's better that we should know about this guy in case he tries to con us," I argue, my pride wounded.

"Who?"

"The lotero."

"I never would have suspected that you would give so much credence to what some Guardia Civil officer says. Good grief! All that business about Pedro el Pastor in the Guardia station in your village, the evil mayor, you, the big rebel, all your revolutionary friends in the university. And now you're all 'at your service Lieutenant Casares, sir.' The only thing we care about here, León, is selling encyclopedias. Visit clients, sell books, and collect our travel allowance. Others can collect the payments and distribute the books. I'm going to give you a bit of advice. Don't talk too much about the clients. That was my client visit, so you keep your mouth shut about it. The less our buyers know about each other the better. That way they won't uncover our strategies, our discounts, or our payment schemes. Understand? Sometimes, we make exceptions for some clients, and we don't want the other ones to know that. Let's see if you can get that through your head. Do not give away our information."

After our long bus ride from Granada, a visit to the beach felt good. A quick sandwich in the canteen and my excitement about seeing the sea help me get over my irritation with Vicente. Sometimes he says and does things just to contradict and rattle me. It seems like I do everything wrong. He's so superior, as if selling encyclopedias was an exact science with secret codes that only top experts can understand. Doctorate in Nuclear Physics and

Encyclopedia Sales! If he were a priest, he'd spend all his time denouncing heresies. But wait, there's the seaside, a palm tree, two palm trees, the port, a navy ship moored at the dock, and endless fishing boats. I'm not going to confess to Vicente that I've never seen the sea before, that I'm gulping in the briny air, filling my lungs with blue bliss that's both contagious and enigmatic. The sea: not ugly, not catholic, but very sentimental. The sweetest salt in the world. When I called my mother yesterday to tell her I was going to Motril, the phone filled with happiness. She asked me to send her a postcard with a picture of the beach. I wonder how I'm going to accomplish that without Vicente noticing. I've had enough of his mocking for one day.

The bus drops us off near the docks, on a street close to the Paraíso Hostel. For someone like me from a mountain village, seeing the seagulls and the ships for the first time is a big deal. It's a different world, with its own fantasies and its own sorrows. It's three thirty and our next appointment isn't until five. What should we do? Vicente tells me to follow him. We walk past an ice factory, across the breakwater that lines one side of the port and head toward the beach. A few low-slung shacks and a vast reed bed look out toward infinity. The improvised, thatched lean-to's are empty and the abandoned beach umbrellas suggest all the holiday makers are at lunch. Get up, eat breakfast, swim in the ocean, eat lunch, have a siesta, go back to the beach, stroll along the marina, eat dinner, enjoy the evening breezes, and then to bed and sweet dreams. That must be the life that Don Alfonso, along with his wife, his children, and his maid, is enjoying right now.

Vicente sets his briefcase on the sand. He removes his jacket and carefully folds it. He finds a clean spot, with no seaweed, tar, or human trash. He sits, takes off his shoes and tucks his socks inside them. He rolls his trousers up almost to the knee and walks off toward the water. When he's almost knee-deep in the ocean, he looks back at me.

"So? You coming in? There aren't any waves."

I'm too embarrassed. I go off to find some shade. No seascapes, no hurricanes, no pirates, shipwrecks, or messages in bottles. My first view of the sea is blighted by the sight of Vicente's bare legs stepping through the ankle-deep water with the articulated gait of a wading bird. Trying to shake that image from my mind, I concentrate on the silhouette of a battleship anchored just outside the port. Is it Vicente or is it me? Is the resentment surging through me because of my own sense of shame because I'm too embarrassed to wade around in the water like an idiot? Or am I furious because of the tenderness I feel for this helpless fellow splashing his lack of pride before all in Motríl, Spain, Europe, and the world? León Egea, in an exercise of introspection, observes himself in the reflection of the sea.

But the sea has its own intrinsic value. Even on calm days, it offers movement and depth. You have to respect ideas and feelings that you can only collect with a net. If you let your imagination run wild, as my literature professor sometimes asks us to do, you can imagine almost anything as you gaze out beyond the miles and miles of ocean or imagine things fifty yards below the surface: a starfish, a sea snail, an island, a dolphin, a mast, a shipwreck, reefs, jetties, the horizon. I'll be there in a minute, I shout to Vicente, and I go into one of the bars close to the pier. When we walked by on our way to the beach, I noticed a couple of postcard carousels in the doorway. I choose one that shows fishing boats leaving the port and heading out to sea. I hide it in my satchel. When I get back to the beach, Vicente has already put his shoes back on. He shakes out his beige jacket as though it were a sail, ready to race toward the horizon. He also shakes out his soul with a smile. He seems happy.

"Life has its happy moments. You have to take advantage of them. Come on, let's go get some coffee."

~⌒~

We're sitting in the same bar where I bought the postcard, when a lottery vendor walks in. He greets the owner, enters the dining room and ten minutes later says goodbye. I tell Vicente that this lotero must be Juan Benavides and we should go talk to him. No, Vicente says, we made the appointment for exactly five o'clock at his house. But maybe we could finish up early, I say. If we want to be taken seriously, Vicente explains, we need to stick to the plan without making any unnecessary changes. Surprises are nothing more than an advance on bad luck. Plus, meeting someone in his home creates a sense of intimacy and commitment that's difficult to undo. In Vicente's head, even the most ridiculous scenarios are based on some sort of logic. For example, he said, we could have brought swimsuits and then we could have avoided the whole splashing around with trouser legs rolled up. We could have gone all the way into the water, even if we were still only wading, like gentlemen. Proper ocean bathing. It had occurred to him, but ….

But, Vicente said, Consuelo wasn't able to find any rooms for us near the port, so we'll have to go back to the town center for the night. Even there, it's doubtful we'll get a shower because they'll probably turn off the water here too. There is no worse summer nightmare than selling books, putting up with clients and waiting for buses with sea-salt stuck to your skin, mixed with the sweat between your thighs, along your back, in your trousers and under your shirt. Vicente explained it all in minute and concrete detail, following his own personal logic. Occasionally when something jolts him out of it, he looks around with the bewilderment of a traveler who's just missed his bus.

By the sea, it's not as hot as in Granada, even at four-thirty in the afternoon. We get a little lost looking for the lotero's house. Vicente stops and asks for directions from a boy hanging around in the street. During the summer at siesta time, the streets belong to the children. When I was a kid and my parents were having their siesta, I used to hang out in the farmyard, in the storage room at the store, in the olive groves, on street corners, in empty fields. Other kids might hang out on the jetty, jumping from rock to rock on the breakwater, or peeking into the ships docked at the pier, their offices, engine rooms or cabins. Each person's solitude is shaped by the conditions that surround them.

"Hey tough guy, what's your name?" Vicente asks.

It would have made more sense to ask for directions in a bar, but Vicente decides to place his trust in this five- or six-year-old boy.

"Luis."

"Luis what?"

"Luis García, sir."

"Do you know a lotero named Juan?"

"Yes sir, he's a friend of my father's."

"And where does he live?"

"Behind the Naval Command headquarters. I can take you. It's not far."

He places the tin can he was carrying next to a tree, and becomes very serious as he walks ahead, leading us. He's silent. We turn at the first corner, walk past the Naval Command, and he points with his finger.

"It's over there, the second house, the one with the dog out front."

His mission complete, he runs off and disappears.

The dog ignores us, which we're thankful for at this time of day when no one's around. Juan Benavides does turn out to be the same lotero who came into the bar earlier. Short, thin, with olive skin and eyes like an eagle's, he laughs at everything he says, everything he sees, everything he hears. I've never seen such agility in a man's face. His eyes are never still, they move like fish darting around an aquarium. I wonder how old he is. Thirty-something? He invites us into the kitchen, the coolest room in the house. We're alone with him. His wife and three children are visiting her sister for a few days in La Alpujarra. If you're poor, it's a good idea to cultivate warm relationships with different family members. You help me today; I'll help you tomorrow. The lotero stayed behind to work the rush of summer vacationers. He offers us water, wine, and sweetened, spiced coffee, boiled on the stovetop. It's all he has, he explains, his eyes in constant motion until they stop, and he becomes all ears. No thanks, we don't need anything.

"We just had some coffee. We saw you come in the bar." I've always considered it polite to justify saying no. "The bar in front of the pier."

"Well, I didn't see you. You don't look like vacationers. I've gotten used to only seeing what I need to see. Faces of possible customers. This line of work makes you half-blind."

"My colleague," Vicente says, "is going to explain how useful this encyclopedia is. You won't regret buying it." He opens his briefcase, takes out a volume and puts it on the table. I curse him silently from the depths of my soul as he hands the pitch over to me. "Go ahead."

"So, Juan—Señor Benavides—what is your eldest son's first name?"

"Juan, like mine."

"The world is full of important things and people whose names begin with the letter *J*, such as yourself and your son, or countries like Jamaica, or animals like the jaguar, or the jay."

"I'm more of a jaguar than a jay, although my voice is as bad as a jay's squawk. I'm tone deaf. My mother wouldn't even let me sing Christmas carols. I was just too off-tune. Go figure."

"Juan, your son, would benefit enormously from having access to this encyclopedia for his homework. He'll make you proud. Spain's history is full of kings whose names begin with *J*, like yours, such as Jaime el Conquistador, or the kings of Aragon...."

"Too many kings," he interrupts me again. "In a poor man's house, it's better to talk of other things."

"Well, there are popes, for example. Juan XXIII, the good pope, recently passed away...."

"He was the less bad pope. There are no good popes. Too many popes."

"Yes, sir, you're right. It all depends on what you believe." I'm struggling to go on and feeling abandoned by Vicente's strict silence. "But an encyclopedia brings you the whole wide world, its past and its future. The pagans believed in Jupiter, the French believed in Joan of Arc, poets believed in Juan Ramón Jiménez. This encyclopedia contains the whole universe in alphabetical order, with *J* for justice ...."

"Or for jerk off."

"Excuse me?"

"Is jerk spelled with a G or a *J*?"

"Excuse me, sir, I don't think I've done anything to disrespect you." Instead of helping me, that bastard Vicente is trying not to laugh. "If you prefer, we can stop now. There's no need to continue."

"Don't get mad, muchacho."

"Well, sir, you are the one who called our offices and asked that we come speak to you."

"Fine, fine. I've decided to buy the encyclopedia. My cousin, a close friend since we were children and also a follower of Juan XXIII—may he rest in peace—runs the lottery office in Motril. I do the lottery ticket street sales for her. Between that and some other odd jobs, and with my wife's help, we're able to take care of our children. And we should have enough to pay the installments on the encyclopedia."

"Of course, you will," Vicente finally weighs in. It's about time. "Shall we go ahead and complete the forms?"

"Yes, go ahead. And sorry, muchacho. I'm too much of a joker sometimes."

"If you are a just man, we can put up with your jokes."

I'm not sure what Vicente meant by that last line, but he quickly moved on to close the deal and he baptized the lotero Juan the Just, a nickname fit for kings or popes. Then he sent me ahead to the bus station to buy the tickets. I go out into the street and take a deep breath. That unpleasant experience was enough to prove to me that I'm a terrible salesman, whether it's encyclopedias or whatever. I've always been ashamed to talk, even when I'm not trying to trick anyone. If I have trouble in a shop, I'd rather keep my mouth shut than start an argument. Anyway, I can't be patient, I can't be humble, I can't stand it when a cretin like Juan the Jay, Juan the Jaguar, Juan the Just tries to be funny. Vicente is fine about it, just another sale. Me? I'm sick of the encyclopedia and all its flora, fauna, historical figures, letters, and battles. Señor Jay is right, we are jerks. In just the last two days I've been called a fairy and a jerk. Some joke.

I want to be a writer and there is the sea. Its blue instantly helps anyone reconcile with his life. It's possible that the whole business with Juan Benavides was some kind of joke that Vicente decided to play on me, a bizarre hazing ritual. Maybe Benavides is a friend, and Vicente got him to play along so they could both laugh at me. That may even be why Vicente ignored the warning from the Guardia Civil this morning. Who knows? Even the most ordinary people can sometimes have their secrets.

The sea is the solution. As time passes, I'll forget my frustration, I'll forget the encyclopedia, I'll forget Vicente. What I will remember about this day is the first moment I saw the sea. My father has never been. He did his military service in land-locked Zamora. My mother hasn't seen it either. I buy two tickets for the six-thirty bus into the center of Motril and, disconnecting my brain from everything else, I head to the beach.

I see children, fully dressed nannies sheltered beneath beach umbrellas, and bronzed women in bathing suits. I notice a redhead who, rising from her towel and crossing to the water, inflames the sand, the tranquility of the sky and the blue of the Mediterranean. I feel lucky to see this blue coast. I am aware the Atlantic is greyer, cloudier, without that almost Caribbean clarity and transparency that I've just discovered in the Mediterranean. I'm lucky to see the redhead. She needs nothing else but to be alive, to be present in herself, just like the sea, aware that each wave, each reflection, each bit of foam belongs to the same plenitude of life. My literature professor says that pretentiousness is a poet's biggest trap. Behind every pedant there's always an imposter. As I watch the redhead dive into the water, I'm ashamed by my ideas about the sea: each bit of foam belongs to the same fullness of life. Yesterday, I was very close to a naked woman. She wasn't even wearing a bathing suit. She was behind an open door, slowly drying herself off, slowly calling to me, slowly disappearing into her room, her towel barely covering her body. I couldn't follow her. It's easier to be a fish than a man. You swim along through the deep, you spot the redhead, you sneak up on her, you circle her, watch her closely, then, if you are a shark, you eat her up without being afraid of blundering, being blamed, or making a fool of yourself.

"You like the sea, do you? You're gawking at her like a fool. Well, I can tell you, she's a bitch." An elderly man has taken a seat next to me and starts up a conversation.

Today is not my day. Even old people are rough on me. A foolish-faced landlubber with a jacket and a briefcase apparently deserves an impromptu lecture on the true nature of the sea, which is not a tame animal and not the private property of summer vacationers. The old sailor got emotional as he recounted how the homicidal heart of those waves had made him suffer. I endured two of his tragic tales, then made my excuses. I'm running late, I say.

"I thought you'd disappeared," Vicente says, waiting on a bench by the bus stop. "Where'd you go?"

"We have our tickets for the six-thirty bus. I went to the beach."

"Did you wade in the water? It really helps."

"I don't like making a fool of myself."

51

"Are you referring to wading in the ocean or your thing with Juan Benavides?"

"Both."

"There's no one on the beach at three-thirty. If no one sees you, you hardly need to ask permission for a little bit of bliss. And don't mind the lotero. He seems to think he's some sort of comedian. We do what we do. Which is to stick him with an encyclopedia."

"Do you know him?

"Yes, I've heard of him. He's a difficult person."

These will be my memories of a summer day by the sea and a night in a hostel in Motril's Plaza de España. We ate a delicious dinner in a real restaurant. We deserve it, Vicente said. Then we went to our double room at the pensión virgen del mar. Vicente's body and the intimacy of sharing a room with another man has had more of an impact on me than my anecdotal sighting of the redhead on the beach. I'm going to confess all of this to Consuelo Astorga.

A month ago, I didn't even know him. And in reality, he's still a stranger. But now I'm watching him hang his jacket on the back of the chair, take off his shirt and trousers and there he is, in his white briefs. He brushes his teeth. Then he makes his way to the bed with his body, not tall or short, big or small. But his pale flesh looks flabbier than ever. I spend five minutes hiding in my bed in embarrassment about my body. I undress quickly, trying to keep him from seeing my underwear. I put on my pajama bottoms, turn on the bedside lamp and open my book. I can't wait to start reading. It's my refuge, and it means I don't have to look toward the bathroom or the other bed. I can disconnect from everything around me.

It's hard to inhabit a space of forced intimacy. Two men, two briefcases. In his, an encyclopedia and a toothbrush. In mine, two encyclopedias and a pajama bottom. I'm embarrassed to see him in his briefs, pulling back the sheets on his bed with exhaustion, staring at the ceiling.

"I'm not going to read," he says. "But the light doesn't bother me."

I try to concentrate on *The Brothers Karamazov*. Every now and then I glance over at Vicente's bed, and I can see him lying there on his back, his eyes wide open and staring at the ceiling. Then I hear his breathing slow and a slight snore. I look and he's closed his eyes. He's asleep. I turn out the light. I reflect that I've never been to a hostel even with my father. We've never traveled. Sometimes I'd go out with him to work in the fields. We'd get tired, we'd find a tree, we'd eat our lunch, and, if it weren't too cold, rainy, windy, or hot, we'd take our siesta under the shade of its leaves. Closing your eyes out in nature isn't the same as in the hostel. The sounds—birdsong, the whisper of leaves, the murmur of water in the canal—all unite you with the world, give you a sense of fullness. The man who sleeps by your side in the countryside belongs to the trees, the open sky, the mountains in the distance, to every corner of the universe, as far away as that may seem. Entering a hostel is like crawling into a den, into a space where breathing is too close. Everything conspires to make you feel the closeness of the person nearby.

My father doesn't talk much. In that, he's like Vicente. I think my father and mother are happy, but their relationship has had to bear all the fear, insecurity, and pettiness of life in a village. My father's silent because he doesn't have much to say. The townspeople know him already, they've observed his life day to day, harvest to harvest. By marrying my mother, he experienced the joy of winning the woman he loved. But it also meant he had to accept a role of inferiority bestowed on him by his father-in-law, the pharmacist, and the village gossips. Maybe he's silent because he feels he's failed, with his in-laws, with his wife, with his son. My mother talks a lot. She's got energy to spare, she's confident and knows what she wants. She doesn't regret falling in love with my father, acting out of love for him. I can hear her now. We may not live in paradise, she says, but we don't have to act like we're in the Middle Ages either. They were planning to marry me off to a rich but ugly man, a brother-in-law of Antonio, the mayor. You don't know him because he left years ago. But I preferred my handsome, hardworking man. And I'm so happy, she says, because you were born, and you are the smartest and most beautiful boy in the village. Don't be too nice, or they'll think you're a fool, she says. I don't care whether we're a farming family selling lettuce or pharmacists selling aspirin. I place my trust in those I love. People who have the least are the most honorable. And who cares what Antonio the mayor thinks anyway? I just thank god that we have money to send you to study in Granada, she says.

My parents have come twice to Granada. The first time with my Aunt Rosario. We spent a Saturday together. They visited the Alhambra, stayed overnight in a hostel, and went back to the village on Sunday after lunch. In a shop near the Palacio de Carlos V, my mother dressed up as a Moorish lady to have her photograph taken. My father refused to dress up. So did Rosario. The second time, my aunt didn't come. My parents got a ride with some neighbors who were coming and only had room for two people. Right now, I'm missing all three of them. I wish I could be with my father in a hotel room, or in a hostel, or in this very hostel, to have him here, we could get up together in the morning, I could take him to the bus stop, buy two tickets to the port of Motril, we could stroll along the dock, among the boats, and I could introduce him to the sea. Father, this is the sea. Sea, this is my father. You are both awesome, although you, Father, avert your eyes too much, and you, Sea, sometimes you become too enraged, and you provoke tragedies like the ones described in novels or by old fishermen. You might just want to limit yourself to delivering seashells and red-headed girls.

Consuelo looks like my Aunt Rosario. Maybe that's why I hung my head when the pipes in Consuelo's apartment started unexpectedly to gurgle. Consuelo stands, walks to the bathroom, undresses, and calls to me. Imagination is a presumptuous friend. It's worth its weight in gold for someone who wants to become a man of letters, but it's still very impudent. It sees, it hears, it touches more than it should. Consuelo undresses. She removes her dress, her bra, and her panties. In the shower she lets the water fall, trickling down her skin as she searches for the soap with her eyes closed and uses it to caress her body, filling with foam its hidden places, wet mysteries, her unfettered breasts, her nipples hardened by the sudden cold, her white belly and pubis, her round thighs, and toenails. The sight of her pubis is like an exploding flare. She sees me watching her and becomes shy but allows me to amuse myself with her back and her bottom, and then she rinses and turns off the water, and with her hand she signals toward the towel hanging on the rack.

I'm obedient, Consuelo. I'll bring you the towel, I'll let you get out of the shower, careful, don't slip, I reach for your shoulders, I feel your wet hair, I gently squeeze your pubis between my fingers, and then I surround you, I envelop you with my arms, I search for your neck with my mouth, I nibble, I seek your breasts with my hands, I squeeze, I continue until you turn, you kiss me, you soak my shirt pressing your wet breasts against me, and then you stand back a moment and smile at me. You're beautiful, Consuelo, like my Aunt Rosario but younger, more mysterious. I'm no longer a boy for you. Give me your hand, take me to your bedroom. Your curtains are fine, but we'll get to that curtain rod later. I'll come back tomorrow, and we'll put up the new one that we've left in the living room. That's my excuse for coming back tomorrow, and the next day. Now you lie on the bed. You watch me take off my clothes. I don't fold my pants, I don't hang my shirt on the back of a chair, everything falls to the floor because I am in a hurry, you are waiting for me, I am the nephew transformed into the lover, the timid boy who breaks out and wants a mad adventure, the body that presses into yours, that opens your legs, that seeks your sex to enter, that becomes yours like water after a drought, like each swell of the sea.

I stir rhythmically in my bed. I glance over at Vicente. A wave of panic washes over me. Fortunately, he's still sleeping. The enemy sleeps, at ease. He's noticed nothing strange, no weakness in the other bed. The last thing I need is for him to see me masturbating nearby, in this sordid hostel rotting by the sea like an old shipwreck. Not a chance. Yesterday, when I got home and went to bed, I couldn't sleep. Not out of desire, but from shame and disgrace. It was that cruel feeling of being ridiculed, the way Consuelo talked about Vicente being homosexual, the sound of the shower, the open door, the shadow of her sex which I never really saw, the stupor of my own paralysis. With this heat, this drought, and at my age; I can't believe I didn't accept that shower in a flash.

"What do you want, Consuelo? A shower? We don't need to shower, let's go directly to bed so I can show you just how much I don't know. I'm going to be a man, since it seems you are looking for a holiday substitute for Don Alfonso, your careless boss who's gone off to the coast with his wife and children. He's left you on your own and isn't thinking of you because he's entertaining himself watching the redheads rise from their beach towels and dive into the sea. I'm here for you, Consuelo, or at least I would be if I weren't such a jerk, with a *J* or a *G*, a jerk who freezes at the worst possible moment, who doesn't get up, who doesn't go into the bathroom as the shower rained down, who doesn't dry you off with a towel, who doesn't follow you to the bed to spread your thighs, to climb on top of you pressing all of my weight onto your body to compose that strange beast with two backs of which Shakespeare spoke. My literature professor says it's possible to cite the classics even when making love.

No, yesterday I didn't feel the slightest twitch of desire. I was alone in my room, the whole apartment to myself, no bothersome witnesses listening to the squeaking box springs or sensing through the darkness the rhythmic movement of a jerk-off. There was no one around to say, "I don't need to know about that," "I don't need to see that," "I don't need to hear that." But now, in this shared room, with Vicente just a few feet away, Consuelo's nakedness is upon me, her mouth, her barely concealed body, her composure; and my impertinent imagination carries me away and is like a woman sinking her fingernails into my back, clasping her legs around me, telling me don't stop, don't think about anything else, don't stop, don't stop.

But I do stop. It's no use. What am I supposed to do? If I have even the slightest suspicion that Vicente has noticed something, how can I face him in our business meeting with the pharmacist and walk back to the bus with him? Shame is like a corrosive sea salt that doesn't wash off with a shower. It lasts months, years. I turn toward the other side of the night, seeking the north. I don't masturbate. I wait as the spider web unravels. I stop thinking about Consuelo. I don't even think about my Aunt Rosario in her intimate solitude, her grief as she prepares my sandwich or declines to dress up as a Moorish lady, or about other strange ladies or Consuelo. I don't need to think about Rosario's coldness or the grimness of death. All I have to do is imagine Vicente's flabby white flesh in its lonely pallor as he brushes his teeth nearby. In his white briefs. Forced intimacy is a difficult sentence to endure. I must resist, focus only of the next curve in the road, nothing else. Tomorrow is another day.

~⊙~

Yesterday, Friday, July twenty-sixth, nineteen sixty-three, I arrived in the office carrying two big pots of geraniums which I bought the previous afternoon in one of the flower kiosks in the Plaza Bibarrambla. Consuelo's look of surprise made it impossible for her to pretend she didn't know they were for her. She teased me, acting as if they were a gift for the office to celebrate our sales success in Motril. But geraniums aren't indoor plants, and in the office, there are no windows or balconies where you can hang flowerpots. I don't intend for them to stay here keeping company with the electric fan. These flowers are much more appropriate on your balcony, amiga Consuelo, I said to her, and didn't need to work too hard to convince her because her eyes had already given her away. She knew they were a present for her. When she finally has curtains on that new curtain rod in her bedroom, she can pull them open and see these flowers on her balcony. And think of me.

Vicente arrived late, weighed down by the sorrow of his shoes. I understand he wants to dress with the seriousness his position demands when we make sales calls to the provinces. He is the businessman, the salesman, the official representative of the illustrious Editorial Universo. He needs his jacket, his polyester pants and black shoes that serve equally to hike in the Sierra Nevada, venture into a Guardia Civil station, or search the ocean for pirates and redheads. But the formality of his office wear is noticeable. Maybe he's too old to wear jeans, like a student. But a t-shirt and sandals would make the paralyzing heat of this summer much more tolerable. It's painful to watch his air of resignation as he arrives, says hello, and gets straight to work. You don't notice it at first. You have to watch him closely to figure out what he's feeling because he tries not to call attention to himself. The humiliation of his defeat is most intense when he realizes one of his shoes is untied.

I continue to perfect my powers of observation. And I write more fluidly. That's another piece of advice from my literature professor whom I obey like the older brother I never had, and I follow as if he were a guide through the jungle. In my first conversations with him, I went on too much about inspiration and great ideas. Ignacio told me to focus more time and effort at the desk; practice, review, edit, rewrite, read the classics and Russian novels. This journal is helping me refine the tools of my trade. It's fun and it's boosting my confidence. Having observed Vicente, I can confirm there is no greater tragedy in his life than an untied shoe. He flushes with impotence in the face of his bad luck and hostile destiny. Looking for the closest chair, he doubles over, uniting his belly to his thigh and slowly works to remediate this affront from the gods. It is only the surprise of the geraniums that finally awakens his interest in the morning.

"What's this?"

"It seems I have an admirer." Consuelo shields herself behind a benevolent smile. "But it's my secret and I'm not about to reveal details."

I was grateful for Consuelo's silence. I was grateful for Vicente's awkward discretion, unable to ask for details. After being mocked in Motril, I didn't feel like getting caught up in any more practical jokes. I want to navigate my own path through this strange combination of excitement, embarrassment, and optimism that Consuelo provokes in me. If anyone had said that to me when I first met her, I would have said they were crazy; it was impossible to even imagine. But now I'm gripped by obsession. That's why I'm so thankful for the silent complicity in her response to Vicente.

The plan was simple. Two flowerpots weigh more than a bouquet of flowers. A little patience, a little dissembling, let the morning unfold, let the clock do its work—the clock is the most important employee in any office—and in the evening, at the end of the workday, offer to carry that heavy load to Consuelo's house. Good works begin when the workday ends. My good deed carrying heavy curtain rods will be re-enacted today with two flowerpots. There is life after humiliation.

All morning I struggled not to spy on Consuelo out of the corner of my eye. I worked the phones more than ever, making it a point of pride to prolong my conversations in the same way that Vicente wields his kerchief and waves his arms. When I finished my sales calls, while waiting for my next assignments, I took refuge in a conversation with Vicente about Dostoevsky's psychological labyrinths. "Isn't that more of a wintertime novel?" Vicente asked. I started to play the pedant, but his question made me laugh. Yes, he was correct, Dostoevsky was too heavy for the hot summertime and for a clock that seemed as dead as a doornail. I kept checking the wall clock in part to avoid looking at Consuelo. It only confirmed to me that time—in its dense, sweat-soaked inertia—weighs heavily. I wear jeans and franciscan sandals to the office, but reading Dostoevsky makes you hotter than wearing a jacket, polyester pants, socks, and shoes with untied laces. You need a lot of towels to mop up the sweat caused by numbers and hours.

When Vicente proposed a coffee break in the Lepanto, I declined, frowning with the face of an anxious university student. Study of the Russian novel is a decisive moment in the formation of a writer, I said. I was finishing a chapter of *The Brothers Karamazov* and preferred to stay in the office, reading and taking notes. I'd have to sacrifice his invitation to coffee. Vicente's eyes widened, his lips pursed, he nodded his head in understanding, and went down the steps to the street. His philosophy of appropriate books for each season went with him.

"Thanks for not telling Vicente that I'm your secret admirer."

"That'll spark his curiosity a bit. He seems so distracted lately."

"He seems listless."

"It's probably the heat. This job is no fiesta either. Anyway, thanks again for the flowers. Please don't think me rude if I don't take them home now. I'm meeting someone for lunch. I'll take one of the pots home tonight and the other one tomorrow."

"I can carry them for you." My voice had taken the curve too quickly and was swerving between offering help and begging. "Besides, we need to put up the curtain rod."

"I don't know. I may go to the movies with a friend." Naughty Consuelo, cautious Consuelo, seductress Consuelo, daughter of Eve, with her necklace of silver roses dipping into her white blouse paired with a blue skirt. Wicked Consuelo. I tried all morning not to look at her, but even so

59

I've memorized her, from her blonde locks and new glasses to her canvas sandals, also white. With her right toe, she nudged the canvas off her left heel, then the left toe to the right heel, and liberated her feet. Her toes leapt free of their cages, for a few moments scampering about the floor enjoying their freedom and fresh air before slipping back into their canvas sheaths. Consuelo is evasive, proud, and predatory. "But I'm not sure. I'll let you know later."

When I came back to the office after lunch, she said nothing. Vicente was already there and maybe she was trying to keep up appearances. But there are many ways to play the spy, a gesture, a few words scribbled on a scrap of paper, a conversation with double meanings, an aside while the potential witness is away in the bathroom. Consuelo, daughter of Eve, seems to have forgotten about the geraniums. Focusing on my phone calls and Dostoevsky, I was able to wait until Vicente said his farewells. And I finally got my answer from Consuelo only after he had shut his briefcase in a pathetic gesture of ending his workday and left the office. It was ten minutes after seven.

"So, are you going to help me with the geraniums?"

Two flowerpots filled with geraniums fit on the tram much better than two curtain rods. We got on at Puerta Real. The Fuente de las Batallas was as dry and as silent as the empty car. When the tram lurched into motion, the pulse of the external world began to match my internal agitation, which was much more attuned to the jangling of the windowpanes and wood panels than the silence of a half-deserted city. Everything was repeating itself, though in a very different way. We skirted the Jardinillos de Genil, passed by the Kiosko Las Titas, and got off at Puente Verde. There before my eyes, like a foretaste of a conquered reality, was Consuelo's street. A second chance. Everything in place, according to plan, fitting and appropriate like an index card from the office, or a cleanly edited page of text.

As we started up the stairs, the stain of my previous failure began to spread over me. Getting up to the fourth floor of number four Calle Transversal de la Bomba was not so simple. It wasn't because the flowerpots were heavy, but because the shadow of defeat grew with each step, like encroaching damp in the walls. The silence was charged with the timid intimacy of unspoken assumptions and doubts because although the game had not yet begun the die was cast.

I know that you know that I know, and you know that I know that you know, and neither of us really knows anything. I suddenly stopped being the intrepid suitor, and was seized by a premonition of disaster, because I've never done it, because I was afraid of looking foolish, of not knowing, of coming too soon, of humiliating myself, again, this time definitively.

"Come on in, let's put the flowerpots on the terrace."

I followed Consuelo to the bedroom. A double bed with no bedspread, white sheets pulled tight and folded over with industrious tidiness, the photo of her parents on the dresser, the mirror, the wardrobe, all in keeping with the soberness of the home. My anxious presence takes them by surprise. I just came to help carry the geraniums, please don't think badly of me, I said to myself as if apologizing to the furniture and to her parents as Consuelo slid open the door to the terrace. It turns out that she was referring to a large terrace at the back of the apartment, not the balcony that looks out onto Transversal de la Bomba.

"That swimming pool belongs to the Falange Sección Feminina. I used to go there a lot with my mother."

"And this is your small garden," I improvised the compliment as I set the pots down next to a wall where a collection of flowerpots was already hanging. Lush ivy had taken possession of the other wall and the railing.

Consuelo kicked off her shoes. She offered me a beer, and we sat on the sofa in the living room to continue our insinuations about Neruda, now animated by the agitation that reading Dostoevsky's psychological dramas can provoke in someone with melancholy neurosis. I was about to ask for a second beer when a jubilant gurgle announced that water, the prodigal daughter, had returned to her domestic life. She's here. Consuelo stood, walked into the bathroom, and left the door ajar. I heard streaming drops of joy begin to pound on the bottom of the bathtub. It's not like I was wavering, but I did wait a minute before getting up so I wouldn't seem over eager. When I entered the bathroom, I saw that she was leaning over the bathtub faucet filling two blue watering cans. They matched her skirt. She had not taken her clothes off.

"One each. You can help me water the plants. They're really suffering this summer."

I was a gentleman. Not a trace of disappointment crossed my face. Scheduled surprises and life's twists and turns would have to arrive by a different path. They would take a bit more time to appear. The watering cans filled, I lifted mine and followed Consuelo across the living room, through the bedroom and back out onto the terrace. She had started with the new geraniums, so I worked on the ivy. As I was concentrating on distributing the water gently across the lush foliage, I felt a trickling down my neck, soaking my back. I turned, thinking I had wandered under one of the hanging flowerpots that was dripping water, to find Consuelo, barefoot, with her white blouse and blue skirt, with her necklace of silver roses, her glasses and her arm raised high to pour water over me slowly, without shampoo or soap, soaking my head and face, eyes open, my chest, my pants, my sandals. Using all the water to the last drop which fell into her palm.

"The water's not that cold. But we will have to dry our clothes."

She drew close and hugged me to soak herself equally, kissed me on the lips and unbuttoned my shirt. Her hands paused at my chest. I knew well the feeling of my own desire but had never experienced someone else's. I saw it in Consuelo's eyes, in her hand pressed against my chest. The desire of another is even more thrilling than our own and sweeps us away into a whirlwind. "Wait," she murmured with her head resting on my shoulder. She took off my shirt and hung it with two clothes pins on one of the laundry lines that crisscrossed the terrace, then told me she wanted to finish taking off my clothes inside the bedroom. I glanced around to see if any neighbors might be watching us. No, no one could spy on us there. The Sección Feminina building and the windows of Calle Escoriaza were too far away. I didn't speak, not a word. I decided to place myself in her hands, the most sensible way of falling into her arms.

My professor says that one day, when censorship here ends, the writers in this country will realize how difficult it is to write about sex. I can report, thanks to Consuelo, that it wasn't difficult for me to experience it, although I did commit the grave error of not bringing condoms. She stationed me next to the bed, gazed at me, unzipped my trousers, and pulled them off. There's no doubt you're happy to see me, she said, and then, leaving her glasses on the night table she pushed me onto the bed and lay down beside me. The moistness of my body concentrated itself on Consuelo's long kiss. My imagination became reality when I felt her hand move down my belly and embrace my sex. I tried to respond and reached for her breasts, but my fingers got caught up in the buttons of her blouse. Wait, she said, and stood up.

She looked me in the eye as she slid the blouse off her shoulders. She looked me in the eye as she removed her bra, revealing round breasts. She looked me in the eye as she lowered the zipper of her skirt so that it dropped to her feet, revealing her thighs and her panties. She looked me in the eye as she removed her panties, revealing the blonde blaze of her nakedness. She looked into my eyes to see her own nakedness in them, and to see my desire, the extreme need in the intoxicated light of my own gaze.

I felt her nakedness along the length of my body. I embraced her, she embraced me. She guided my hand between her thighs, we rolled across the bed until I was on top of her. It was then that she told me to put on a condom. I confessed, fearful I had committed an unforgivable error, that I had none. That's something the man's supposed to take care of, she protested gently, and quickly gave me the information I needed. They sell them in Cuesta, the pharmacy in the Plaza del Carmen. This was invaluable information, especially because it confirmed the possibility of another date, another opportunity.

She let me enter her. But be careful, don't come, she warned. I remained long enough to feel the desired and oppressive heat, the strange intimacy of being inside another body, being another, erasing for a moment the limits of existence itself, with other arms and other legs, emerging from the vertigo of reality itself. To be inside and out, in yourself and in the other, in the mind and in the flesh, very close and very far. Don't come, she repeated, moving to detach herself. Wait, she said, and turned me onto my back. I felt her kisses on my chest, on my belly, on my sex. There, she stopped, and each sensation multiplied with anticipation of the next until containment became impossible.

I embraced Consuelo, we were silent, time passed, the last embers of the sunset faded, night fell, we resumed our kisses.

"If you had condoms, we'd go again. But since you don't…that wouldn't be fair, would it?"

"I'm going to spend all of my commissions from Encyclopedia Universo on condoms."

"If you want this to last, don't go talking about it. It will only work if you keep it secret. Ok?"

"Ok. Promise."

"I don't want any problems at work. It's best for us to go underground with this. No more flowers in the office."

"No more flowers."

"Condoms. Papelería la Cuesta. Next to the Plaza del Carmen. That's the best gift."

Consuelo is younger than I thought. She's thirty-seven. She looks older when she's all done up like the perfect secretary. If someone in the office had told me her real age, I'd have thought they were shaving a few years off. Some women lie about their age because they're afraid of getting old, as if manipulating words and numbers could change reality. For them, each year is a sin for which they seek absolution. Writers are not the only ones who want to change their lives with words. My mother says she's forty years old, and so she's forty, not forty-two. My mother is spirited, strong, decisive and yet she skims years off her real age. My Aunt Rosario is immersed in her silence, has little strength, isn't proud and she doesn't skim any years off her age. My father laughs when the age issue comes up. You two better get your story straight, he says, because in this family now the little sister is older than the big sister.

Consuelo's nakedness is irresistible. In bed, lying next to me, after I've seen her with no clothes on, I believe in her sincerity. Thirty-seven years, seventeen more than me. Her skin, her breasts, her hips, her thighs seem much younger than when she's dressed up as the perfect secretary. The first time I saw her in the office I thought she was fifty. Then, I looked more carefully; I saw she was a single woman but not a spinster, a mature woman of about forty. Her words and her nakedness strip away another decade. Fifty, forty, thirty, counting down toward me. She's giving me this gift, the best days of my life.

I don't have to express all of my musings as literary theory. It's enlightening to think about them that way, but if I try to articulate them, the words seem out of place. I wouldn't dare try to argue in class, for example, that a novel is like a chance encounter on the Corto de Loja train, or that a poem is like pillow talk. The professor's only response to my analysis was a silent smile. Most of the other students—the bookworm from Málaga, the priest from the Escolapios School, the two cute girls from Calle Recogidas, and Pepe el Cantautor—would roll their eyes. They'd think, there he goes again, the hick acting like a know-it-all.

This may not be an appropriate topic for literary theory, but it's the honest-to-god truth. Learning about sex is not just a body-to-body thing, but a complicity of shared understanding, a partnership that fills the home, the game of sharing a shower when the pipes sound the alert that water's arriving, the trust in sharing the last bottle of beer in the fridge, and the curious openness of pillow talk. It's an honesty that reminds me of poetry, whispering, exposed, your heart in your hand. Each word is a choice. In a novel, anything is possible, like a trip on the Corto de Loja train, riding along with the stories of strangers who are born, baptized, grow up, fall in love, get married, celebrate the wedding with drunken guests, produce descendants, go to the doctor, pay debts, take out loans, bury their relatives, give away their children in marriage, enjoy grandchildren, get old and die. The end.

Consuelo's taught me about making love and about pillow talk. She's taught me how to speak the truth. Beds are full of lies, she warned me. That's why they end up being problems. I'm very old, you are a boy, she told me, we are not going to fall in love, you will tire of me when you are sated, you will frighten me when I stop to think about what I'm doing, life will go on, and this will become a warm friendship, a fond memory belonging only to a young man who weaves illusions and a single woman of a certain age who no longer believes in anything she's been taught. I don't trust what I read in the newspapers, what I see in the streets, what I hear at the office.

"You don't believe in anything?" I ask. She lowers her voice even more, as if dragging the words out, and murmurs that she believes in other things, and then she asks about my studies, my father, my mother, my Aunt Rosario. I don't tell Consuelo that she looks a lot like Rosario because my aunt's face has been erased from my memory. When I think of my family, I see my mother, my father and Consuelo Astorga dressed like my Aunt Rosario, with blonde locks that have never been to the village, and a body so close by, so precise, that it confirms word for word all the ideas and confessions of our pillow talk. Words sound different when they're enveloped in the warmth of the body that speaks to them.

I confessed to her that at first I was too embarrassed to go into the Cuesta to buy the condoms, that I waited half an hour for the shop to empty so I could go in without being seen, that the first day I was at her apartment I felt like an idiot when I left without having dared to grasp the situation, that the following night in the hotel in Motril I was consumed by the memory of her nakedness in the shower and I had to make a tremendous effort not to masturbate in my bed with Vicente Fernández Fernández nearby, that the day after that I was terrified of walking up the office steps because I didn't know how to start, what to say, how to behave. I confessed to her that I can think of nothing else, but I was afraid of being a nuisance. I don't want her to tire of me.

I told her about my quarrels with the mayor of my village, the story of the infamous punch. I needed to be with her, naked, in bed, to realize that many of my own reactions have to do with my father's self-doubt; he's a man who says sorry even when he's buying cigarettes at the pharmacy. In Villatoga, I'm not the chemist's grandson, but my father's son, which is fine by me, the son of my father and my mother and I wouldn't have it any other way, but it doesn't mean I'm worth less than a chemist's grandson or the mayor's son. Those who seek me will find me the same wherever they look: in grade school, in high school, on the farm, in Pedro el Pastor's shack, and now at the University, with Ignacio Rubio, with students who study Latin and talk politics. I'm the smartest one in the room. I can't stand the tone of defeat and humiliation in my father's voice each time he implores me to be more careful. History is not on our side, he warns, and I hear the church bells, and I see Rosario's mourning, and Sergeant Palomares' abuse of detainees in the Guardia Civil station. And I see Vicente as he mops the sweat from his brow and says, I don't need to know about that.

What is it that I don't need to know? I didn't ask Consuelo about our office boss, Don Alfonso. I don't want to tarnish my relationship with her, transform it into something ugly and dominating. Protecting yourself from lies doesn't always mean demanding the truth, at times it's knowing what not to ask. Consuelo was born in Granada. She lived here until she was seventeen while her father, Lieutenant Astorga, was stationed with the Tenth Infantry Regiment of Córdoba. Then she went with him to Madrid. She didn't just study typing, as she first told me, she got a degree in philosophy and literature. She's already graduated with the same degree I still have four years to work on. She never considered teaching, she wanted to be a librarian. She stayed in Madrid when her father got orders to return to Granada. She studied, she dreamed, she had a fling with a classmate named Pedro, she graduated, ended the relationship, studied for the exam to get a job in one of the public archives or libraries but never took it, had another relationship this time with a painter named Alberto Toledo, and that didn't work out either, though it lasted four years, the two of them in Paris, immersed in the bohemian lifestyle that Vicente dislikes so much. Things went wrong, she broke up with the painter and ended up working in a high school before returning to Granada. Here, she found a job at Editorial Universo thanks to Don Alfonso, and that's why she stayed in Granada when her father was promoted to captain, transferred to the reserves, and retired to live permanently in Madrid. Both her parents live there now, and she visits them often. Their Granada home on Transversal de la Bomba is practically the same as they left it: uniform and ready for inspection. That's where the sober furniture comes from. I'm old, Consuelo says, but not that old, and silently she begins to kiss me again, and I take advantage of the moment to slip my hand between her thighs.

Don Alfonso is an intruder in this kiss, in any kiss. I am a boy, she is a woman, our relationship is not going to end in a wedding, according to Consuelo, but ours is a lovely story, a better story than cuckolding the boss by stealing his girlfriend. Our affair isn't about taking advantage of his vacation and inattention. Now I'm furious with myself for imagining things about Consuelo's private life. Life's not always about creating literature, pushing the limits of your imagination like I have with Consuelo's supposed resemblance to my Aunt Rosario, a fairytale about Consuelo as a soulless spinster too old to marry who falls routinely into the arms of her boss, a fine family man who leaves behind leftover business for his anonymous staff during the summer holidays. The calendar in the Café Lepanto is paralyzed, life is ugly, catholic and unsentimental, there is no running water in this part of the world, but my trysts with Consuelo are not dirty: they are clear, clean and powerful, like the water from the shower we take when the pipes make their announcement and we run to the bathroom, embrace under the streaming water, balancing ourselves so as not to fall, and our thighs pressed together, I feel my sex responding and I know that no cold, no fear, no Don Alfonso will separate me from her. July has ended, August will end, but this can never end.

What bothers me the most is having to pretend in the office. It's hard to be near Consuelo and act as if there were nothing between us. Glances at the clock, telephones calls, conversations about how hot it is at night, confirmation of new orders, additions, subtractions, are all worthless exercises in distraction. I take advantage of Vicente's occasional departures or moments of inattention to approach her, speak to her, steal a kiss from her like someone stealing a pen or a calculator. I didn't want to ask if she was afraid Don Alfonso would find out, so once I approached the question using Vicente as an excuse. Why do we have to pretend in front of him? I'm not ashamed of him knowing, I say. He's not your father, you don't owe him any explanations. We could emerge from secrecy stating simply that I'm alone in Granada, you're alone in Granada, and we're just friends, I argue. We could go out, go to the movies, spend our evenings together. Vicente's not going to be scandalized.

But Consuelo demands absolute secrecy. We live in Granada, not in Paris, and, she says, hammering the point home, these are the times we live in, our fate, especially for women, who have it much worse. Don't you understand? How many women call in to buy an encyclopedia? How many women do you speak to when you go to the villages on sales calls? How many women hear your pitch on the glories of Istanbul, the heroism of Spanish warriors, or the characteristics of the Spanish fighting bull? A lot of them probably listen to the radio, read the newspaper, help their children with their homework, and think about buying an encyclopedia, but it's the husband who calls, who asks questions, who signs the contract. Women are better off acting in secret, Consuelo insists, appealing to me to go unnoticed by her neighbors and keep my distance from Vicente. A relationship that society would forgive in me as a youthful folly, could end up destroying her. This is the reality we live with.

I don't ask about Don Alfonso, and I do as she asks, because she's right. People talk, they watch, they can hurt you. She's right and I don't want to sully our story, our shared solitude in the house where she is queen, where she plays with me, undresses me, shows me how to move my tongue in her mouth, and unveils for me the unique intimacy of pillow talk.

Sometimes we play music while we make love. Radio Granada is full of programs that play popular songs, with announcers breaking in to broadcast greetings and dedications. Consuelo has a record player, and some vinyl records she picked up while living in Madrid, and others that she bought at the Olmedo Department Store on Calle Ángel Ganivet, very close to the office. Music is another form of shared understanding. On the sofa, as an amusing prologue, we listen to Gelu singing her song, "Siempre es domingo." To the words: "...no me preocupa ni me asusta el porvenir," I seek Consuelo's mouth. To: "...poder vivir y poder soñar y aturdirme con la velocidad," I continue to Consuelo's breasts. This new dance called the twist, however, is crazy, it's a joke. Yesterday, Consuelo put on a record by Mike Ríos, the Spanish King of Twist, and she made me dance in the middle of the living room, while she sat on the sofa in front of me like a judge for a talent contest. It was a disaster. I was more like a contortionist than a dancer. But in the end, I didn't mind because then she changed the record, put on a ballad by Paul Anka, and led me by the hand to the bedroom.

⤙⚬⤚

There was a surprise waiting for me when I got to the office this morning. The boss's door was open. A door defines space and time, especially when it stays shut. Doors delineate our space, our routines, the contours of the playing field, the area off-limits to workers and the worries of day-to-day life. Our office feels less secure with Don Alfonso's door wide open. It was the first time I'd seen it like that, and it scared me, provoking my fear that any change could destabilize a situation that has favored me immensely. I looked at Consuelo. I walked across the office to her desk. Beyond the open door, Vicente's voice was reporting the summer's progress. Everything was going better than expected: more orders, more sales calls, more commercial activity, and that didn't even include the brilliant deal sealed by the boss himself. The salesman's forced enthusiasm bathed the statistics in optimism.

Consuelo told me that I should go in, the boss wanted to meet me. I don't know why I sensed a trace of worry in her expression. I knocked on the door. I saw a photo of his Excellency Francisco Franco, Jefe del Estado, on the wall and furniture of a higher caliber than the rest of the office, as if this space were an extension of the government. Vicente was seated in a black wooden chair with red upholstery, leaning forward with a solicitous smile that extended from his mouth all the way down to the order book resting on the floor at his feet. A large window looked onto a sunlit street, filtering the distant bell of the streetcar. From behind a desk free of papers, file folders or pens, I was greeted by a man with combed-back ebony hair and a trimmed and diminutive mustache, wearing a light blue shirt and an air of jovial maturity.

"So, this is our young colt. Good morning, León. It's a pleasure to meet you. Consuelo has spoken highly of you and Vicente says you're an efficient helper. Are you happy here?"

"Yes, sir."

"Well, everybody's happy then. Smooth sailing. Where are you from?"

"Villatoga."

"That's in Jaén, right? I've been hunting there once or twice. It's a good area for partridge and hare." (How old are you, Don Alfonso? How many years on you, you old geezer? I was trying to get used to his face, his charm, his chatter, his ability to harmonize the movements of his mustache and his hands. And I was really wondering about his age.) "I know some guys there who own a lot of land and a jewelry shop on Calle Reyes, De la Chica is their name. Do you know them?"

"No sir. But I think they were friends with my grandfather."

"Good people. Nice house. When they were younger, they organized a lot of hunting parties. Now they're half dead and they won't budge. They've gotten old. And you are studying...?"

"Philosophy and literature."

"But that's a girls' major. Antonio's daughter, the one at the Cafetería Birrambla, she studies philosophy and literature. You might know her. Dark-haired, a real beauty." You can always come up with an excuse for passive obedience when you have to. Mine was Consuelo and avoiding any problems that might separate me from her world, distance me from the routine that had led me to her home. I thought of my father and lowered my gaze. "Law school, now that's for men."

"I want to be a writer." And as I spoke, I felt a flush of fear that the boss wouldn't consider literature a manly career choice.

"I know many writers and aspiring writers who studied Law. But, no matter, enough said. In fact, that's even better for us. Philosophy and literature benefit culture in general. That's good, that fits right into the sales strategy Madrid is developing. Encyclopedias for everyone, buyable in easy monthly installments."

Fifty-four. Don Alfonso is fifty-four years old, I thought then. I'm about to turn twenty. Consuelo is thirty-seven, seventeen years older than me. If we add another seventeen to Consuelo's age, we get fifty-four. Consuelo is exactly in the middle of the two of us, equidistance, seventeen years of separation on either side. Face to face, north to south, mountains to sea, the beginning of youth and the beginning of old age. Maybe it was wishful thinking, but I felt sure I guessed his age right.

He spoke about Torremolinos, that bustling village on the coast of Málaga that for him was the perfect place to spend summer vacations and cultivate friendships. Long dinners, parties, complicities, evening breezes that unite business with pleasure. Then, Don Alfonso spoke about the amazing deal he'd just struck with the central government's Education and Recreation Department to supply encyclopedias to local libraries, tourism and cultural offices, and worker production centers. I didn't ask him what he meant by worker production centers. All I knew was that we had hit the lottery, all of us: Editorial Universo, the local Granada office and its employees. Next, he spoke of the twenty-third Traineras Regatta rowing competition in honor of Generalísimo Franco, to be held on August fifteenth in La Coruña. That's why he paused his vacation. From Torremolinos to Granada, from Granada to Madrid, from Madrid to La Coruña, where he'll attend the regatta as a personal expression of gratitude to his friends in Education and Recreation for such a lucrative business deal. Of course, he's going to take with him Ramón López Bravo, Editorial Universo's director general and leading voice. And he told us that the Caudillo would also attend, along with General Augustín Muñoz Grandes, the vice-president, and Manuel Fraga Iribarne, minister of Information and Tourism. Don Alfonso's conversation was starting to sound like one of the government's NO-DO newsreels. The names did not tremble on his tongue. In conclusion, after describing his friends, adventures, projects, travels, and events, he sent me out to buy cigarettes. But the worst task was reserved for Vicente.

"Listen, León. Do you mind going out to get two cartons of Goyas in the tobacco shop on Calle Reyes Católicos? And Vicente, I'd like you to go to Calle Duquesa to pick up something for my wife. Ask Doña Concha for the package for Doña Cecilia. I think it's two blouses and a summer skirt. More clothes for my missus. Sorry about the request, but I'm not going to have time to pick it up. This morning I'm completely booked. I have to call Madrid, Coruña and the Education and Recreation office. What a hassle, a complete hassle, right when things were so nice at the beach."

We went out onto the street. Vicente said nothing about Don Alfonso's request. It didn't seem at all unusual to him that the boss was using company employees as errand boys. I grew up running errands for my mother and Aunt Rosario. The best thing about when we opened our own family grocery store was that I didn't have to suddenly run out to buy salt, wine, oil, milk, or sugar anymore. But it didn't really matter. I was a kid, and they were family errands. But this was different because of the ease with which Don Alfonso chose to use his office for personal business. Vicente declined to criticize this abuse, probably because it didn't matter to him that the boss was in the office alone with Consuelo. I wonder what Don Alfonso requests from Consuelo. I see the strategy: you, go to one place, you go to the other place, and I will stay here to explain to Consuelo that my train to Madrid doesn't leave until tonight and we have all afternoon free together.

"It looks like we're all going to get at least a token commission from the deal with Education and Recreation." (Vicente was more interested in sales than what might be happening back in the office). "Not bad. The deal is worth a bundle. Whatever trickles down to us, even if it's just a quarter of the normal commission, should be good money."

"Why did he send us out to buy cigarettes and pick up his wife's skirt?"

"Just because. Who do you think you are? This is normal, just the way things are in the business world. The only unusual part is that we are getting a share of the commission."

"How much?"

"A lot, I already told you. And because of it, your father won't have to pay nearly as much tuition for you this year. So, this is how they keep us happy. Hey, did you know the boss was coming. You're wearing a clean shirt and shoes instead of your sandals."

I didn't respond. There was no way I could explain anything to Vicente. It was Consuelo's doing and so it fell under our agreement of secrecy and complicity. Yesterday she gave me the shirt that I wore today to the office. After spending the afternoon in bed with her, I was getting up to dress when she went to the wardrobe and pulled out a shopping bag from the Olmedo Department Store. It was a present, a green shirt, my size, that she insisted on helping me try on—here, let me help you—as if making up for the toenail prank she had played on me. We'd showered, we'd dried off, we'd made love, we'd enjoyed some pillow talk about Madrid, Granada and Villatoga, about her parents and mine, about the University, which she is familiar with and I'm getting familiar with, whispered words about everything and nothing. And just as I was looking for an opportunity to begin again—kisses, caresses, neck, breasts, pubis—suddenly Consuelo sat up, folded her pillow to support her back and, leaning against the headboard, began to paint her toenails. It was another episode of intimacy. Naked and meticulous, she showed me how to paint first the big toe, then the other toes, finally the little toe, then let them dry and move on to the other foot.

I didn't protest when she started to paint mine. There is pleasure in abandoning yourself, letting others do things for you, a gift, like someone stroking your back, removing a splinter from your skin, giving you a foot massage. Of course, sometimes the outcome can get ridiculous. Suddenly, I found myself with the toenails of my right foot brightly painted, as if they were Consuelo's toy.

"How do I get this off?"

"Let's see how long you can stand it. It will be our secret. Are you embarrassed?"

"Yes, actually. It's not very presentable."

So, this morning I showed up with a new shirt and shoes. No more sandals. It's one thing to allow your toenails to be painted, but quite another to wander around the city displaying them like a degenerate. I didn't dress this way out of respect for Don Alfonso, but in honor of Consuelo. I wanted to show her that I was keeping her secret, that I left my house and was moving through the world with our secret intact, my painted toenails, without anyone noticing, going about life as normal, going to the office, speaking on the phone, accompanying Vicente to the Café Lepanto to have coffee and talk about soccer, unnoticed wherever I go. Don Alfonso, feverishly at work on his business projects, was anything but unnoticed. After buying his cigarettes, I spent the rest of the afternoon eavesdropping on the conversations escaping from his office. The door remained wide open. I had to listen to his jokey phone calls, details of his comings and goings across Spain, his expressions of satisfaction, his orders, his flattery, his yes, of course sir, you know you can count on me, on us, and tomorrow we'll talk on the train, we'll celebrate in La Coruña, see you soon, yes sir, see you tomorrow. And it culminated with a general invitation to all:

"Come on, let's go. Everyone to the bar."

Towing Consuelo along with him, he got all of us to enjoy two rounds of beer, a plate of Serrano ham and some boiled shrimp, which he ordered from Marcelo, the widowed barman. We sat at a corner table, under the abandoned calendar. Marcelo asked Don Alfonso why he had come back from his holiday in Torremolinos.

"It must be something important because you've never worked a day in your life," he said, with a strange tone of familiarity.

"Careful Marcelo, don't go too far. Have a drink on me. I'm going to the Regatta del Generalísimo in La Coruña."

"It used to be called the Regatta del Caudillo. How Spain is changing!"

"Ok, back off, Marcelo. We've been friends a long time, but there are some things I'm not going to take from you. You're a red, a commie."

"You're friends with all the waiters in Granada. If I were a red, my dear Alfonso, I wouldn't be speaking to you so freely. Shall we compare our military service records?"

Don Alfonso raised his glass. Familiarity breeds contempt, he said. He toasted Marcelo, then he toasted us, ate the last slice of ham, mentioned that his car was parked nearby in front of the Cine Regio, and offered to give Consuelo a ride home, since her apartment was right on the way, and he disappeared with her down the tunnel of an endless afternoon.

I stayed in the bar with Vicente and my thoughts. When we left, I asked him about Marcelo. Was he a red? What was in his military service record? How did he become Don Alfonso's close friend? Vicente responded, as ever, we do not need to know about that.

⌒

I was afraid to go back to my apartment and spend the rest of the afternoon twisting in the wind. My house keys stayed in my pocket. The stairway was too dirty, too dark, too lonely. I turned around and retraced my steps to the Café Lepanto. In any case, it was lunchtime, I had to eat something. That's life. You hunger for many things, but reality is a demanding machine. It seeks food, love, sex, glory, wisdom, information. Only the dead have no needs.

The bar was empty. Marcelo was listening to the radio and washing glasses to keep himself busy until closing time. From four until six I close the blinds, even if a whole cavalry regiment appears to drink my bodega dry, he said, as I ordered a tuna sandwich and a beer. I began to chew carefully on the bread and the conversation. We spoke of the unbearably hot summer, August just as bad as July, tomorrow an exact copy of today. A round of applause and good luck to those fortunate enough to escape the city and spend the hottest months in Torremolinos or in La Coruña. We spoke about Editorial Universo, about books, about buying things on the installment plan. Don Alfonso had given Marcelo an encyclopedia set as thanks for his logistical support and for being a good neighbor. We spoke of my village, my studies, my job, the bar, the University, the paralyzed calendar, and of his wife.

I ordered another beer. With the sandwich half-gone, I asked him about his friendship with Don Alfonso. They met in nineteen thirty-six, when Marcelo arrived in Granada, fleeing from Málaga and the Civil War. After Franco won, Marcelo exchanged his weapons for a waiter's serving tray and white jacket in Granada's Café Suizo. Don Alfonso hosts a tertulia there every Tuesday, a gathering of friends who share stories about their battles, infidelities, and business deals. In nineteen fifty-four, Marcelo declared his independence from the Suizo and opened the Café Lepanto which showcased his wife's great cooking. We served the best tapas in all of Granada, he said. After she died, his menu was reduced to toast with olive oil or butter in the mornings, plates of Serrano ham, fried potatoes, and boiled shrimp at midday and in the evenings, along with a discrete selection of sandwiches.

When Don Alfonso mentioned one day that he was thinking about opening a local office of the Editorial Universo in Granada, it was Marcelo who told him about the office space on Calle Lepanto very close to the bar. At first, Don Alfonso focused on stocking all of the local bookstores with copies of Washington Irving's *Tales of the Alhambra*, with its descriptions of Granada's famous medieval Moorish palace. Then he made good money taking advantage of the first wave of foreign tourists coming from Madrid and from the new highways along the coast, and selling them guides to the city, its Moorish monuments, the cathedral, and the royal chapel. All that and a few textbooks compiled by professors at the University of Granada, kept him in business until that stellar moment the encyclopedia arrived.

"It seems like he's doing well for himself. I'm glad."

"Me too, I'm learning a lot at this job. Although sometimes they seem like pranksters. Why did Don Alfonso call you a red?" I dared to ask because I could see he was enjoying our conversation in the almost empty bar.

"Because he can be an ass sometimes." Marcelo didn't seem to mind talking about his personal life to me, a regular customer perched on a stool with the last piece of tuna sandwich still resting on his plate. I've been having my breakfast at his bar every day for the last month and a half. "My father was shot by the reds in Málaga, and I escaped on the run. I did my war service in Granada when I was just twenty years old. Real war service, along the front lines in Motril, then later in the capture of Málaga and Almería. Alfonso, yeah, he was a big hero of the rearguard, away from the front lines, all talk and no action. I don't think he exposed himself even once to being shot by a red. When enemy soldiers fell into his hands, they were already defeated and on their way to the firing squad. I, on the other hand, was wounded twice.

"So, it was a joke then?"

"Yes. A bad one. There are people who come into this world to work, and others who are born with a flower up their ass. War or peace, it's always the same. I made more friends among the Germans than the British. I put in three years, battle after battle, and now I'm happy just to get up every day to serve breakfast to the neighborhood. The medics from the Casa de Socorro are welcome, the workers from the Granada Club de Fútbol are welcome, the civil servants from City Hall are welcome—café con leche and a big piece of toast for all. There are other guys, though, always chasing shady business deals, bar hopping, picking up women. Me, I don't see the world that way. I'm a romantic."

"Sir, you're a good man."

"Every man bears his burdens and hides his sins. Except your boss who's got his on display."

"But Don Alfonso is a good husband, isn't he?" I defended him just to keep Marcelo talking. I wanted to keep the good information flowing and gave the impression, I think, of defending company honor. "This morning he asked us to pick up some dresses for his wife at a boutique. He seems very attentive to her. Do you think he has other women on the side??"

"Oh no, of course not. A model husband, you bet. The gifts are part of his campaign for forgiveness. Now, look who's just come in the door. Just what we needed. Speaking of gifts."

A bootblack who looked like a gypsy was entering the bar lugging his box, his wooden stool, and the stench of the day's heat. Like a vulture, he scanned the empty tables, registered the lack of any potential customers, and shrugged in silent understanding with Marcelo. Too much drought, too much summer travel, too few tourists and too much ruin. He was furious to hear that Don Alfonso was back from Torremolinos and had dropped by the bar. Another customer slipped between his fingers. He's a good customer and a friend, I clean his shoes all the time, the bootblack said, casting his predatory eyes on my shabby shoes.

"Those shoes could use a touch up. They seem a bit worn."

"No, thanks a lot though."

"I can take care of them for you. Won't take a second. I'd be happy to."

"No really, it makes me too uncomfortable." The truth was that my shoes needed a good cleaning. I hadn't found anything in my apartment that removed the accumulated summer grime. What really horrified me though since my arrival in Granada was the sight of a man squatting on a stool slavishly swiping the dust from stranger's shoes. And that's what the gypsy bootblack, who in a flash had pulled out his implements, was already doing. "Please, no ...."

"Don't send me home with empty pockets. It's shameful. Sir, c'mon, don't be lame."

The widowed barman was enjoying my discomfort. "I thought you could defend yourself better than that. You better start learning. What an odd duck you are. Come on, come on, Manolo, I'm about to close."

This gypsy bootblack, smoothing black polish across my shoes, wondered out loud at my socks. "If this fancy young gentleman doesn't take off his wool socks, he's going to spark a forest fire. In this heat!"

If Ignacio Rubio, my literature professor, were in town this summer, I would have walked myself and my shiny shoes over to his place to have coffee, talk about Russian novels and ask his advice. The best moments of my first year in Granada have been listening to him talk about his theories on esthetics and the contemptible political situation in Spain and confiding in him my doubts and my ambitions. But until September, he and his wife are at her parents' house in Santander. That's a long journey, too far for me to walk. My shoes would get really dirty. So, I left the bar and walked aimlessly, first toward Puerta Real, then up to the Carrera del Darro, then back toward the Paseo del Salón. Marcelo's words left a deep impression on me, not only because they suggested the boss was a Don Juan. Hey Chelo, come on down to the bar with us and have some beer. He called Consuelo by her nickname with an intimate familiarity. For Don Alfonso, she was Chelo, not Consuelo. It makes a difference.

I was also impressed by the widowed barman's war memories. What did I know about the Civil War? I knew a bit, but I was more affected by what I didn't know. Ignacio Rubio and I had spoken about the death of García Lorca, the exile of Antonio Machado and Rafael Alberti, of Miguel Hernández's imprisonment, of verses, books, and songs of the era. But after Marcelo exposed such personal details of his previous life, I suddenly realized how little I knew of my own history, and that of my family. My grandfather José, my father's father, died in the war. But I don't know how, or even which side he was on. Neither my father nor my grandmother Elisa have ever told me anything. It just wasn't discussed. And what about my other grandfather Felipe, the pharmacist? And my father's adolescence? How were the roles distributed in my family? Who were the heroes of the rearguard, who took enemy fire in the trenches, who faced the firing squads? What did they see as children, how did they experience the Second Republic, the uprising against it, and the military victory that followed? What about the British and the Germans? What do they have to do with the life of a waiter on Calle Lepanto, with my parents' lives, with my own? I know my family horizontally, but not vertically. I've lived on the surface, in silence. I realize I've grown up in the present tense.

Where did we come from? Where are we going to? The great Rubén Darío contemplated these questions. As for me, for the moment I was coming from the Café Lepanto and going to Transversal de la Bomba, by way of Jardinillos del Genil. Life was turning me into a spy. What better way to bring an end to the afternoon and my agitation than by spying on Consuelo's apartment? I wanted to see with my own eyes Don Alfonso leaving her apartment building, confirming my doubts and speculations with the miserable truth. However, her treeless street with only one parked car offered little in the way of camouflage. It would be difficult for them not to spot me if they left the building and walked toward the tram station. Better to wait at my post near the corner of Paseo de la Bomba. I positioned myself there to observe Consuelo's apartment while pretending to be the boyfriend who's been stood up, planted like a tree at the street corner, who couldn't make up his mind to leave as the minutes passed because he harbored the hope that his love would appear at any moment pleading for forgiveness with a convincing excuse for being late.

The motorcycle repair shop closed. The pharmacy closed. The nannies who'd been strolling with their charges up and down the Paseo disappeared making way for the kisses of young couples. As the daylight faded, so did my peace of mind. It suddenly occurred to me I might have it backward, that Consuelo and Don Alfonso could come up behind me catching me by surprise spying on her building. If his family was in Torremolinos and he had to pack his bags for the event in La Coruña, it was likely that the lovers had decided to go to his house. I was pained by the thought of Consuelo, naked, folding his clothes and organizing his suitcase. Another pair of pants, two more shirts, socks, underwear, shaving bag, a comb to tuck in his inside jacket pocket. And what if the couple decided to stop by Consuelo's apartment before going to the train station? It would be so easy for them to discover me at my post by the corner. A humiliating moment, with awkward and befuddled excuses, the ridiculous spy, the employee given his marching orders, the lover exposed, the bumpkin put in his place, forever separated from Consuelo. Of course.

I decided to change positions. In the end, it didn't matter if I surveilled the doorway to her building or the entrance to the dead-end street itself, so I crossed over the Paseo de la Bomba and took up a position by the tram stop at the curve by Jardinillos del Genil. It was a good place to lose myself among the crowds. It was two trams and twenty minutes later when I spotted Vicente at the end of the Paseo, with his weary walk and aching feet. He was not wearing a jacket. As he got closer, I could see that a pair of sandals had replaced his shoes. From my hiding place I could easily observe his trajectory. He turned the corner and walked straight up Transversal de la Bomba, waving hello to one of the neighbors as he entered Consuelo's building. This was one too many surprises for a single day. Life is a bitch.

But I decided to wait. Maybe it was a last-minute assignment or order, a phone call from Don Alfonso, a special request from the office. If Vicente was there on business, he'd be out in a few minutes. I'd see him come down the street and walk across, by himself or with Don Alfonso, or with Consuelo and Don Alfonso. I sat on a bench in the Jardinillos. I started to feel more like the watched than the watcher, scrutinized by the stone mermaid in the waterless fountain. Darkness seized the Paseo, and no one left the building. The sickly light of the bulbs strung through the trees was a good reflection of my state of mind.

"Hello. Got a cigarette?" A man of some fifty years, with a green shirt, white pants, and a belt cinched very tight, smiled at me.

"Sorry, I don't smoke."

"Mind if I sit here with you?"

"No sir, not at all, please sit down. I was just leaving."

"You don't want to stay just a little longer?"

"I think there's been a misunderstanding." I remembered Marcelo's advice after falling prey to the bootblack. I had to learn to defend myself, but without losing my dignity. "Goodbye sir, have a good evening."

"I just thought that since you were sitting here, so young, so handsome."

My literature professor says that distance and irony are fundamental tools for writers. I understood the concept quickly enough, the theory, the literary trick. But tonight, as I write, I'm discovering just how difficult it is in practice to stay calm when reality takes an unexpected turn and crushes your heart. Writing with irony and distance is a lie when your life has collapsed around you.

~⊙~

I've been out of sorts all morning. I decided to disguise my dark mood and treat Consuelo the same as always, following the unspoken rule of keeping everyone at a distance when you're hiding a secret. Unfortunately, I'm now hiding three secrets: my relationship with Consuelo, my suspicions about an affair between Consuelo and Don Alfonso, and the shock of Vicente's surprise nocturnal visit to Transversal de la Bomba. It turns out that the staid office worker, the salesman of books on easy installment plans, our cowed and mediocre colleague who doesn't want to know about anything, is also hiding his own mysteries, weaknesses, betrayals, and vices. What difference does one more adulterer make to this world?

Three secrets are a lot for just one person. Three such grave secrets would threaten to destabilize anyone's literary effort to observe the panorama of the human condition. Obsessions are like the blades of an electric fan; they spin around and make a lot of noise. It's been hard for me to stay calm. What I really felt like doing was going up to Consuelo, calling her by her nombre de guerra "Chelo" and asking her point blank about Don Alfonso and Vicente. I also felt like telling Vicente he didn't fool me with his beige jacket and shoes, that I'd seen him in the street in his sandals and shirt sleeves, that I knew about his indiscretions and that very soon his wife would be receiving painful anonymous messages about the liberties being taken by her hypocritical husband. All of this I recounted in minute detail in my journal, my ally in revenge. Literature is also good for that, to settle accounts. Yes, to vent my rage and denounce the hypocrites.

After my bouts of indignation passed, while Vicente was on the phone and Consuelo was going over the distributor's report on July sales, I began to feel ashamed of myself. Who am I to stick my nose into Vicente's life? The only right I do have is to a frank conversation with Consuelo and some sort of explanation. But I don't have the courage and I fear I'm condemned to play the fool for my last month and a half in this office. My journal will become my only confidant, a confessional filled with doubts and exercises of introspection. Another benefit of literature: it gives you comfort and a lifeline when you need it.

The desolate grief of the day thickened when Vicente told me I had to travel with him that afternoon to Maracena, a small city north of Granada.

The san joaquín Cultural Association decided to award some encyclopedias to its affiliates during the village's summer festival. The initiative was launched by Carlos Cid, a Maracena local, the Association's secretary and the owner of the Bar El Colorín. The festival's cultural program included a film screening with a colloquium, a flamenco performance, and a public presentation by Encyclopedia Universo. A must-see, Vicente said. But we needed to proceed carefully, be cautious, avoid political trouble. Everything's been checked, everything's under control, Don Alfonso told Vicente, but still, keep your eyes open.

Villages have a habit of baptizing their residents with nicknames, and Carlos Cid's was "el Colorao," the Red, because of his political convictions. In addition to nicknames, villages also typically have a pharmacist, a doctor, a mayor, a Guardia Civil corporal, a tailor, a priest, and an official red. For years the Association's secretary and his family were known by the affectionate nickname of the Redtops. But the slant of Carlos's political opinions led the town to trim the nickname back to the Reds. The local authorities at the time were not thrilled about letting him build the bar. But with time, everything calmed down, and the revolutionary was apparently not so dangerous after all. And it was the priest who called Editorial Universo to organize the presentation in Maracena. The secretary of the Association must be a good guy if he had the support of san joaquín and the church. Some people talk tough but underneath they're like lambs.

Before accepting the invitation, Don Alfonso informed himself down to the last detail and then explained it all to Vicente. As I listened to my colleague's blather, his apologies for not letting me know about the trip sooner, my thoughts wandered. This was yet another missed opportunity to see Consuelo, for her to invite me home, to speak with her, to explain myself, to renew our intimacy amid running water, songs, and nakedness. Maybe Vicente's nocturnal arrival at Consuelo's apartment had to do with this visit to Maracena. Was it a special request from Don Alfonso, some sort of last-minute commitment?

So, the day darkened even more without a single cloud appearing in the crisp city sky. I was in no shape for more sorrow. I'd already added to my emotional pain by taking up smoking. Last night after I finished writing, I felt an impulse to start. Sorry, I don't smoke, is what I said to that gay guy who tried to pick me up in the park. I was sitting alone on the bench, like an idiot, vulnerable, with no justification for being there, no pack of cigarettes, no box of matches. I thought of Consuelo in her apartment holding a lit cigarette. I wish I would have stood up from the park bench with dignity, and said to him, here, have a light, you can keep the matches, but do me a favor mister and don't touch me, do me a favor Don Alfonso and don't touch Consuelo, and you, Vicente, do me a favor and never go back to Paseo de la Bomba. Keep the matches but leave me in peace.

The truth is, I don't know anything about anything, I have no right to judge. But I remembered the pack of Celtas that Jacobo, one of my roommates, left in his bedroom. Entering someone else's abandoned space is like having a lover with a lot of visitors. It turns espionage into a religion. While my roommates were off enjoying wonderful summer holidays with their families, I'd discovered many secrets in their closets, shelves, and desks. So, I went in search of that pack of cigarettes, I lit one, and sat down to read Maxim Gorky's novel about spying, *The Life of a Useless Man*. The combination of Russian literature, cigarette smoke, lack of experience and the August heat provoked a knot in my stomach. It was a disaster, which reminded me of the time when I was a boy and the cobbler's son and I made ourselves sick trying to imitate the grownups. This time I would stick with it, I promised myself. I wanted to become a smoker, to buy cigarettes in the tobacco shop, offer them to others to facilitate conversation, and to provide me with company in my moments of solitude. And to incinerate my insides.

I waited several minutes, read three pages of Gorky, and lit another. I decided to suck the smoke in deeply, in all its abundance, the way one should drink in life. The second drag wrenched me to my feet. I ran for the bathroom, propelled by retching, and afterward stumbled to my bed. I'd never been so drunk. The nausea overwhelmed me until I became an invalid. It transformed my life, my apartment, my bedroom into a torture chamber. That was yesterday. This morning my resentments weigh heavily, as do my legs, my arms, and my head. But by the end of the day, I scored my first big professional success.

At five in the afternoon, Vicente's friend Antonio Mendoza picked us up at the office. He parked his SEAT Seiscientos in front of the Casa de Socorro. Mendoza's from Maracena, where he works in a car repair shop. Every now and then, his boss lets him use one of the cars. It's like this, he explained while driving us to his village, after you fix the car, you have to test drive it. This one's working great, just like new, he said with expansive pride and personal satisfaction. Antonio Mendoza is older than Vicente. His self-promotion from mechanic to driver seems to be his way of helping the community and collaborating in the organization of the festival. Short, friendly, agile, he has the face of a squirrel and the hands of a pianist. The elegance of his character is concentrated in his fingers, which are whiter than his skin and longer than the rest of his physique would suggest. He must work on engine parts with a surgeon's precision.

From the back seat, I watched Antonio drive as I listened in on his conversation with Vicente. We don't expect much in the way of sales, Antonio said, maybe two or three encyclopedia sets, one for a guy named Marcial, another for Felipe Casanova, a friend who'd done well in construction, and another for the priest's school. That's the one the Association agreed to pay for. But it was still a good idea to go and be introduced, meet the people of the village, soak up the atmosphere. An event like this in the middle of the san joaquín festival will boost the prestige of Editorial Universo, the Association and El Colorao, he told Vicente. You'll be amazed.

"I don't like public speaking. This is crazy," Vicente said.

My annoying colleague didn't seem convinced. The indifferent and disinterested of this world have distinct ways of showing they're nervous. In Vicente's case, he asked a lot of questions. He wanted details on the location, the assistants, the schedule of speakers, the plan for afterwards and the journey home. Don't worry about it, Antonio Mendoza protested, trying to calm his friend's concerns. After it's all over, I'll take you right to your front door in this very car, he said. I haven't quite finished testing it yet.

I was surprised that Vicente wasn't more excited about today's event, if only out of curiosity. When I first got into the SEAT Seiscientos, I was immersed in a life crisis and shattered by a tobacco hangover. I was dispirited, disillusioned, with no future and no patience. But now, I surrendered myself to Antonio Mendoza's pale hands and eager optimism.

There were a lot of people seated at the tables and standing at the Bar El Colorín, better known now as El Colorao. More than fifty, the owner announced. Carlos Cid was a corpulent man. He spoke and walked with power. By way of greeting, he placed two bottles of beer on top of the bar.

"I haven't met you. Are you the new guy?"

"Yes, he's helping us at the office. His name is León." Vicente answered for me as he surveyed the situation. "When do we start?"

"Take your time. Drink your beer. There's no rush."

"Has anyone come from City Hall?"

"The mayor can't make it, but a couple of council members are here. They're over there, talking to the priest."

They'd improvised a small platform with three chairs at the back of the room. When we stepped onto the stage and took our places, the chatter died away and the room focused on us. I thought it was going to be hard to get the audience's attention, but you could have heard a pin drop as Carlos Cid began to talk about how the san joaquín Cultural Association began, you know, as a collaboration with the, uh, village festival, you know, and how interesting the movie and the animated discussion were afterward, um, you know, and how good the flamenco singers were going to be at the closing ceremony, you know, and how appropriate it was to include the, uh, book presentation because knowledge, you know, is what makes men free. The Association thought it was a great idea to take up a collection among our friends and affiliates to provide these great works from Encyclopedia Universo to the parish school, you know. And who better to tell us about it than Vicente Fernández, the man some of you already know, who is responsible for the Granada branch of Universo, you know.

No, I didn't know. I didn't know that Carlos Cid and some of his friends knew Vicente, maybe from a previous disastrous meeting. Above all, I didn't know what tone my poor tongue-tied colleague was going to take to sell the encyclopedia to that group. I suddenly understood why he was nervous.

"It's truly a great honor for me to be invited to join you here today." His words echoed like the official speech of an ultra-patriotic government official. A salesman has to be a chameleon, blending in with his surroundings, shifting away from the intimacy of the naming strategy in living rooms to different forms of public speaking for great national knowledge projects announced at small town festivals. "As Carlos Cid said, culture is the backbone of any village. Culture and knowledge are as important as bread, they nourish our ideas, our sense of duty and commitment. A country without culture is a jungle, a land without honor."

The audience was attentive, eager to listen and learn, to appreciate a more dignified way of life. Vicente was speaking formally and well, but I began to feel that surge of discomfort, that whisper of fraud that haunts me during every sales session. Our sales calls and promotional visits during the first two weeks of August had been fruitful. But I've been learning that beautiful words can deceive, disguise the truth. Hidden behind those lofty phrases we use to praise culture, community, ideas, duty, and commitment are lucrative bits of business for Alfonso and his friends in Madrid but miserly commissions for the salesmen. The admiration I felt for Vicente's ability to adapt, to recalibrate his tone of voice and vocabulary, intermingled with my distress at the intimate damage caused by fraud.

"Knowledge influences modest day-to-day events as much as the great affairs of history. History is embodied in names. Take Carlos Cid for example. With the Encyclopedia Universo, you can learn the story of one of the greatest Spanish medieval warriors, el Cid Campeador. You can also learn about the bravery of Carlos III, the Enlightened Monarch, the king who brought modern education and economy to Spain. You need go no further than the C of Carlos or Cid to understand the characteristics of that charming redheaded songbird called the colorín." A burble of giggles began to surface across the room, a prelude to the tumult about to break out. "And you can also learn about the wealth of meanings behind the word Colorado." A surge of guffaws. "Words are like deep wells which we use without realizing how much is in them. Colorado means many things. It can refer to something more or less red." More guffaws. "A mountain in Bolivia and two rivers in the United States are called Colorado. It's also a state in North America. And the conservative party of Paraguay is called Colorado...."

"What? Conservative?" The voice of Antonio Mendez sails like a dia-
bolical arrow over the heads of the attendees.

"Yes, conservative, nationalist and anti-communist. It was founded by
General Bernardino Caballero...."

"That's bullshit!" Carlos Cid shook his head incredulously.

"Hey, Colorao." Mendoza readied his bow for a second arrow. "Maybe
you're a fascist instead of a pinko!"

"Shut your mouth, or you'll get what's coming to you."

"You're a fool."

"A fool? Me? You miserable piece of ...."

"Actually, if you consider the history of Spain...," I found myself suddenly standing on the stage talking without thinking, propelled by the aggressive tone of the conversation and the tension in the air."... Los Colora-
dos were the liberals who fought against totalitarianism. And don't forget
that colorado is what you call someone who is blushing with shame, which
is what christians who hoard their wealth and allow their fellow citizens to
die of hunger should be doing. That blush of shame should also be felt by
those who forget the three sacred words of modern times: liberty, equality,
fraternity."

Vicente gestured at me to shut up so he could continue his own comments, but it was too late. Led by Carlos Cid, the audience had broken
into a standing ovation, even the priest joined in. Only the two city council
members stayed seated. They displayed neither pleasure nor concern. They
seemed happy enough to just finish off their beer while contemplating the
uncertain boundaries between religion, culture, history, and politics.

"My colleague, the university student León Egea Extremera, speaks
with the passion of youth. Knowledge embraces all things. That's why the
Encyclopedia Universo is open to suggestions from the public. I've come to
ask you for information about the history of Maracena. Unfortunately, in
this edition of our encyclopedia there is very little historical information
about this beautiful village. But I know that great events have taken place
here. For example, very near to where we are right now, on the plains by
the Acequia Gorda, the fifteenth-century nobleman Don Martín Vásquez
de Arce, the famous Doncel de Sigüenza, was found dead during the War

of Granada. And I also know that Rey Alfonso I the Warrior, in one of the most glorious battles of the Reconquest, was in this very area in the year eleven hundred twenty-five. And in the year fourteen ninety-two, Ferdinand and Isabella, the Catholic monarchs of the united Spain, were also here to consecrate their definitive victory over the Arab occupiers. We have come here today to officially request information for future editions of the encyclopedia."

Timid applause marked the end of Vicente's comments. Nothing compared to the spontaneous ovation for my support of Carlos Cid, El Colorao, who'd been treated so unfairly by the political history of Paraguay. I'd acted spontaneously, wanting to calm the situation, but Vicente's pride was wounded. His assistant, a simple apprentice, had stolen the limelight. He invented all sorts of objections when Antonio suggested we stop at a nearby roadside inn to eat dinner. What with the commotion in the bar, attendees wanting to greet and speak to us, and congratulations for me from Carlos Cid's friends, we hadn't had a quiet moment to order even a sandwich. The corpulent frame of Carlos Cid himself made its way toward me as we were about to go; he shook my hand and held out a pack of cigarettes.

"Hey kid, want a cigarette?"

"Yeah, sure. Let's smoke." And each drag felt good to me because it represented standing ovations, warm embraces, and friendly greetings.

The conversation at the inn was one-sided. Antonio Mendoza, holding forth over wine, sparkling water, tomato in vinaigrette salad, fried eggs, and potatoes, analyzed the proceedings in positive terms. A unique event for the people of that village. Great atmosphere, lots of attendees, good participation, and a few unexpected sales. The priest's purchase was already covered of course. A total success. Vicente was silent; he refused to be swept up in Antonio's gush of enthusiasm. He seemed insecure. It was probably bothering him that this clumsy youth, the same one he'd pranked with the lotero in Motril, had so quickly bested him. But I was in no mood to feel sorry for him after the hypocrisy both he and Consuelo showed toward me. What goes around, comes around. If speaking at a public event for the mayor's office frightened Vicente, that was his problem. Don Alfonso didn't do me the honor of consulting me about it.

Vicente rose and asked Antonio for the car keys. He dug around in the SEAT Seiscientos and came back with his briefcase. He pulled out the first volume of the encyclopedia.

"Here you go, take this as a gift from Universo for your taxi service today. Read the whole thing, front to back. The explanations are in the envelope."

"And the other two volumes? Only on the easy installment plan?"

"We'll give them to you in payment for other services. When you finish reading that one, pass it along to El Colorao to see if he shows any interest. You're right, he is a fool."

As we entered Granada, our driver asked me where I lived. He muttered to himself *Realejo* three times while stroking his cheek with his pale fingers, made a mental calculation and decided it would be easier to drop off Vicente first. Lo and behold, I was finally going to discover where he lived. But it seemed that my colleague wasn't too happy about that idea. He started arguing with Antonio, insisting on a different trajectory.

"This boy is very young. He needs more sleep than I do. Take him home as soon as possible."

Vicente won in the end. Some losers are sore losers, and that's worse than the defeat itself. I walked up the stairs to my apartment hopeful for a shower and some time to read. I hope the water is still on, I thought. It was. Another thing that worked for me today.

It's a pleasure to open my journal in a good mood. Confidence helps you recount events more effectively. Tonight, the only thing I found tiring, believe it or not, was my obsession with writing church names in lower case: san joaquín, virgin, god.... But I keep up the effort, I persist. My literature professor says that discipline and willpower are indispensable.

⁓◯

A vacation within a vacation is one too many vacations. No classes at the university, no work at the office, no courage to knock on Consuelo's door, have turned the walls of my bedroom into a prison. I can emerge from my bedroom, walk around the apartment, sneak into Jacobo's room, snoop around in Jesus's boxes, but the prison follows me. I could lose myself in a Russian novel, avail myself of the Russian steppes, a battle, a love story, but the prison is still with me. I can open the door, walk down the stairs, go out into the street, stalk around the city with the insolence of a wild dog, but the prison still follows me. Wherever I go, it's with me. You'd have to lock every minute of the day behind bars if you wanted to break free of your obsession with time while waiting for an encounter with someone, whether or not the encounter was desired.

The August festival of la virgen de la asunción is a national holiday, but in my village it's not a big deal. In Villatoga, we invest all our religious fervor in our local festival, the día de santiago, the twenty-fifth of July. The solemn mass, Don Bartolomé's sermon, the procession, the brass band from Jaén, and the fanfare of that day dress up the summer heat for a party. August fifteenth, on the other hand, lacks vim or vigor, among other things because our parish priest Don Bartolo always abandons Villatoga mid-August for his native León in the north for two weeks of vacation with his family. When I was a boy, he used to tell me that anyone who had the same name as his beloved home city was duty-bound to behave correctly, better than anyone else. I think at first, he liked me because of my name. Later, he started to watch me more carefully, like he did with everyone else. The truth is he enjoys scolding people and likes to force people to respect him, but he also has a good heart and is kind to the unfortunate. My mother always says that Don Bartolo observes things and speaks to people with more wisdom than our mayor does. When he's out of town, the diocese sends a replacement, a clip-on priest, an adornment for the parish. The faithful make their way to church on Sundays out of duty, then afterwards forget their commitments. Their fear of sin leaves for vacation on the same bus as Don Bartolo, and returns with him as well, neatly folded in his suitcase among the priestly robes.

This completely unnecessary long holiday weekend has split in half the month of August, leaving me idle, unable to make any short-term decisions about my life without knowing where I stand with Consuelo. I stare at the walls, let the hours slip by, I start to get used to the apathy, I fidget like boiling water, I imagine, I contemplate, I reflect, but ideas escape me.

The only episode worth recounting is my conversation with Marcelo, the widowed barman. I already knew something about his history, based on his occasional comments and confessions in between serving me breakfast or beer. Just a few scraps of information about his life here and there. But today, he told me everything.

"How about a glass of cognac? Wait a bit until these French tourists leave and we'll close up."

I'd left my apartment at lunchtime to grab a tuna sandwich at the Lepanto. This was a strategy to feel closer to my normal life and schedule, and to my anger toward Don Alfonso, Vicente, and Consuelo. Marcelo was glad to see a familiar face among the tourists. With his regular customers gone for the holiday, legions of overheated foreigners trooped through his bar. Too many blonde people, too many beautiful but untouchable young women for a lonely man weary of watching the days slip by.

"For every one of them who'll chat with me, there are a hundred who won't. I couldn't pull a word out of them with a corkscrew."

When the last French couple left, he tidied up their leavings, turned on a light, shut the blinds, took away my coffee cup and placed two glasses of Soberano on one of the tables. Marcelo must eat on the run, grabbing whatever's in sight or at hand. I got there at three, exactly at lunchtime, and I didn't see him make lunch for himself or even grab a sandwich. So, it seemed odd to me that he would drink cognac after the tourists left.

"I'm feeling a bit melancholy, muchacho. We all have our secrets and our crosses to bear. Tomorrow will be fourteen years since I first met my wife, Angustias. She was twenty years old."

I immediately realized that I'd appeared at the perfect moment to hear Marcelo's confession. His stricken face, his manner of speaking, the closed bar, the glasses of cognac left no doubt. A happier person than I might have thought it was some sort of trap, but I was grateful for this strange opportunity for a shared solitude. I was also grateful that my role was to listen, rather than talk. You can be generous sharing stories about your past, but when it comes to talking about the present, you're better off biting your tongue because otherwise you have to live with the consequences.

Marcelo met Angustias Cañas in August of nineteen forty-nine. It was a Sunday during an outing to Pinos Genil, a small village near the Sierra Nevada wilderness, for lunch in a country inn to wind up a weekend of partying with the guys. Since I'd recently become a specialist in calculating the age difference between spouses, I did some quick marital math. I remembered that he was twenty-two when he left Málaga in nineteen thirty-six, so in nineteen forty-nine he would have been thirty-five. He was fifteen years older than his wife, eerily similar to the age difference between Consuelo and me. Although so much calculating quickly became a waste of time because numbers and reality don't always add up. A husband fifteen or sixteen years older than his wife is considered normal, but a woman who falls in love with a man fifteen or sixteen years younger? Scandalous.

"She was practically a child. At our wedding, my friends from the Café Suizo asked me forty times if I didn't feel sorry for her. They were just jealous, making jokes at a happy wedding, although she really did look a lot younger than she was."

Angustias was orphaned by the Civil War at the age of seven. Her parents were anarchists and very involved in village politics. They fell quickly. Her aunt and uncle, Don Juan and Doña Maria, took her in. They owned a restaurant near the river in Pinos Genil, and that's where Marcelo found the beautiful Angustias, polite and well-mannered, a walking treasure who helped in the kitchen and waited on tables. With obsessive punctuality, he began to frequent the restaurant every Sunday for lunch, sometimes alone, sometimes with friends. He became the suitor of Pinos Genil, and his prestige in coming from the big city of Granada facilitated his victory over local suitors.

When Marcelo learned that Angustias' parents were reds, he worried about his own past, disguised the details of his family story, reinforced the least compromising memories, and decided to hide the side on which his family had fought in the war. For Angustias, he didn't mind sacrificing his own political ideals and even the memory of his father, arrested and executed by the reds in Málaga in the early days of the military uprising. But he soon realized he wouldn't need to make that sacrifice, because his fiancé's aunt and uncle were conservative people and had raised her with piety for and devotion to the sacred mother church. Marcelo had found a religious and chaste girl. They married in nineteen fifty-one.

But it wasn't what Marcelo had done in the past that he needed to change for Angustias, it was what he was doing in the present when he met her. His real secret was the disreputable life he'd been living as a retired soldier, waiter, and friend to a gang of upper-class cads. On Saturday nights, after he'd hung up his uniform, the white waiter's shirt and jacket, black pants and bow tie, he would plunge into Granada's alcohol- and temptation-filled nightlife. The day he met Angustias, he'd woken up next to a sulking and decrepit girlfriend-by-the-hour in a house in the Albaicín neighborhood of Granada. The morning light had removed the better part of her charms. Pedro Aguilar, another Suizo waiter, was asleep in the next room, and Don Alfonso, my boss, was in a third. In those days he didn't have enough money to leave the city during the summer.

The group's desire to continue the party changed Marcelo's life. After they wasted the morning having breakfast, saying farewell to their lady friends, having a second breakfast, delaying the trip home, coming up with a plan, and rejecting the plan, Don Alfonso finally proposed going to Pinos Genil for lunch. After the previous night's poisonous atmosphere, coming across Angustias was a revelation, a different kind of poison, a kind of spell, a translucent enchantment, like the crystal-clear water of a mountain stream. On the spot, he renounced his previous lifestyle, his Sundays, and his fame as a dissolute former combatant, trading it in for a life alongside the girl at the inn. And he got his way. It's lucky, if you think about it, to have something to renounce for love. That's not my case, that's for sure. What do I have, what could I sacrifice, what could I give up, for Consuelo or for some other woman? I'd be hard-pressed to murmur in her ear that I'd transformed my life out of love for her. My anecdotes of life in Villatoga, my University routines, my ambitions to become a literary writer don't amount to much. I think Consuelo is the one who'll have to renounce her past life. Farewell Don Alfonso, farewell Vicente, from now I'd like to be a different person.

But these kinds of changes aren't so easy. The devil may spend two weeks hiding in Don Bartolo's suitcase, but the rest of the time he's on the job.

After two years of happy marriage, Marcelo began to relapse, taking up the night life again, and on Saturdays staying out later than he should have. True love is not incompatible with temptations of the flesh and the influence of friends. Pedro Aguilar reclaimed Marcelo's participation in his nocturnal adventures, though just once a month. It was a rite between old friends.

"It was a fatal error. Angustias thought I was indifferent toward her because she wasn't getting pregnant. But I wasn't indifferent, really, I wasn't. I was just stupid, too easily influenced by my friends. We were hoping for a boy, then a girl, then another boy. We were excited about the idea of a large family. Damn, life is complicated, León. You have no idea. Tomorrow it will be fourteen years since the day I met her, and this calendar is stuck on the day that she died."

The cross Marcelo bears was the work of the devil himself. Angustias made a vow to rise early each Sunday and go to the seven o'clock mass in the church of san matías. Some women are unlucky and get pregnant by mistake; others have to make vows, light candles, and pray to the virgin and the saints. Marcelo will never forget that cursed day, as he arrived home at six thirty in the morning to find Angustias just leaving the house. She'd risen at dawn to keep her promise. A loved one's pain can cut deeper than an insult. Angustias didn't protest. She greeted him with "good morning," and went on her way to church. Young and dignified, beautiful even in the feeble light of dawn, she moved past Marcelo with her prayer book and her veil as if accepting the inevitability of her disgrace.

"Life is such a bitch, León. I was so ashamed, so broken, I decided to give up my partying, get away from Pedro, find a different job. But the damage was already done. From that moment on, our fate was sealed."

He was silent a long time. I was loathe to interrupt with untimely questions. He seemed to be contemplating his wounds, the curse that had paralyzed his private life as well as the calendar at the Café Lepanto. Then he rose, grabbed the bottle of cognac, and refilled our glasses. Sometimes reality tricks us, he said, picking up the thread of his story, we think that everything will be ok, that the danger's past. He quit his job at the Suizo, decided to make use of his wife's skill in the kitchen, and opened his own bar in nineteen fifty-four. The best way to avoid more mistakes is to distance yourself from temptation and unite work and family. The business was a success, it began to draw regular customers, and then Angustias got pregnant. Fair winds favored us for a few weeks, but luck, in the hands of the devil, is a fragile thing. Angustias suffered a miscarriage at five months and lost our baby boy.

"That was the first sign of the curse. We should have given up our idea of a large family. Neither god nor the devil was going to forgive my sins."

Her second pregnancy didn't go well either. She took every precaution, she stopped working, she didn't over-exert herself, but at four months she had another miscarriage. Marcelo again felt marked by the curse that had fallen on them that day they crossed paths in the doorway at six thirty in the morning, she, on her way to the san matías church, and he, coming home from a night in a brothel.

In September of nineteen fifty-nine, just after turning thirty, Angustias learned she was pregnant for the third time. She was extremely careful, spent hours in bed, followed the gynecologist's instructions to the letter, made it to the delivery day and gave birth. But she was weaving the cloth of her own ruin, her own shroud, because there would be no forgiveness. The following day, she died, at six thirty in the morning on the nineteenth of April, nineteen sixty. Their baby girl survived.

"I'm afraid to raise her myself, León. She's being cared for at a nunnery in Almería. I love her, I visit her as often as I can. She's my daughter, my wife's daughter, but I know that if she's living under my roof, something terrible will happen to her. We all have our secrets and our crosses to bear."

He pulled a photo from his wallet that showed him holding the little girl in his arms, and then he was silent. After several minutes, he rose, saying that it was after six and time to open the blinds for afternoon customers. He thanked me for listening. I left with a sunken heart, sad and gloomy. Unnerved by the curse that hovered over Marcelo, I realized I needed to be careful with my own emotions and obsessions. This city, my apartment, my bedroom, and my books didn't seem like a prison anymore. Best not to tempt fate.

⌒◯

Is it possible to be angry and happy at the same time? It's like being a melancholy optimist, an honest charlatan, a silent chatterbox. That's Consuelo this whole afternoon. Angry and happy at the same time.

I spent the whole holiday weekend, from the fifteen to the eighteenth, in meditation, and also climbing the walls. I decided that when I saw Consuelo again, I'd keep my distance, an extreme distance. I wouldn't look at her from my desk, I wouldn't stay in the office alone with her when Vicente went to the bar, I wouldn't send her secret love notes, and I wouldn't linger at the end of the day hoping for an invitation to her place. I'd even planned an act of protest. At mid-morning, I'd stand up from my desk, ask her for the disinfectant, then empty the entire bottle in the toilet as an aggressive demonstration against the foul smell in the office. A declaration of war.

But when I got to the office, my plan collapsed before my eyes. Consuelo was wearing a dress that made her impossible to ignore. The devil in a tight white dress with red flowers and a plunging neckline. She was curvier than the road to Motril and when I hit one of those curves, I had no choice but to contemplate the next one. I couldn't stop looking at her all morning. On the other hand, I didn't want to give up my café con leche in the Café Lepanto. I accepted Vicente's invitation. Not to punish Consuelo. It was more like a ceasefire, a pause to get my breath back, to develop a self-defense strategy. No peace, no indifference, no disinfectant.

The clock in the office had to work harder than ever to get to two o'clock. It seemed to have forgotten how to count the seconds, minutes, hours. I couldn't take my eyes off Consuelo. As I walked home, ate lunch, forced myself through a broken siesta, and returned to the office, my mind was making a thousand bets, wondering constantly whether she loved me or loved me not as I mentally pulled the petals off five hundred daisies. Will Consuelo come back this afternoon in the same dress? Yes, no, yes, no, yes, no. Would I be able to maintain my dignified distance? Yes, no, yes, no, yes, no. Would we end up at her place waiting for the rush of water to greet us? Yes, no, yes, no, yes, no. My literature professor says talking to yourself is a sign that you have a rich inner life and are well-suited to the profession of writing. Never before have I talked to myself so much.

I bought a pack of cigarettes and a box of matches and walked up the stairs to the office. Consuelo and Vicente were both there. Vicente, in his jacket and weary-man shoes, said hello. Consuelo, in that same white dress filled with flowers and curves, greeted me like a bullfighter going in for the kill. But I lit a cigarette and sat down, prolonging the opening ceremony of the bullfight.

"You're smoking?" Consuelo's voice sounded amazed and amused. "Since when do you smoke?"

"Smoke equals success." Vicente's voice responded with pained irony. "Last Wednesday, he had a big success and he celebrated it by lighting up."

"Everyone smokes at the University. But I only smoke every now and then." My voice rang with idiotic self-importance.

Everything that begins must eventually end. Often, that unavoidable ending is for the best. Vicente reviewed the last letters of the day, answered the last phone call, gave some last instructions to Consuelo, and said goodnight. The clock showed five minutes after seven. I remained firmly at my post, as if I weren't waiting for anything, as if I didn't feel like leaving, as if I were a silent chatterbox, after not having been an honest charlatan. And I was barefoot, with my painted toenails on display. I'd bared my feet for her, to show that in this world there are those who are true to their word and keep their promises. It took a while for Consuelo to notice. Finally, I heard her stand up. I looked toward her. She went to the door of the office with the keys in her hand and locked it from the inside. She sat on my lap, said hello, and gave me a kiss. Some conversations are worth postponing, and at that moment I almost renounced forever the conversation I'd planned with Consuelo. And I was grateful I'd decided to tuck some condoms in my wallet.

Consuelo had been unavoidable all day. Now she was close and unavoidable. I pulled her dress down over her shoulders, pulled her arms from the sleeves, and removed her bra so I could be alone with her breasts. The maneuver, amid contortions and protests, was worth it. Easy, wild man, easy, you're going to tear my dress. Unavoidable and definitive was how she looked at me as she pulled her dress up to her waist and sat astride me, pressing against my chest and my mouth. Unavoidable was how we ended up on the floor, my back on the hot tiles, her curves seated on top of me like a powerful destiny, her dress in disarray and covering only her belly, her movements and murmurs progressively deeper, darker, more ragged, extending the truth of flesh and of life, over the saturated file cabinets of Editorial Universo. The climactic laments, hers, mine, ours, gave lie to the authority of bureaucracy, the noise of the electric fan, the tedium of the hot summer and the mediocre routine, and filtered out into the air around Calle Lepanto. The city no longer felt like shoes with worn out soles. Now I do feel like I'm at the center of the universe, I thought, and I'm so glad.

I was so happy I completely forgot about the conversation I'd planned, which I'd imagined as an interrogation, but which ended up as a confession. If the office workers of the world did their jobs naked, if, like adam and eve in paradise, they wore no clothes while they answered the phone, filled out forms, signed certificates, and approved records, reality would change direction every half hour. Naked people may want to be wicked, but they never stray far from their innocence. Tailors and dressmakers are the agents of order. But history comes full circle. It's a trick. They say that the serpent made adam and eve lose their innocence and cover themselves. That same serpent made Consuelo and me end up naked in the office and afterward I fell into the trap of the innocent, and I told her everything. My innocence might get me expelled from eden.

It started with a game in the office. She thanked me for my bare feet and painted toenails as a testimony to our complicity, our shared secret. I paraded my bare feet before her, walking around the room, into Don Alfonso's office, across the room to the entrance and back to my desk, I picked up my telephone and began a cruel imitation of Vicente in an imaginary conversation with a potential client. *P* for polish, *T* for toenails, *N* for naked, and here we have an example. If you visit us at our local office on Calle Lepanto my colleague will tell you all about the unforgettable experience of having your toenails painted and my other colleague will be pleased to show you her spectacular thirty-seven-year-old body, round breasts, hard nipples, firm thighs, round hips, a very fine nude, sir, because after all, fine nudity is the backbone of a nation and the honor of our land. Have no doubt.

Consuelo followed my lead. She sat at her desk and observed me as if we were at work, showing great interest in my mad sales pitch to the imaginary encyclopedia purchasers. When I finished, she congratulated me on my sale and the ease with which I had closed the deal, and then she added that Vicente was a good man. That was the hook. And I took the bait. Yes, I told her, I figured you were good friends since I had seen him go into her house one night. Learning that I'd been spying on her, that I was in the Jardinillos and at the tram stop, surveilling her building, like an idiot, to see if she would go in or come out, didn't upset her too much. But when I told her that my jealousy of Don Alfonso had led me there, when I confessed, imbecile that I am, that I was pained by the suspicion that she was the boss's lover, when I said I couldn't help imagining her with him, she stood abruptly, like a train screeching to a halt after someone's pulled the emergency brake, and paradise came to an end. She put on her panties, her dress, her shoes, she warned me to hurry up and get dressed if I didn't want to get locked in the office, she waited, irritated, then locked the door, walked down the stairs, and set off down the street at a blistering pace without a glance in my direction.

Running alongside her, I tried to explain my actions and the fears that precipitated them. I've never had a love affair, I said. I've never been with a woman before, I said. You've become the center of my life, I said. You're wonderful, I said. So beautiful, I said. A gift, I said. The best thing that's ever happened to me, I said. I have no experience, no common sense, no worldliness, I said, and an overly vivid imagination. I'm so sorry if I offended you, I said. It was not my intention but my weakness, my clumsiness, my confusion, I said.

Is it possible to be angry and happy at the same time? As we continued through the Plaza del Carmen, Calle Ganivet, Puerta Real and Carrera de la virgen, she didn't say a word, but I began to notice that she was angry and happy at the same time. She didn't respond to my questions or challenge my explanations. She didn't smile or look at me, but she didn't tell me to be quiet either, or to leave her alone, or to go away. She began to slow down. She put up with my monologue along the Paseo del Salón and the Paseo de la Bomba. We arrived at Transversal de la Bomba, and she let me follow her into her apartment. She kicked off her shoes, got two beers out of the fridge, put them on the coffee table in the living room, and told me to sit down because she had three things to say, and she was only going to say them once.

"One: I'm sorry to have to confess that I'm flattered by your jealousy. Deep down, I'm glad I make you feel this way. Two: do not ever spy on me again or try to control my life. You have no right to know what I do or don't do. I have enough of that with my neighbors. Three: If you have such a rich imagination, use it to put yourself in my place, to understand the world from my point of view. It's going to take a lot for me to forgive you. I'm no one's kept woman. Is that clear?"

"He called you Chelo in the office."

"One more thing. Four: You are an idiot."

Then she came close and kissed me. She had organized her emotions as though they were encyclopedia entries. The attributes of a nation, a biography, and even a human heart can be organized into groups of four. I understood her words, or in any case, I interpreted them as favorable to me. Saying it'll be hard to forgive me means she's willing to give me another chance. I didn't dare ask her any other questions, but I was grateful that she now seemed to feel like sharing some details. She'd replaced her stubborn silence during our walk with a desire to talk. She's known Don Alfonso since she was a girl. He was a friend of her father's. He'd always treated her kindly, and she was grateful, but there was never anything untoward or insinuated in their relationship. Rich playboys are not my type, she said, I prefer idiots. And she added a compliment that made me happy and calmed my jealousy: don't be silly and underestimate yourself. I don't go to bed with the first man who comes along.

Vicente is having a tough time right now, some personal problems, she said. He and his wife aren't getting along. The dark circles under his eyes and the apathy he brings to the office each day aren't just from the unbearably hot sleepless nights. The marriage is failing, and his wife wants to leave him, go back to Madrid to her parent's house. Consuelo has become his shoulder to cry on. Every now and then, they have dinner together and he unburdens himself; she listens, understands, offers advice. She is jealous of her privacy and doesn't want any of this to reach the rumor mill. That's why they meet in secret, without mentioning it in the office. When I saw him entering her building, she was preparing to dress the salad with vinegar, olive oil and the salt from his bitter tears.

Consuelo was happy and sad. I used my imagination to put myself in her shoes. That's a piece of advice my literature professor never offered me, and it's arrived not from the theory of literature but from the lips of an angry woman. But it is great advice for an aspiring writer. You can't limit yourself to amplifying your own fantasies. You have to use your imagination to understand the feelings of others, to live for a moment or two in their hearts. It makes sense that Consuelo was angry. My relationship with her had led me to imagine shameful events, in a shameful era, with shameful people, shameful themes, because I was unable to understand her past, her nature, her heart, her decisions. And my shameful thoughts have also sullied our relationship.

I complain about not knowing enough about my past, the death of my grandfather, family stories about the war. But do I really know my own mother? And my Aunt Rosario? My imagination can't reach into her emotions. The love of my mother and Aunt Rosario, their indulgence of my every whim, has been so completely unconditional since I was born, that I've never felt the need to imagine myself inside their skin. Instead, I've imagined my father's self-doubt, the mayor's arrogance, the motivation behind Pedro el Pastor's defiance and then submission, and Vicente's shoes as he walks through a city of silent calendars and aching feet. But I've never felt the need to put myself in my mother's shoes or those of my aunt. And the truth is the only thing I've been able to imagine about Consuelo is her falling into the arms of a rich playboy.

Vicente needs to make a promise to his wife, to try to understand her. Broken hearts can lead to promises. I made three promises to Consuelo as I started to undress her again. One: I would continue to feel jealous of any man who came near her. Even though I know she's not mine, and she's right, we aren't going to get married, the age difference is insurmountable, and the best outcome would be for us to end up as good friends, with a shared memory of a wonderful summer. All that, but with jealousy too, because life is a contradiction and emotions are never coherent. Two: I would not spy on her any more or try to control what she did or didn't do. And three: I would put my imagination to work to understand her better. And then I added a fourth: I will never forget how lucky I am to work at Editorial Universo, how lucky I am that she noticed me, my glances, my obsessions, and decided to put up with me, how lucky I am to have won the lottery of being chosen.

The memory of our nakedness in the office is a powerful one. I don't think I'll forget it as long as I live. The sun had gone down, and now Consuelo wanted to give me another unforgettable memory. Instead of getting in bed, she spread a blanket on the terrace. Eating and drinking under the open sky are in themselves invitations to joy. Making love under the stars is our return to paradise, with two humble potted geraniums playing the role of the tree of knowledge of good and evil. With the same sincerity I used to confess my sins, I told her about my success in Maracena, and how I inspired people to think about liberty, equality, and fraternity. I told her that I was thinking about getting involved in politics, maybe getting in touch with some of the student groups at the University.

"My literature professor speaks beautifully but he prefers analysis, and now is the time for action."

I rambled on for a while about the situation in this country and how something had to change. Consuelo was worried, she told me to be careful. She reminded me that I have a tendency to be impulsive and that politics in Spain were no joke. The police are even less forgiving than an angry woman. These are dangerous times, she said.

We slept on the terrace. The sun was already up when Consuelo woke me. Fragile shafts of light were beginning to expose our presence. My back was aching, but the night there with Consuelo was worth it. We sought refuge from the impertinence of the new day inside the apartment. At seven the water was still on. We showered. She made breakfast. Consuelo and café con leche, Consuelo and orange juice, Consuelo and toast with olive oil. The radio, laughter, and Consuelo. After listening to a radio commercial, I decided to demonstrate how easily I could now laugh off my jealous anxieties. The commercial was for champagne-cider El Gaitero, not just for New Year's Eve but for summertime too. For those special moments, the ad went, ask for delicious champagne-cider El Gaitero. It's a friendly drink, soft, bubbly, and good for you. Young people prefer it. Adults demand it.

"I don't prefer it. Don Alfonso and adult friends in Torremolinos must demand it."

"Maybe, but they probably prefer French champagne. They can keep their friendly bubbles. And you, don't ever be too soft."

Consuelo's lighthearted laughter brought us even closer together, but she insisted we leave her apartment separately. To avoid gossiping neighbors, it was best to hide our relationship. Women who violate social norms become outcasts, she said. Plus, who knows, there might be some idiot spying on her outside the building or at the Jardinillos tram stop. I took the joke on the chin and a kiss on the lips.

Consuelo had a plan. She would leave first; I'd follow fifteen minutes later. Seemed good to me. And I did not break my promise about spying on her. Poking around is not the same as spying. For the next twenty minutes I opened her wardrobe and verified the organization of her intimacy, the world of her dresses and her shoes. In her lingerie drawer, underneath her bras and panties, I found a record titled *La mauvaise reputation*. I've never heard of the singer, Georges Brassens but I do recognize the name of the man who signed it: "I love you. This is our music, Alberto Toledo, Paris, nineteen fifty-seven."

I closed the drawer and jealousy punched me in the gut, again. It wouldn't be the last time. I'm hopeless. Life is hopeless. I decided to turn the page by inspecting her library. You could tell that she'd studied philosophy and literature in Madrid. I found Ignacio Rubio's *Manual de Literatura*, published by Editorial Universo, and a small press edition of an article that Ignacio wrote about Antonio Machado that I've never even seen. The dedication Ignacio Rubio had written on it made me envious: "To Consuelo, with gratitude for her patience and the things she has taught me. In warm friendship." I imagined the careful collaboration he'd had with Consuelo when he was preparing the book, the delays during the final preparations and the corrections, the phone calls to discuss details, work meetings. It had never occurred to me that a close friendship could exist between Consuelo and my literature professor. But the dedication written on the article was proof.

I plan to borrow Consuelo's books, her memories, and much much more.

⁓

The big news over breakfast at the Café Lepanto that morning was the kidnapping of the Argentine soccer player Alfredo Di Stéfano in Caracas while he was playing for Real Madrid in a tournament in Venezuela. The commotion had altered the tournament, our national life, and the summer routine on Calle Lepanto. Hundreds of news reports, official statements and inquiries were streaming out of Venezuela and around the world. Di Stéfano had been held captive over the weekend, and his release was expected soon.

"They think it was the communists," said one of the medics from the Casa del Socorro.

"On the news they said it was a Venezuelan terrorist group," the widowed barman explained.

"It's their local communists. They've got balls," summed up the bootblack. "They're protesting against the assassination of Julián Grimau."

"The Grimau thing wasn't an assassination, it was a death sentence and execution," said the widowed barman, explaining again.

"You better not make that mistake again, or I'll report you to your friend Don Alfonso," one of the bureaucrats from City Hall warned the bootblack.

"Maybe we should just let him speak." Marcelo didn't look angry; he didn't raise his voice, but the tone of his words was biting. "Because if we don't speak up, we may all die of thirst. You haven't read the newspaper? Yesterday, they opened another dam in Cataluña, this time in Vilanova de Sau. Almost two thousand gallons of water per second for Barcelona. They know how to speak up there, ask for what they need."

I hadn't heard about the new reservoir, and I didn't know anything about the rumors, reports, and denials surrounding Di Stéfano's kidnapping, so I avoided those conversations. Instead, I told Vicente about my trip to Villatoga. I hadn't been home for eight months, since last Christmas. When

Consuelo told me she was going to visit her parents over the weekend, I decided I'd do the same.

A family visit which, including travel time, would only last from Friday afternoon to Sunday evening, seemed a bit ridiculous, especially after having wasted the long holiday weekend of la virgen. But in the end, the heart rules, and my reconciliation with Consuelo had given me the courage to go back to my village. The ways we spend our time can be as improvised as the placement of posters on a student's bedroom walls. But what about Consuelo? Why didn't she take advantage of the holiday weekend? But then I stopped myself, avoiding the impulse to once again poison my thoughts with my vivid imagination. The wasted days of imprisonment by my wild fantasies about Consuelo, Don Alfonso and Vicente were still too recent. So, I decided to imitate her, to visit my family too. I accepted life as it was and went off to Villatoga without another thought. Consuelo left the office on Friday afternoon to catch the train to Madrid. She booked a round-trip sleeper car, so she could arrive back in the office today, Monday, exhausted, beautiful, and punctual.

Villatoga is much closer to Granada than Madrid, but also much further away. Since Christmas, I've been separated from my home by an uncomfortable bus to Jaén, a second, even more uncomfortable bus with an unpredictable schedule to my village, and an existential discomfort that's hard to define. When your life changes, your memories of an earlier time can fuse with an unshakeable feeling of apathy. I love my parents, my Aunt Rosario, and my grandmother, I have no complaints about them at all. But I did feel very distant from the life of the village. If it hadn't been for Consuelo's discipline in visiting her own family each month, I wouldn't have even thought of seeing mine. It would have made more sense for them to come visit me in Granada, to take them walking in the hills around the Alhambra again, to thank my mother for insisting on cleaning the apartment, mending and ironing my clothes, to listen to Aunt Rosario's testy refusal to dress up as a medieval Moorish woman for a tourist photo. It only took one school year, one summer break and one summer job to turn me into a city boy.

So, I was surprised at how happy I was to be back in the streets of

Villatoga. The first feeling was a sudden surge of gastronomic joy. I was a bit nauseous from reading Thomas More's *Utopia* on the bus, the book I'd borrowed from Consuelo. But that disappeared as soon as I set foot in the plaza. After almost a year of eating student sandwiches, cheap tapas, and poorly prepared meals, I couldn't wait to get back to my mother's home-made gazpacho, marinated partridge, and roasts. My stomach led the way as I happily turned down my street, entered my house, my room, and my bed. I was eager to greet the neighbors, and to celebrate my mother's tears of joy, my grandmother's kisses, and my father's silent embrace.

They sent me to surprise Aunt Rosario and invite her to a family dinner. My aunt does not look like Consuelo. I don't know what I was thinking. They have completely different facial expressions, speech patterns, smiles, and silences. I try to think of some similarities that would explain my first impression of Consuelo; maybe the forehead, the nose, I don't know. It's a mystery.

I barely spoke as I devoured my food. Enjoying your favorite dish is an affirmation of self-awareness and of life itself. It's all you need to feel satis-fied, at least for the hour or so while the meal lasts. My mother dominated the conversation and filled me in on the comings and goings in the village. Then, after wolfing down two slices of watermelon for dessert, I began to talk. I spoke about the University, the coming school year, the process for getting my military service deferral, and my work at Editorial Universo. I held forth as if I were a hero returning from an overseas adventure, a man steeped in the literary world of Parnassus and the business of books. But I must not have been very convincing because my Aunt Rosario's only re-sponse was an offer to buy an encyclopedia from me.

I was very tired and had no interest in going out in search of anyone or anything. Sometimes you can leave the house in peace looking for friends; others you're hunting for enemies. I just wanted to walk Aunt Rosario home and come right back. Falling into my bed would reaffirm my home-coming. But there was one more thing. I was still waiting for my mother to surprise me, as she always does. When she came in to say goodnight, she saw me underline a sentence in *Utopia*. She didn't approve of my writing in the book.

"You mustn't damage books."

"I'm not damaging, I'm underlining."

"But you're cheating," she said, as if she had caught me in the act.

"What are you talking about?"

"When you study, you need to memorize things. If you don't work to make the information stick, you won't be able to use it later."

"But I just want to highlight this one sentence."

"You can't carry that book around everywhere. You have to use your brain instead of your pencil." That's my mother and her gift for having an opinion on everything. "Sleep well. We're so happy to see you!"

After breakfast, I offered to help in the store. I always liked interacting with the neighbors, selling them sugar, flour, potatoes, or soap. But my mother said no. That's nonsense! She was not about to see me spend the few hours I had in the village working behind the counter. Better to go for a walk with my father. My father and I obeyed. We walked up the road toward the Fuente de Ciprés. I'd forgotten about our shared silences. His silence next to mine says it all without words. He didn't say that he was happy to be walking with me up the hill in our village, or that he was proud of me for finding a summer job. You have to learn to earn a living with your own hands, I imagined him thinking. He didn't tell me he was happy that I was studying in Granada, or that he dreamed of the day they would hang my graduation photo on the dining room wall, just as my mother had already placed my postcard from Motril on a shelf in the store. He didn't have to say a word. Or if at some point it had been important to speak, it wasn't anymore. Living at a distance had helped me know him better, to understand the things he wasn't saying, that he couldn't put into words.

Near the fountain, we ran into Pedro el Pastor and his flock of sheep. I don't know how old he is; I've never really wondered. We embraced. He was older, shrunken, but his sense of humor was intact. He asked me about the flocks of goats and sheep in Granada, and how they cross through the city navigating stoplights, buses, and tram lines. He offered to roll a cigarette for my father.

"I smoke too," I said.

"Life goes on," Pedro said.

My father nodded and lit his cigarette. The olive grove extended outward, spilling down the side of the hill toward the village and the road to Villacarrillo. The sun was still low on the horizon. From afar, Villatoga looks like a splash of white across the landscape, a picture postcard of placid whitewashed houses. But the reality inside the village is another thing altogether. I didn't need a vivid imagination to know what life is like for the people of Villatoga, their routines and their histories. I didn't dare say anything to Pedro el Pastor about his new dog, or Sergeant Palomares, or the mayor's son. Neither did he. Within an hour, the heat would start to become oppressive. Time to get moving. We said goodbye.

Lunchtime. My mother takes nourishment watching me eat. Just as Pedro el Pastor frets over his flock, my mother frets over food and worries about cheap restaurants, junk food, and poor nutrition. By the time I finished my flan, all I wanted to do was to thank her and head off to my siesta. During our morning walk, I'd wanted to ask my father about the war. Sensing his silence, I decided it was better to wait. I also considered bringing it up during lunch, so that Aunt Rosario and my mother could talk about their family, my grandmother and my father about theirs. Sensing the joy in the women around the table as they watched me dive into a platter of deviled eggs, I again decided to leave it for later. Everything can be left for later.

That afternoon, I had an unfortunate encounter at the bar. And I left that one for later too. The mayor's son and Don Diego's son showed up looking for me when I was smoking a cigarette and having a beer with my friend Pablo Osuna, the cobbler's son. They weren't there by accident. They came looking for me because someone told them I was back. It might have been Mercedes in the tobacco kiosk. The mayor's son had gotten fat. He was dressed like a rich dandy, uglier and stupider than ever and was looking for revenge for that punch I gave him.

"Well, well, well. Look who's here. I can't believe he dared to come out," he said. They'd positioned themselves on the far side of the room, like they were in Western. Instead of pistols, they shot off their mouths trying to impose their bravado on the entire room. "Last Christmas, he didn't even show his face."

"Yeah, and we were so hoping to wish him a Merry Christmas," Don Diego's son threw in.

"He was with his mommy. He was probably afraid. Granada's turned him into a chicken."

I didn't want to make trouble for Pablo. Or for me. The mayor's son was a coward. He'd go running to his father after the first blow. Don Diego's son was tougher, but nothing a beer bottle to the head or a kick in the nuts couldn't fix. I could see Pablo was getting nervous and I asked for the check.

"Can you give us the bill please and include the first round for those two," I told Ernesto, the barman, who was struggling to stay calm.

"For us? Don't even think about it," yelled the mayor's son, taken aback.

"Don't worry about it. You know me, we go way back. And I'm picking up your bill, so you don't have to beg your father for money."

"Say that again and I'll break your face," he threatened.

But his plan had crumbled. He wanted to humiliate me and provoke me into losing my temper. He was trying to make me look ridiculous or create a motive for his father to report me to the Guardia Civil. My first reaction to his insults was an intense desire to beat the shit out of him. But it can wait. I considered Pablo's anxiety, my mother's joy as she set the deviled eggs in front of me, my father's silences … and Consuelo, who would be back from Madrid on Monday morning. No one was going to stop me from getting on Sunday's overnight bus to Granada.

"Thanks Ernesto. Goodbye gentlemen." Even I was surprised by the strength and calm of my voice. It seems that learning the art of selling encyclopedias has instilled in me some self-control and strategic thinking. "Let's go, Pablo. I'll walk home with you. We can go by the church and the convent, smoke a cigarette, and enjoy the cool of the evening and the quiet of the boulevard."

But we didn't follow that plan. Pablo wanted to take the shortest route. We walked straight along the Calle santo domingo. We didn't know if the mayor's beloved boy and Don Diego's son would be waiting to ambush us somewhere, but when you humiliate the enemy, it's always better to be cautious. My dinner, my bed and my *Utopia* were waiting for me. Life in easy installments.

On Sunday, after lunch, my parents and Aunt Rosario walked me to the bus. There they were, the three of them, watching me enter the dilapidated spaceship heading toward the future. For them, the future lies in shopping bags full of cheese, chorizo, olive oil, sausages, my studies, a graduation photo in the living room, a son with a lot of books in his head, some happy grandchildren to come visit them in the village during vacation, a life free from unpleasant surprises, and little else, allowing time to pass without any major misfortune. And me? I spent the bus trip thinking about my relationship to Villatoga. I no longer think of my village with unshakeable apathy, as a place I needed to flee to seek my own destiny somewhere more open, a city where I could search and fight for my own future. That was my turbulent mood a year ago when I planned this trip. But now my village seems like a refuge, a home where I can retreat from each and every kind of hostility. Both your memories and your vision of the future depend on a combination of fiction and personal experience. It's all an exercise in self-preservation. I'm going to dream about Villatoga, my family, my friends. I'm betting on Thomas More and his optimistic vision of the future.

Distracted as I was, daydreaming about my past and the dark circles under Consuelo's eyes, Di Stéfano's kidnapping seemed like a minor event that morning. If the Venezuelan terrorists release him safe and sound, their ploy would go down in history as a masterpiece of political propaganda. The Franco regime uses soccer to pacify the masses, which means soccer is a powerful tool. Watch out for soccer. That's what my literature professor says sometimes on Mondays when he comes into class: you must respect Di Stéfano's goals and Paco Gento's plays. And now, the communists in Venezuela are also using soccer to awaken the masses. An eye for an eye, a tooth for a tooth.

"Hey kid, I'm gonna clean your shoes. It'll just take a second." Manolo the bootblack placed his stool at my feet.

"No, sorry, I have to go up to work." I rose and headed for the door. "Vicente, pay for my coffee, would you? Thanks."

⌒

My literature professor has sent me a letter. He wants me to tell him how my job is going. But this isn't a great moment to answer his questions. I don't know what to say; it would have been better to write to him a few days ago. How am I doing? Well, good and bad, much better, or much worse than expected, with wins and losses that have little to do with work trips, sales calls, and encyclopedia sales. Vicente? Before I met his wife, I was much more certain of who he was: an unhappy man, a good person, a mediocre person, a pedestrian whose shoes pinch his feet. Consuelo? Well, it's anyone's guess Ignacio, because I understand nothing. I can't imagine what I can tell you, what I can explain, or what is going to happen between her and me. It's too much sadness and silence for a letter I'd really like to use to thank you. Thanks, Ignacio, thanks a lot for finding me such a peaceful, simple summer job.

Today, Friday, I went to the cinema. Consuelo practically ordered me to go. It was just like the scene from the movie starring José Luis López Vázquez, where he twists himself in knots trying to impress a beautiful woman with his submissive repetition of "your admirer, your slave, your friend, your servant." I feel like I'm the one constantly saying those same words to Consuelo, while I study, walk around town, meet up with school friends who have come back early for September exams, go to the movies, get myself organized, and cool off. Since she got back from Madrid, she's had this idea that we should cool off our relationship. Just when I thought things were full steam ahead, everything has suddenly become distant and limited.

On Tuesday, I surprised her by showing up at her house with a Black & Decker drill to finally put up the curtain rods. I'm her admirer, her slave, her friend, her servant, armed with the latest model of electric drill. For the last week, construction workers have taken over the apartment next to mine. They wake me up with the noisy hammering of a much larger project, repairing the pyramids of Egypt, for example. The foreman apologizes when I leave for work in the morning.

"Too much noise?"

"Don't worry about it. I have to go into the office early anyway."

"The thing is, if we start much later, it's too hot."

When I saw him with the drill, I remembered the curtains. Be careful with this, my brother brought it for me all the way from Germany, he said, after agreeing to my request and explaining how it worked. He loaned it to me as payback for the blast of morning hymns sung courtesy of his crew's tools. I told him my girlfriend was redecorating her house. We'd be eternally grateful if he could lend us his drill for a few hours. He who sows sympathy, reaps favors. It's easy to do things well if you have the right tools, and the right words. I was doing everything well. I was using my imagination to work my way into Consuelo's soul. I was using my new social skills to surprise her with my dedication and efficiency. In less than half an hour, the curtain rods were installed with no damage to the walls.

Consuelo was amused to see me in the role of a construction worker. I think I might dress you up each day as something different, she said, taking the drill from my hands and kissing me. One day you're my office colleague, the next a construction worker, then a doctor, a priest, a chauffeur, a milkman, the electricity collector, she said. I accepted without complaint. What is a student after all? Someone who hopes one day to disguise himself as something else, so I envisioned myself as a writer, enveloped in Consuelo's arms. Full steam ahead. I buried my face in her hair, searching for her earrings with my lips.

But later, our pillow talk turned tragic. With gentle words, much kindness and care, trying not to disappoint me, wound me, anger me, offend me, or deceive me, Consuelo said that we should cool off our relationship. Some words make bigger holes than a drill. She reminded me of her warnings at the start, of our age difference, my family's feelings, the pain of people criticizing us, the danger to her reputation, my struggle to accommodate an impossible love affair that would distance me from my school friends, from women my own age, from the world that should be my world, the life that should be my life. We mustn't turn our moment of gratification, a beautiful, shared history, into an obsession. It wasn't good for me to come to her house every day, to act as if I were her husband, watering the plants, installing the curtain rods, going out to pick up cigarettes or beer for dinner.

Without wounding me, with kindness, she placed limits on our friendship, and I accepted them, as her admirer, her slave, her friend, her servant, as she rose, naked, and walked across to the bathroom to retrieve the nail polish remover, returned to the bed, took my foot in her hands, and to cool off our relationship, telling me how handsome I am, giving me a kiss, she removed the polish from my toenails, kissing me again, pleading with me to understand, she was really only thinking about me. Or thinking about the two of us, but in a potential future of friendship. She began to talk about looking toward our tomorrows, and I started to get irritated with the whole tomorrows thing. What's the big deal about tomorrows? Just when you think the future is now, suddenly you have to start thinking about to-morrows. Consuelo doesn't want me to be distressed if we bump into each other in the street. She doesn't want to interrupt my studies or disrupt my normal existence.

She didn't want to wound, offend, or disappoint me. She wanted me to get my life back. I should call other friends, go to the movies, go for walks, live my own life five or six evenings a week. She wasn't breaking up, just adding a little ice to the shower and the electric fan in the office. It made more sense to meet up every now and then to talk about books, have dinner and some laughs, and yes, make love. A woman of my age cannot permit herself the luxury of losing a lover, she said. But we need to do things right, she insisted, and she gazed at me, kissed me, and ravished me. Pillow talk is something you learn to do. You can also learn that it's possible to make love with sadness, as if each embrace were a loss, each kiss a premonition of distance, each caress a farewell, the sheets a platform at the train station. Desire doesn't always surge with joy, its natural ally. It can also arrive with confusion, fear, melancholy, and bitterness, and with inescapable facts of life like clouds, dead leaves, and autumn. You can learn about so many things in bed. And, out of fear, you accept them. The León who left Consuelo's apartment was young, weak, and pacified. He hadn't been blown away, but he had taken several bullets. He wouldn't protest about the treasure he'd lost, but he wanted to make very sure he could hold onto the small prize still left to him. A heart ripped in two, then mended.

Write, read, walk, and go to the movies like an admirer, a slave, a friend, a servant; that seems to be my new mission. The movie *Atraco a las tres*, a comedy by the director José María Forqué, is playing again at the Cine

Aliatar. I didn't see it when it was first on during the school year. With my mind set on Operation Discipline and Cooling Off, it seemed more appropriate to watch a movie than to immerse myself in Russian literature. In the end, I laughed more than I thought I would at the movie's protagonist, Fernando Galindo, a bank clerk. Played with hilarious obsequity by the actor José Luis López Vázquez, he plots with his downtrodden colleagues to rob their own bank as revenge against the owners. The would-be bank robbers are bumbling, naive, and humble, like Spain. They try to think about their tomorrows, but they end up portraying our present, the reality of our needy nation, where even our dreams are impoverished and hope is nothing more than a tentative friend, a dripping faucet.

In this country, the powers that be try to close the door to the future, but they've failed and it's still open just a crack, enough for a bit of hope to filter through. In the movie, you get a glimpse of that hope in the modest list of needs the would-be robbers draw up when considering how much money they'll get from the heist. The actress Gracita Morales, as a bank clerk, deploys her trademark screechy voice to list her humble hopes: enough cash to buy six pairs of pantyhose, pay off the installment plan on her television, buy a new spring coat, and purchase a hearing aid for the deaf housekeeper in her building. Of course, there's the one person in the group who goes for broke and asks for enough money to buy a beach house in Torremolinos, in the hope of spending summers far from the city and close to Don Alfonso and all the foreign tourists, the French, or the franchutes, as Manolo the bootblack likes to call foreigners whether they were born in Paris, London or Stockholm.

I'm going to tell Consuelo that sacrificing all of our upcoming afternoons for the sake of tomorrows is absurd. I should turn myself into a professional thief so I can hold up the bank of time and live life without losing a second. I see no difference between "tomorrows" and tomorrow afternoon. Anyway, the only way to get to tomorrows is with easy installments by the day, like Sunday afternoon, Monday afternoon and Tuesday afternoon. September, for example, is a perfect month to buy a tv or an encyclopedia which you can enjoy, minute by minute, hour by hour while you pay your installments. Isn't the future more than just an encyclopedia or a tv? Of course. But the point is you have to start enjoying it today. It's absurd to sacrifice the present so that in ten years we can be good friends. I don't accept the arguments about our age difference, obsessive gratification, my family's feelings or those of my classmates. But I obey. I read, I write, I go to the movies, I leave my weekends open. I postpone lecturing Consuelo about tomorrows until Monday, then until the following Friday. But I'm going to tell her what I think, though it will be as her admirer, her slave, her friend, her servant.

If you're paralyzed by the fear of tomorrow's disaster, the disaster will only come find you today. So instead, I decided to have a laugh with José Maria Forqué's movie about amateur bank robbers, an apt reflection of the cowed Spain we live in today. But the distraction didn't erase my unease. With gentle words, with kindness, without offending, Consuelo has invoked a tomorrow that condemns me to disaster five days of every week. I don't doubt her, and I'm not going to bring up any more suspicions about Don Alfonso. I've used my imagination to put myself in her position and understand her fears, her unease, her fatigue. But I do want to talk about it, to debate this dilemma of tomorrows, to defend my vision of a happy future in easy or not-so-easy installments.

My vision of a happy future in easy or not-so-easy installments! What a concept! This journal is turning out to be a real literary workshop. I organize my desk, open my notebook, begin to write, remember my professor's advice, try to be intelligent, exhaust my imagination, deploy irony, step outside myself then dive back in, practice introspection, search for adjectives that build my capacity for observation and fill up the pages with writing. I'm a diligent student, but I'm afraid it will be impossible for me to show off my improved writing skills to Ignacio Rubio. It would be wrong, reckless, and indiscreet to let the eyes of others observe my world with Consuelo. There's only one person who has the right to read this story: Consuelo herself. Maybe that's a strategy to explain myself, to help her understand what I feel.

Look at me in the mirror, Consuelo. Let's make fun of me together. What do you see? A pedant, a braggart, a fool masquerading as an intellectual, a victim of Russian novels, of poets, of philosophers, an idiot who tries to measure up to an ideal, but who only writes worthless drivel because he's powerless to describe the only thing that really interests him: I love you; I've fallen in love with you.

I'm tired. I'll leave the rest of this story for tomorrow. A twist in the plot is crucial if you want a novel, and a life, to be successful. As I left the movie theater, I bumped into Vicente and his wife. She's very beautiful, very dark, very different from the type of woman I imagined as the perfect companion for my maestro in the art of selling encyclopedias. I had imagined an older woman, heavier, less striking. Vicente introduced us, we said hello, we spoke about the movie, and we said goodbye. But that's not the end of the tale, because, being an amateur spy, I decided to follow them, a gangster "a la española." I wasn't ready to go home and lock myself in my apartment. My cooling off with Consuelo had made solitude a fearful thing. I needed to find some entertainment so I wouldn't have to go home right away. And as a result, I now know where Vicente lives. I'll write about it tomorrow after I finish the letter I still owe to Ignacio Rubio. This much is true, these confessions are going to take on a whole new tone. My colleague's life is full of surprises. I'm going to erase the noun *mediocrity* and replace it with the adjective *lucky*.

~⊙~

Vicente's wife liked the movie. Vicente liked it too. But more than the movie itself, he seemed to like that his wife enjoyed it. A couple's thing. He saw things through her eyes, laughed through her lips, shook my hand through her hand. It wasn't exactly him, but the illusion of being with her. What a surprise, he said, it's good to see you. He must have been glad that we bumped into each other in such favorable circumstances. For two months I've been sharing trains, buses, hostels, and an office with him, but I hardly know anything about his wife. The little detail I do have is from Consuelo. Given that Vicente's in the middle of a matrimonial crisis, it must have been a relief for him to play the role with his wife of a normal, happy couple enjoying a Friday evening stroll, a glass of beer and a movie at the Cine Aliatar.

117

He introduced us. León, meet my wife, Marisa. Marisa, this is León, a colleague from the office. Vicente was a bit stingy with his introduction. He could have said, León, this is my wife, a dark-haired beauty with her tresses pulled back in a tight ponytail, very pretty, as anyone can easily see, much more vibrant and taller than me, with large eyes full of smokey light, and Marisa, this is León, an office colleague we've run into by chance, a collaborator in selling encyclopedias who can hardly believe what he's seeing. I loved meeting Marisa, and Marisa loved *Atraco a las tres*. The bewilderment of the good-hearted thieves who are swindled in the end was nothing compared to my own confusion. She had the classic beauty of southern Spanish women as depicted in paintings by Julio Romero de Torres, but her s's danced on her lips in a completely different way than ours do in the South.

Marisa's fashion sense didn't jibe with her husband's beige jacket, polyester pants, and shoes. Her large, red, youthful handbag draped like a smile over her purple dress, making her look more like a university student than the wife of a dull office worker. Vicente seemed happy. He was celebrating his own happiness and my awkwardness. We commented on a few scenes, praised the actors' performances, and when we reached the corner of Calle Recogidas and Puerta Real, said goodnight. As I watched them walk away, I felt an abyss open up inside me as I started to think about Consuelo's cooling off idea, and Jacobo's presence in my apartment. My roommate had just returned to Granada to take his Natural Law exams. When you're in a state as fragile as mine, it's better to be alone than in unwelcome company. So, I decided to write the next scene of that comical, criminal movie: I began to follow Vicente and Marisa. After all, exploring themes of crime fiction is part of a writer's education.

They followed Calle Acera del Casino to the tree-lined promenade Carrera de la virgen. The evening was humming with activity. It was easy to disappear among the strolling crowds, and I kept my distance without losing sight of them. I froze when they stopped to read the billboard on the Teatro Isabel la Católica, then maneuvered behind another couple when Vicente and Marisa turned and started toward the County Council office. Marisa's head was nestled against Vicente's shoulder as they started down

118

the Carrera. The gesture of affection upset me all over again. Who knows what goes on inside a marriage, the ups and downs of a relationship, the fabric of their day-to-day commitments, the cause of a crisis, a breakup, or a reconciliation. If Consuelo was really worried about the emotional distress of our friend, she could dial down her concern. That head resting on Vicente's shoulder looked more like peace than war. There seemed to be no danger of abandonment any time soon.

They stopped again at the Cine Madrigal to read the billboards. They moved from cinema to cinema, just because Marisa really loved going to the movies. From Monday to Friday, her husband belonged to Editorial Universo. He distributed knowledge and information about the big wide world to mayors, teachers, farm workers, parish priests, and the Guardia Civil. But when the clock in the office gave its gift—seven in the evening wrapped up in a weekend—Vicente belonged to his wife. He strolled with her, and they went to the movies, where they enjoyed the love stories, the farces about regular folk, the bad guys with pistols, and the histories of kings and vampires, all promoted with colorful posters on the billboards. It was then that I understood why Vicente always seemed lighter on Fridays. He had the same jacket, the same shoes, the same aching feet, but he left his briefcase behind, and he was a little happier. Instead of going home, he met his wife in a café or at a movie theater.

Vicente belongs to Marisa. Who do I belong to now? To Consuelo. Following Vicente was, in a way, like following Consuelo, to extend the world of our office and our conversations across the city. Vicente was the friend I had seen go into her apartment, the colleague who greeted her every morning from Monday to Friday; he formed part of the universe that brought me close to her, and following him lets me thaw, from a distance, the chill that she's trying to impose. Following Vicente and his wife was a way of maintaining the fiction of an existence centered on Consuelo. My literature professor says dialogs that are too profound or philosophical can become obstacles. They make normal characters seem less believable Marisa's appearance makes my portrait of Vicente—the mediocre office work—implausible. Just two days ago, when we visited Guadix, I could barely contain my laughter when the pharmacist who'd called us refused to buy an encyclopedia, even after a brilliant, hour-long exposition about the *C* in chemistry, the *L* in laboratory, and the *P* in prospectus. Apparently, the contraindications outweighed the benefits, and Vicente ended the meeting looking like a poor man with aching feet. Not even Manolo the bootblack could put a shine on that disaster. But tonight, Vicente was walking like a man with a treasure, the owner of a safe-conduct pass that would protect him from any calamity. Marisa was like a just, intimate, and unbreakable shield protecting Vicente from any and all threats.

During any surveillance operation, it's a liability to get lost in your thoughts, whether they're superficial or profound. You can't follow two suspects when your eyes are turned inward and your head flees to a corner of your heart. Distracted by my worries about Consuelo, I didn't notice the couple had moved on, no longer in front of the Cine Madrigal. Fortunately, I spotted them again quickly near the virgen de las angustias. I followed them, camouflaging myself behind the banana palms, until we got to the Paseo del Salón. There, it was easy to go into the Jardinillos and hide behind the aviary in front of the library. No one would see me there. The birds were enjoying the darkness, resting on artificial branches from their day job as public birds. I was enjoying the darkness and a break from my spycraft under cover of the night. Vicente and Marisa were enjoying a long kiss in the dark. They'd paused in this dark corner of the city to act like besotted teenagers without a room. If I were a detective, I would make the following note in my report to Consuelo: Vicente is fooling you, there is no emotional crisis in his life. In my life, yes, but not in his.

From there, they crossed the Río Genil on the Puente de los Escolapios. Following them there would be risky; footsteps on the bridge would echo through the night and all they'd need to do was turn their heads and I'd be discovered. Vicente knows where my house is, so it'd be difficult to explain away my appearance behind them as a coincidence. Any excuses would be ridiculous. Oh, I just happened to be here, at the scene of the crime, because I remembered there was something from the office that I needed to tell you. Don't forget to call Antonio, the mechanic from Maracena, on Monday. Or, oh, I just happened to be here because I like this part of

Granada, where sometimes a stranger will approach you in the park and invite you to join him on one of the benches and chat about life. But don't worry, I haven't seen a thing, I didn't see Marisa's head resting on your shoulder, I didn't notice how you paused in the most secret corner of the Jardinillos to share passionate kisses like two clandestine lovers. Crazy, unjustifiable, pathetic explanations. It's better just to avoid mistakes, let them cross the river while I observe their movements from the other side, then pick up the thread of my pursuit from there. They turned onto the Paseo de Violón heading toward the Sociedad de Tenis.

Following someone through a city is sort of like reading philosophy. You follow each step of the argument, then something catches you by surprise. You stop, you're confused, you try to clarify, then you reorient yourself, and set off again. But you're always at the mercy of foreign thinkers, whether it's Plato, saint agustin, Descartes, or Kant. A pursuit is like required reading. You have to keep going, to persist, though you pause when there's an interruption, and then you take off running when the chase is back on. I waited patiently until Vicente and Marisa entered the dark undeveloped plots of land south of the river. Then I raced across the bridge like a fugitive, and in my rush, I caught the humid scent of the Genil, a ribbon of water that bisects the sand.

As they pass through Granada, the Genil and Darro Rivers have more letters in their names than water between their banks. There are times during the year when the two rivers fill and surge and party like bad boys to justify all those letters. At those times, the water rushes with the fury of a thunderstorm down from the Sierra Nevada mountains, causing floods. But mostly these rivers are idle and sleepy as a siesta. If I were a classical poet, and I had to come up with a human embodiment of the Rio Genil, I'd choose Don Alfonso, with his mustache, his slicked back hair, and his affable charm. He's more attentive to his friends than to his business. People always seem to invest more energy in examining the lives of others than their own; we celebrate their failures and suffer from their successes. There isn't a neighbor in this world who doesn't monitor who's going up the stairwell, who's going down, who's going in Consuelo's apartment and what can be heard behind her walls. I'm lost in my thoughts again, and while they're accurate and true, they're not at all convenient as I pursue my colleague and his wife through the night.

Just before they got to the Sociedad de Tenis, Vicente and Marisa turned left into a dark alley. No people, no trees, just high walls along the length of the street. To continue my pursuit here would be mad, an act of blatant self-destruction that would ruin my last month at Universo, and my coexistence, in the office at least, with Consuelo. I would rather lose track of my quarry than be discovered. I let them disappear into the shadows and lit a cigarette. I counted to thirty, added another five seconds just to be safe, then I threw away the cigarette and followed them into the alley. Maybe I'd catch sight of them again when I came out the other end.

But no. The long walls ended, and the black night was empty. Music from a street festival filtered out of the darkness. It was coming from some houses at the other end of one of the empty lots. I knew it was inside the city limits because I could still see the lights of the Barrio del Zaidín. I'd been to that neighborhood three or four times to visit a classmate who used to live there. It was hard going walking through the half-finished streets and shrub-choked empty lots interspersed with small family gardens. But I refused to give up and followed a narrow path through thickets of scrub toward the music, heading away from the more developed area as I followed the sound. Maybe Marisa and Vicente had decided to go dancing for a while before heading home. The buzz of a nighttime street festival is tempting for lovers. That's what I thought anyway, but it was another trick of my imagination, pure poetry, because as soon as I got closer to the houses, I unexpectedly picked up the tracks of my victims. They were walking down a brightly lit street to the right of one of the few paved roads in this area. They were a long way away and I ran after them like a rat, scuttling from shadow to shadow through the city. I was lucky. I didn't trip on a rock or fall in a ditch. No mishaps impeded my mad dash. I was also lucky because I got there just in time to see them go into a building. Vicente opened the door, ushered his wife through, and disappeared inside behind her.

Calle Comandante Valdivia, number three. From this building Vicente walked out each morning to go to the office or to Consuelo's apartment. It was here that he hid Marisa, the protagonist of a false marital crisis, the woman you would least imagine in Vicente's kitchen, shower, or bed. Despite his desire and efforts to go unnoticed in everything except his work, I now knew where he enjoyed his private life. My adventure as a literary bad guy who follows his victim, or as a fictional cop who pursues his suspect, had culminated in complete success. I'd crossed half the city following a couple without being discovered. What an achievement! I decided to celebrate and headed to the street festival.

The music led me to the Sociedad Hípica, the high-end equestrian center that doubled as a concert venue. The sound of the Dúo Dinámico singing their popular song: "Quince años tiene mi amor, le gusta tanto bailar el rock," was escaping from behind the Center's wall and cypress trees. A couple was making out on the street corner. The gatekeeper invited me inside. Don't bother buying a ticket, he said, I'll sneak you in. I thanked him but was suddenly afraid of inserting myself into such an unfamiliar atmosphere. Enough investigating for one night. I'll leave the chapter about the young rube fascinated by upper-class leisure for another time. I asked the gatekeeper how to get back to the city center, this time along a road with streetlights, and I headed home.

It was a smart move. Five minutes later a lightning bolt split the night. The sky thundered and warned that rain was finally on its way. Things happen when you least expect them. Hopefully, it signaled the end of the drought, the water rationing, and the oppressive heat of this dense summer. Caught up in the movie and my pursuit, I'd failed to notice the clouds gathering above my head. Things build up right in front of us and we don't notice, or we're incapable of interpreting the signs. Struggling through the tangled undergrowth of life, we lack the time and the wisdom to notice a hidden toad, a dead bird behind a hedge or the good-luck gecko. As I was crossing the Plaza de Mariana Pineda the skies opened. By the time I got home I was soaked and immersed in thought about a song. "Quince años tiene mi amor" as the Dúo Dinámico sing. Your love may be fifteen, but mine is thirty-seven, and you can't really say her face is rosebud pink like the girl in your song. Is there a problem with that? Yes, a big one. Consuelo's right. These are not good times for a boy of twenty to forge a formal relationship with a woman of thirty-seven. If neighbors, parents, professors, fellow students, and co-workers found out, it would be a full-fledged scandal. Although, taking advantage of a pretty, capricious fifteen-year-old girl, delicate as a flower, seems like a much bigger sin, to me. She may be the star that shines its light on the Dúo Dinámico when the sun goes down and the beautiful people are dancing at the Sociedad Hípica, but fifteen is too young to be out that late at night.

~⊙~

As soon as I walked in the door, Jacobo started going on about a weekend excursion. And in the end, I said ok, fine, just so I could escape into my bedroom for the night to write up my experiences as a gumshoe on the streets of Granada, pursuing a couple past movie theaters and through vacant lots. He barely gave me time to dry myself off and change out of my wet clothes before he announced his perfect plan for Sunday. All Jacobo's plans are perfect. He always organizes the best experiences, with the best companions, and the most interesting circumstances with such intensity that it's impossible to say no. During my first months in Granada, he dragged me from one event to another with unshakeable conviction. It was more the life of a law student than one in philosophy and literature. Eventually, I learned how to turn down his invitations without offending him, and I ended up accepting one out of every five adventures, fiestas, movies, lectures, plays, pool halls, or other excursions. So, since it was September and I hadn't seen Jacobo all summer, and Consuelo had given me leave in the form of an order to distance myself for the whole weekend, I said yes. Ok then, let's go to the river.

My roommate had engineered an excursion to the Sierra Nevada with Mariví, his girlfriend, and her very cute cousin, Elena. Everything had been conjured up to make it the best, the happiest day ever. Let me sum it up, he said. One: it's not as hot outside anymore. Two: it's been raining, and the swimming holes along the Genil are brimming with clear water. Three: Mariví's parents are the owners of the Pastelería Pintor Velázquez bakery, so she's going to prepare a picnic basket filled with delicious sandwiches, ham and cheese rolls, and pastries. Four: since he has to go to mass

124

with his parents at nine anyway, we don't have to get up early. We can take the noon tram. Five: the noon tram will take us on an amazing journey through mountain gorges into the heart of the Sierra and drop us off next to the swimming holes on the river, to enjoy our food and our companions. Without a doubt, the girls will charm us with their heavenly bathing suit-clad bodies. The bikini beaches of Torremolinos don't even come close. Six: Jacobo was sure it wouldn't rain, it'd already rained a lot, and Sunday would be sunny. Seven: Elenita, Marivi's cousin, was starting at the University this fall in philosophy and literature, and she was very eager to meet me. One, two, three, four, five, six, seven, plus don't be stupid, he said, don't wreck my plan, plus I need you to take care of the cousin for me, plus you'll definitely be glad you went, plus you could fish too, plus thank you very much, plus I knew you would do it.

I already knew Marivi. She was short and dark, with a face as sweet as the confections baked in her family's shop, a perfect match for Jacobo. She embraced all of Jacobo's plans with enthusiasm, and then did everything possible to make them work. When she appeared in the station at quarter to twelve, she wore an expression of joy and a pair of modern navy-blue pants, and she brought with her a basket full of parcels from the Pastelería Pintor Velázquez and a cousin full of ideas about me. Marivi had explained in detail that her boyfriend's roommate is a true intellectual, a devourer of books, a student of philosophy and literature tirelessly devoted to becoming a writer, the next Cervantes. My best way to escape Jacobo's constant invitations is to invent a schedule full of vague and difficult writerly tasks, so he ends up imagining that my vocation consists of closeting myself away in a constant struggle with adjectives and the profundities of being. Jacobo passes along these musings unfiltered to Marivi. So, he introduced me to Elena as if he were granting her an audience with Don Miguel de Unamuno.

Elena is very pretty. She's taller than her cousin and not as sweet, her cheekbones are as chiseled as a work of modern architecture. Her eyes observe and react, her mouth speaks, smiles, debates, and together her features combine into a dignified and distinctive beauty. I got up this morning thinking that the excursion would be a bit hellish. When your head's in another place, another room, another bed, thinking of flowerpots, water pipes, and another body, it's hard to be friendly to those around you, to participate in the conversations and enjoy a picnic in the countryside. My sorrow was confirmed as soon as we got to the Cruz de los Caídos, at the end of Jardinillos where the tram to the Sierra starts and right next to Transversal de la Bomba, where Consuelo lives. She's nearby, not far from the banana palms, the stone columns with chains that adorn the Cruz, the waterless pool where the boys play soccer, and the platform where Jacobo and I sit on a bench next to other expectant travelers, waiting for Mariví and her cousin to arrive. Jacobo is a prisoner of his enthusiasm, and I of my ruminations about Consuelo.

Elena's arrival improved my mood. It wasn't like I swooned at her feet, or forgot about Consuelo, but it was pretty easy to play the role that Mariví had written for me. After the introductions and some opening jokes, I launched directly and with gusto into project Unamuno, ready to display my erudition by leaping across topics ranging from the natural sciences to the mysteries of the soul, from the secrets of verse to strategies for the study of philosophy and literature. I was careful not to offer practical advice. I didn't speak about the dance of course selection, which classes to avoid, which ones were easy, so-so or a cakewalk. I didn't reveal which were the easy or tough professors or how to steal books from the department or from the library, or strategies for copying an exam. I didn't recommend any of the bars that surround the department; each with its own clientele and atmosphere. I took the high road. It seemed better to focus my energy on more transcendental topics, such as the future of the Spanish University, the rivalry between Humanities and Sciences, the debate between reason and faith, and between the timelessness of the Russian novel and the mission of today's youth in a nation as sad, cowed, and backward as our own. As I write this, I realize that irony doesn't always fit. It's easy to add a touch of humor to my stories about exams, the bars in the literature department, or encyclopedia sales. But Spain's situation today, and Consuelo's new distancing and weekly schedule for cooling off, aren't a joke.

The conversation held up through our journey on the tram and our snacks at the swimming hole. You're still the total intellectual, murmured Jacobo, as he geared up for his joke. But at least you're a bit less pedantic.

It does you good to have these kinds of conversations with a woman in a bathing suit. After making his little wisecrack, he disappeared with Mariví into the woods around a bend in the river. He thought I was still that shy student from Villatoga, incapable of staying calm in the presence of a woman. The theme fed all his teasing during my first year at school. A nervous, tongue-tied, and inept lion among lionesses. A León Egea without a mane.

Jacobo was pleased that his plan was unfolding perfectly. A great day with great food, great company and great weather. Elena is very pretty. Her long legs and breasts imprisoned in her bathing suit asserted themselves with authority each time she got in and out of the water. I swelled with pride to see how intensely she focused on my words, scrambling to keep up with our serious conversation. She's only a year younger than I am, but her childlike respect for wisdom remains intact. She hasn't yet learned to distinguish between voices and echoes, wise men and con men. It's fun to play the role of the experienced student.

What Jacobo didn't suspect was that I enjoyed my sudden intellectual prestige more than Elena's body. When he and Mariví disappeared into the woods, they were children playing a game. With an air of condescension and superiority, I imagined their maneuvers; an embrace, two kisses, three caresses, four refusals, no, no, watch that hand, stop, five promises for bright tomorrows, and Jacobo, patient but about to explode, becomes the heir to the Pastelería Pintor Velázquez, after an engagement, of course, and a wedding, god willing. These were my first feelings of condescension. Normally I'm consumed by inferiority or anger. Elena was sitting next to me; her body was remarkable. Two months ago, I would have been flustered just talking to her, sensing her legs close to me, her arms, the moistness of her swimsuit. But now I have the heart of an experienced man, thanks not to last year's classes but to my memories of Consuelo, the image of her in the shower or in bed, the way she would seize me and then abandon herself to me, the way she would entrap me with things that were beyond any quotidian game or courtship.

I hated to admit that Consuelo was right. Her house had become a bubble in which I could forget reality, a ship isolated from the rest of the world. Ageless, with no thoughts of the future, with eyes only for our own intimacy and nakedness, caring only about a shared pleasure so recently discovered, I poured myself into her, I locked myself up with her, abandoning all my other responsibilities and ties. And I missed the authority and wisdom of her age. Playing the role of Elena's teacher didn't appeal to me. Feeling Consuelo's power over me did, I hungered to be trapped in her web. The expression pussy-whipped is not very poetic. But I have to admit that I'm pussy-whipped by a woman seventeen years older than me. I don't care about the distinctions between love and sex, what's appropriate or inappropriate, possible or impossible, sensible or irrational. Elena is great, but I don't feel like being anything but a respectful gentleman with her. I don't need to try anything except to keep up the intellectual tone of the conversation. As I observed her legs, bronzed from the sun at a pool or beach somewhere, as I felt the presence of her body separated by a short distance and a few well-chosen words, I also knew that she would never become the object of any nocturnal masturbations.

"Should we stop for a beer somewhere before everyone goes home?" When we stepped off the tram in Granada, Jacobo was not ready to call it a day. Mariví agreed and sought Elena's agreement with her eyes. "It feels like we still have a lot to talk about."

"I'll buy. I know a bar on Calle Lepanto that serves the best tuna sandwiches in Granada." I was thinking it would be good for Marcelo, the widowed waiter, to see me with my friends. "Lunch was great but swimming in the river made me hungry again."

The bar was very quiet. There were two couples in their Sunday best, and a disoriented French tourist seated at the bar. No sign of the usual faces, those coffee and beer fans who arrived on weekdays from the Casa de Socorro, City Hall, and the office buildings nearby. Marcelo was working to keep up the weekday energy of the bar, with help from Manolo the bootblack, who, as soon as he saw us come in, made a beeline for Jacobo. My roommate didn't protest since the clay and mud puddles of the Sierra were noticeably persecuting the dignity of his shoes.

"Hey, where have you guys been?" Manolo was eager to justify the necessity and difficulty of his job. "It looks like you just came out of the jungle, right? Since León is the king of the jungle."

"Almost. We were at El Charcón," said Jacobo, settling into Manolo's efforts while I went to order our sandwiches.

"It's a shame to go to the Sierra in these nice shoes. They're top quality." He raised his head and nodded toward Mariví. "I think I know you, Miss."

"Me?"

"You're Alberto Salas' daughter, the owner of Pastelería Pintor Velázquez, right?"

"Yes, that's right."

"I've known your father since you were a little girl. I shine his shoes three times a week. And the other señorita, is she from Granada?"

"Of course, that's my cousin." Mariví was enjoying playing lady of the manor.

"What's your father's name?"

"Pedro Salas," Elena said. She was much shyer than her cousin.

"The notary? I work with him too. I know his shoes like the back of my hand."

When Manolo finished the dominical purification of Jacobo's shoes, he came for me. I declined. I was wearing sandals; it didn't make any sense to shine them. But in Manolo's philosophy, shoes and sandals were all the same, especially when worn by two young men accompanying girls from such well-off families. And it goes without saying that decent young ladies deserve respect, he was telling me, and that he knew their parents well, that he was the kind of person who watched out for his friends and his friends' daughters, that it would never even occur to him to question my good intentions or those of my friend, that he trusted me, but ... that, well, well, well, that river, that mud, those shoes. Boys are always careless, and young ladies today put on pants and go wild. But, he said, we're friends aren't we, so no problems. I could stay right where I was on the barstool finishing my tuna sandwich, barefoot, while he took care of shining up my sandals, which were of significantly lower quality than the sandals of a law student but deserving of respect nonetheless.

And that's what he did. It seemed best not to resist him. The widowed barman didn't interfere but sentenced me to a wry grin that lasted several minutes even as he collected the bill from the disoriented French tourist.

I'd never learn, I'd never be able to defend myself from Manolo the boot-black. I looked at Elena and Mariví, I put on my clean sandals, I paid the bill and said farewell to the Café Lepanto until the next time, or until the next assault by the bootblack. His insinuations about our intentions and the need to show respect for the Salas family were as false as Jacobo's gentlemanly behavior. Once out on the street, Jacobo and Mariví conspired for me to walk Elena home, and don't come back to the apartment for as long as possible please. Jacobo had no intention of leaving things for any tomorrows. Good intentions are not incompatible with payments on the easy installment plan, credit, and an advance on your paycheck. Despite this city full of catholics, church bells, prying neighbors and questioning bootblacks, Jacobo was determined to give the future a little shove to help things along.

I walked with Elena up the Gran Vía de Colón until we got to the Plaza del Triunfo and came out onto the Avenida de Calvo Sotelo, a beautiful boulevard lined with lush banana palms. As I spoke to Elena about the University, about my work at a prestigious publishing house, I was thinking about how I'd be coming back to this spot very soon. There's a train station not far from Elena's house, and Vicente and I had set up a meeting there for the next day with two railway workers interested in the encyclopedia. It would be the same area but a very different kind of walk, no discussion of literature, no fantasies about my role as an expert at Editorial Universo, no imagining that I'd be turning into Miguel de Unamuno or Miguel de Cervantes. And no Elena with her admiration, her affection, her skirt, her legs, and her cheekbones.

"Those trousers look good on Mariví. But I like your skirt better."

"That's my father. He doesn't like me to wear trousers."

Your imagination can often get ahead of itself. It captures what will happen tomorrow or the next day and lets you see it today, and you enjoy those things in a way that makes their subsequent reality a simple repetition. Did I imagine myself with Elena, on a future Sunday evening, embracing, strolling hand in hand along the Gran Vía and Calvo Sotelo? Did I foresee that future, a formal engagement, this traditional gesture of walking her home? If the daughter of a pharmacist can marry a farm worker like my father, then why couldn't I marry the daughter of a notary? But no, definitely no. I knew I was coming back soon to this boulevard of palm trees and houses, but it would be a completely different situation and with Vicente, not Elena. All I could think about was the office, the meeting with the railway workers, and my chance to be alone with Consuelo. I was thinking about my way back to Transversal de la Bomba.

Despite all that, I confess that I felt a strange chill go up my spine when Elena opened her front door, kissed me quickly on the lips, and disappeared inside. Her joy and my bewilderment exploded like a silent detonation in the middle of the street.

~⌒~

Vicente was tired and instead of walking, he wanted to catch the bus to the Plaza de la Caleta, near the train station. Plus, it was going to start raining any moment. This he pronounced as an expert on city weather. Farewell drought, soaking September is finally here. Raindrops splatter against the office windows, sketching the visages of unknown visitors. It's strange to work in the office without the whir of electric fans. It feels like something's missing from the phones, the conversations with potential targets, Vicente's gestures, my glances toward Consuelo, the stalled hands of the clock on the wall. The boss is about to return, his door will open, and change will begin at Editorial Universo, in the city, and in my life. Any day now, the streets will lead me only to campus, to my university routine. My priority for this school year will be to ensure summer shifts smoothly into fall, merging Consuelo and my studies, desire and routine. An impossible task. I have to make sure that Consuelo's distancing project doesn't become permanent.

Another strange development is the new atmosphere at the Café Lepanto. The calendar in the bar is still suspended on April nineteenth, nineteen-sixty, but the number of clients has multiplied at the end of August, nineteen sixty-three. The public employees, the office workers and the medics are back, breaking the spell of those obliged to work in the city during the summer. I knew there'd be a lot of umbrellas and sweaters in the Café Lepanto this morning, but the crowd at the bar and the widowed barman's rush to get the coffees and hot toast to the tables was a surprise. Of course, Marcelo still found time to tease me.

"Well, here comes our young wolf in sheep's clothing. That's quite a girlfriend you have, beautiful, tall, and rich."

I tried to explain to Vicente that Elena wasn't my girlfriend, but the cousin of my roommate's girlfriend. No luck. The widowed barman's definition has become the catchphrase of the morning. Life needs to be beautiful, tall, and rich. Good business deals are beautiful, tall, and rich. A great vacation and an encyclopedia are as dazzling as a woman who is beautiful, tall, and rich. It doesn't matter if she's blonde or brunette, as long as she smiles at us like a woman who is beautiful, tall, and rich. Honestly, I don't know why I brought my friends to the Café Lepanto. Maybe I just wanted to give them a glimpse into a small part of my prestigious editorial job, which I'd been lying about all day. Or maybe I just needed to show the residents of Calle Lepanto, the occupants of our office building, and Marcelo that I had another life beyond my miserable existence as an intern selling encyclopedias on the installment plan. The only thing I hadn't considered was the possibility that someone would tell Consuelo I had a girlfriend. That's the only thing that worried me when Vicente started teasing me as well. The only thing. Human beings are rational animals that think carefully about things …except the things that matter the most.

"Your wife is the tall and beautiful one, Vicente."

I'd tried to change the subject with flattery. Well, bring her in and introduce her to us, Marcelo said, as Vicente and I headed toward the bus stop. The number eight bus took us along Calle Reyes and the Gran Vía to Avenida Calvo Sotelo. From there, we walked through the empty lots by the train station. Vicente explained that our contact was a railway worker from Burgos who'd been in Granada for three years and was the coach of a youth soccer team. The children of the railway workers compete each year in a game against the children of the tram workers. The annual encounter is the climax of the season and sparks intense rivalries between the two sides. Which is better, the train or the tram? A bird in the hand or two in the bush? Long distances or short distances? The installment plan or cash upfront? To each his own.

"Hey coach, if I steal the ball, who do I pass it to?"

"You're playing defense, Pepe. Don't make things complicated. Just kick the ball. If you can hit the side of that train parked over there, even better."

Ramiro Martín was in the middle of a soccer lesson. The boy, twelve or thirteen years old, looked at his coach very seriously, internalized the order, then went running off to his teammates. Pass it here, here! Come on, pass the ball. That was a foul! Come on, come on, come on ... the shouting raised everyone's level of excitement and happiness in the open field. The coach was blowing his whistle, adding to the tumult. They only had one goal, and the boys were doing drills in how to attack, defend and shoot. I watched them as we walked through the rail yard in their direction, but Granada's splendid panorama was distracting me. I was reminded that Granada is a historic city, a unique place above and beyond any of my own experiences. Behind the silhouettes of the Alhambra and the church spires, the clouds had parted to display the Sierra Nevada. The vast landscape and clean air were stunning. I had a hard time pulling myself away from the beautiful city view to watch the pandemonium of boys trying to emulate their favorite soccer stars. In place of a real soccer net, they used two stones and some sweaters. I assumed that this led to heated discussions each time someone scored. Childhood is the same everywhere: in my village, the boys played soccer in the street. Searching for the truth without a goal is an exercise destined to fail. It was in! That's a lie! It went in! No, it didn't! It was too high, come on. Two-nil, one-one....

Ramiro Martín was tall and handsome with stylish black hair like a movie star in a railway worker's uniform. He looked good in his grey outfit, which was a bit disheveled from the soccer practice. He'd look good in any color. His face screamed descriptors like ladies' man, playboy, cocky, pretentious, conceited. But it was his voice that most reminded me of an overwhelming men's cologne. His deep, resonant tone overpowered the introductions and his strategic instructions to the boys. His perfectly pronounced s's mocked our local pronunciation. His words amplified the vanity of his eyes, nose, and lips.

"You've got to play smarter, much smarter. You've got to hustle. Pepito, I told you, clear the ball, get it over to the other team's half and let them run it back toward us. Hi Vicente. We'll go in just a moment." Go where, I thought. Where's Vicente going?

"You got it backwards," Vicente said, extending his hand. He was discreetly disagreeing with Ramiro but made it seem like he was laughing along.

"Ok, in that case, no."

"Are your friends coming?"

"Two of them. We're meeting in the freight car." He was talking like we were in a spy movie, meticulously playing his role as the heroic leading man. "Hold on a second. Hey kids, I'll be right back. Leave the ball for a while and run some laps. Just jog but do it with style. Like you're horses not mules."

A joker. The handsome hunk was a joker. Alarm bells started going off as I remembered the prank with Juan Benavides, the lotero in Motril. I sensed a strange connection between my colleague and this slick soccer coach. Vicente and his friends, gearing up to mock the dull boy. Some hunk in a railway uniform who thought he could treat me like a mule. And with an audience, in front of a couple of friends to applaud the trainee making a fool of himself. But this time I'd be prepared. By now I was an expert in telephone calls and sales visits. After my success in Maracena, I've shed my scruples. Vicente was right to feel jealous of my directness and efficiency, achieved after only two months and without all that pitch protocol of words, names, history mashups and geography salads. Sales calls were no longer torture, and I produced the goods. All this emotion around my role as an encyclopedia salesman was nothing, a silent and secondary aspect of my life, compared to other important matters like my relationship with Consuelo, her plan to cool things off, and my definitive and demanding desire for her, because there was no longer any doubt; I knew it was love, obsessive love, despite our age differences and any hostile glances from the neighbors. Vicente and his pranksters had better watch out. This time, I was ready.

Ramiro's two friends, one dressed in a railway uniform and the other in street clothes, were smoking by an old passenger car parked on a sidetrack, a good distance from the main lines through the station.

"Vicente here is a representative from Editorial Universo in Granada.

Vicente, this is my friend Agustín and my colleague Pedro. And this young man is Vicente's assistant. Sorry, what was your name?"

"León Egea."

"Well, my boy, I hope you don't roar too much. We don't want you frightening the passengers."

We entered the dilapidated railcar. Two cats leapt from the windows with alarmed agility. I almost stepped on the remains of a pigeon stuck to the floor. The place smelled of grease and rot. Ramiro invited us to take our places on the four still functional seats. The railway worker called Pedro had a wide and generous smile plastered across his face. Come on in guys, please, come on in. He was the last one to get in the railcar and the last one to sit, as though he were observing some extreme form of etiquette. He was so sorry that the normal meeting room in the station was booked today due to a director's meeting. Agustín remained silent and stunned, like someone led to the slaughterhouse by a friend.

"Right then. We are interested in an encyclopedia. What do you two have to say?" Ramiro's voice rang out like he was chairing the Council of Ministers or the inauguration ceremony of a new school year at the University.

"We'd like to explain all the advantages of owning an encyclopedia. Why don't you start, León?" My esteemed colleague abandoned me to my fate in front of this jokester railway man and his friends.

"The Universo Encyclopedia is extremely high quality. That's the main reason it sells so well." I went straight to the heart of the matter, bypassing Vicente's theatrical method. I wanted to demonstrate my conviction and efficiency. "A team of experts has compiled select information, an authentic summary of human knowledge. I don't know if you have children, but this is an excellent homework tool for students. No household should be without one. They're easy to consult when looking for historic events, geography, literature, science… even practical advice. It's a good deal because it's cheap and you can pay it off in easy installments."

"Ok. Is that all?"

Ramiro Martín's "Is that all?" confirmed my suspicions. After making a clear and concise presentation, I'd stopped talking sooner than anyone expected, no rigmarole. Vicente looked at me with surprise, almost disappointment. The logical next step would be for Ramiro and friends to ask some questions about the price, the payment plans, delivery date, but not just say "Is that all?" like someone invited to the circus and disappointed by the simplicity of the performance.

"Yes, that's it. If you would like, sir, I can show you the three volumes so you can see them for yourselves." The awkwardness of our meeting space in an abandoned third-class passenger car, without the proper atmosphere and a desk, made me forget that Vicente and I had divided up the three volumes between us. I was carrying the last two. Vicente imitated me involuntarily and opened his briefcase. Nestled next to his paper-wrapped sandwich was the first volume. Ok, if you gentlemen would like, we can give you a few examples that will demonstrate the precision of the entries. *Handsome*: physically appealing. Ostentatious in form of dress. Boastful. Cocky. A man who pursues a woman and has affairs with her.

Ramiro was quick to control the flash of surprise and discomfort that crossed his face, but he couldn't stop himself from casting a suspicious glance toward Vicente. No doubt he got the hint. But in case he hadn't, I succumbed to the temptation of continuing my little fiesta of language and its hierarchy of nuance and diversions.

"Let's see, maybe here, no, let's see, what was I looking for? Here we go, for example, the word *pretentious*: a person who shaves very carefully, is overly meticulous, affected, excessively spiffy, slick." Agustín continued to show no emotion, paralyzed. But the alarm that had begun to flash in Vicente's eyes, together with the wild happiness that still seemed to dominate Pedro's silence, encouraged me to push my routine to the point of no return. "Vicente, hand me your volume. Let's see now, let's see. The word *baritone*: a masculine voice between tenor and base. After many years of being grouped under the base, the baritone progressively emerged thanks to the musical innovations of the German composer Christoph Gluck, to the French opera composers, to the great Italian composers subsequent to eighteen thirty, and to a railway worker from Burgos named Ramiro who is handsome but may or may not be pretentious." I closed the book and raised my eyes toward the indicated party. "I think, sir, that this encyclopedia could be of interest to you."

Pedro's guffaws managed to shift Agustin's expression of shock to one of infinite confusion. Vicente had become serious, angry. But Ramiro's reaction was best.

"So, now you've got clowns working as encyclopedia salesmen, is that right Vicente? Very funny, this kid. Do you sell many books with an assistant like this?"

"He doesn't do too badly," I jumped in with my response. "We jog more like horses than mules, and we love jokes. I bet you do too, sir, don't you?"

"Yes, of course I like jokes." Ramiro had frozen his smile to keep it in place. He looked at Vicente. "Apart from this performance by your apprentice, did you bring any documentation that explains the conditions of purchase?"

"Yes, here you go. It explains everything." Vicente took an Editorial Universo envelope out of his briefcase and handed it to Ramiro. I noticed that Vicente was having a hard time keeping a straight face, and in fact was on the verge of breaking out into bigger guffaws than Pedro's.

"Fine, now get lost. This session is over, and I have to go back to the soccer practice."

As we headed out of the vacant lot, we heard Pedro's voice calling out to us. We could count on him to be a client for sure, he said. He loved our revolutionary sales technique.

"No way, seriously. I know that was a prank."

"I'm telling you no, it wasn't a prank. You blew it."

"Then why are you laughing?"

The skies had cleared. Our session with the railway workers ended up being shorter than we expected and we had some extra time, so we decided to walk back to the office. Vicente set the pace with his indigent feet. He was silent, eyes straight ahead, refusing to look at me, choosing our path through the scrubland toward the distant hum of the city. I soon realized he was trying to keep from laughing. When I asked him if he was mad at me, he did just that, answering through guffaws that yes, of course he was mad, that I had messed up what should have been an easy sale, and that I was rude and impertinent. But this time he didn't pull out all his cheap philosophies of life, his consecrated, mushy meditations on prudence, acceptance, and fate. He didn't lecture me from his manual of good office worker behavior. Just the opposite, he kept stopping and setting down his briefcase to laugh again.

"How can I not laugh? Didn't you see the look on the baritone's face? Damn, was he surprised. It stopped him in his tracks."

"It was one of your pranks."

"No, it wasn't."

"Yes, it was, just like in Motril with the lottery guy."

"That wasn't a prank either."

"Then why are you laughing?"

"Because it's funny. I don't like some of these clients either. I can see them coming. Anyway, this summer we've already made a lot of money off the commissions from the sales to Education and Recreation." He burst into a new spasm of laughter. He glanced back toward the train station with a look of joyous spontaneity in his eyes that I had never seen before. "It's true, that railway guy was hilarious, and so was the look on his friends' faces when you called him handsome and pretentious. Look, I'm not an ordained nun of the church of Editorial Universo, and I haven't taken any vows of chastity. I laugh when I feel like it, even if it sinks the sale. But I'm warning you, if you try another trick like that, I'll have to report you to the boss."

"It's not like I have that much time left anyway. The summer's almost over. It went by in a flash and in October, this job is over and I'm back at the University."

"Hold on. Think about this, muchacho. Yesterday, I overheard Consuelo talking on the phone to Don Alfonso and she suggested that he offer you a part-time job going forward. Given how well we've done and all the orders we've had, it doesn't seem like a bad idea."

The news turned my glow of triumph into a knot of terror in my stomach. Consuelo was trying to arrange for me to stay at Universo during the school year, and from out of nowhere I had lashed out at a potential client simply because I suspected Vicente was playing a joke on me. Consuelo was watching out for me, Consuelo didn't want to distance me, Consuelo was trying to make it possible for me to carry on with my normal life with my classes and my friends without losing contact with Universo, or Calle Lepanto, or the kings of the fifteenth century, or the Polynesian Islands, or with her. Vicente may have laughed at my performance, but in reality, I'd acted like an idiot.

"Listen, is Ramiro Martín a friend of Don Alfonso's?"

"No, I don't think so.

Suddenly, the yelps of a desperate dog brought me back to reality. We were in the middle of a demolition site. Vicente had decided to head toward Calle san juan de dios and wanted to take a shortcut through the abandoned fields and empty lots. A chorus of boys and a barking dog blocked our path. Something bad was happening. As we got closer, we saw a white dog tied to a tree, barking rabidly, trying to defend itself from an attack by a tall boy, maybe fifteen years old. The boy, cheered on by his friends, was trying to hit the dog with a long stick. Both the boy and the dog moved with cautious violence to avoid entering enemy territory. Fangs versus stick.

"Be careful, he might bite you." Vicente offered up the warning to win the sympathy of the gang leader. "What's going on?"

"It already bit me and I'm going to make it pay."

"That's a lie, he didn't bite you." Another boy, smaller, blonde, his eyes red from crying, confronted the tall boy. "You're a liar. You just want to kill my dog."

"It bit me yesterday. It's not your dog and I can kill it if I want."

The tall boy, almost as tall as a grown man, bent down, picked up a brick and threw it straight at the dog. The animal's yelps of pain returned quickly to howls of fury. It looked like it might strangle itself in its frenzied pulling against the rope.

"See that? He wants to kill my dog. He says he's going to get a can of gasoline."

"It's not your dog."

"Hello son, is this your dog?" Vicente took a handkerchief out of his pocket. "Here, dry your tears. What's your dog's name?"

"Blanco, and he is my dog." The small boy found courage in Vicente's support. He quickly wiped his eyes and returned the handkerchief. Feeling supported by a grownup he had stopped crying. "I feed him, and he comes to me when I call him."

"Well, we better untie him then."

The tall boy wasn't about to have his authority questioned in front of his gang. First, he threatened Vicente and me for sticking our noses in his business. Then he took measure of his situation and shifted his strategy. He was clever. He didn't speak with that voice of cowardly arrogance that the mayor's son in my village uses to talk to his gang. His cockiness had been cultivated in the streets, hardened by the elements, and perfected in many episodes just like this one. It was the arrogance of neglect, the hubris of those who have nothing behind their own fear and their own audacity. I remembered my literature professor and his lectures on *The Struggle for Life*, by the novelist Pío Baroja, who wrote about misery and brutality in the impoverished outskirts of Spanish cities in the late nineteenth century. Little has changed.

The tall boy had shifted from threats to contemptuous superiority. He warned Vicente that the dog was rabid and would bite him. I was thinking he was right; we shouldn't be getting mixed up in this affair that has nothing to do with us, and it was crazy to go near the dog. But I was also thinking we couldn't abandon the small boy, and we couldn't leave the dog tied to the tree waiting for the blow of another brick to hit him or a shower of gasoline. Vicente opened his briefcase and took out his sandwich, then asked me to hold the briefcase for him. I was grateful to be given something to do to help, because I was frozen with fear. I hadn't done anything or said anything since we arrived on the scene. I was acting like a coward.

"So, this is your dog, right son?" Vicente took the small boy's hand and started walking toward the tree. The dog had stopped barking, but he was watching the situation closely and not looking very friendly. "Let's liberate him."

Together, they advanced toward the dog. When they reached the danger zone, they stopped. Vicente pulled a breaded cutlet out of his sandwich. He gave it to the boy with instructions to throw it on the ground, halfway between them and the animal. Come on, Blanco, eat it, we're going to save you, Vicente said. I glanced at the tall boy out of the corner of my eye to see if he was going to cause trouble, but he was still. He seemed to think it was better for the dog itself to punish Vicente for intruding. I was thinking that would be exactly what would happen, that the dog was not going to obey, that we'd all be paralyzed here forever, that Vicente shouldn't take one step more, that the dog's fear and bluster were also born of the streets, and that the dog's intuition and survival instinct led it little by little toward the cutlet. The small boy tried to go to the dog, but Vicente held him back. It was Vicente who took a knife out of his jacket pocket and walked slowly forward, spoke to the animal with forced serenity, and, when he came up beside it, reached down and cut the rope from its neck. When the animal sensed it was free, it spun around and sprinted away, ignoring the cutlet. The small boy took off after him, without a word of farewell.

And we didn't say farewell to the tall boy either. The event seemed to be over. Vicente put away his knife, took his briefcase back from me, and we resumed our walk toward the city and a kinder world. I was in the middle of confessing to him how much his actions had impressed me when he suddenly cried out in pain. A rock had hit his head. I looked back and saw the tall boy and his gang running away through the abandoned lots.

"Damn that bastard! You're bleeding."

"Yeah, he got me good. Asshole."

It wasn't a large cut, but it was deep. A puncture wound. Vicente took out his handkerchief again—thank goodness the small boy gave it back after drying his tears—and pressed it against his head. We started off again, more quickly this time, in the direction of the Casa de Socorro. I carried his briefcase.

"I'll need stitches for this one, for sure."

"Yeah, it's quite a gash."

"My rotten luck. A war wound."

"I didn't know you carried a knife in your pocket."

"There's a lot you don't know about. It's better that way."

Vicente's patented "you don't need to know about that." But this time it didn't sound cowardly. It didn't even bother me to watch his awkward stride, holding the bloody handkerchief to his head. Vicente's misfortune, his headwound and his compassion toward the small boy filled me with newfound respect. I admired his calm authority while controlling his fear of the dog, and in accepting the incident as fate. We should report him to the police, I said. Don't be silly, Vicente responded. But we have to find a way to get back at that son of a bitch. Yeah, and who's going to go back there to look for him? We have enough to deal with as it is, he said. Every single jerk I've ever met gets a kick out of abusing dogs, I said. If only it was just dogs, he answered.

In the Casa de Socorro, Vicente got four stitches. He explained to the medic, a regular at the Lepanto, that some of the kids in the neighborhood had been messing around throwing rocks at each other. One of the rocks hit his head by accident. Bad luck. Sometimes they break the streetlights, sometimes they break tram windows, and sometimes they break someone's head. Afterwards, Vicente invited me for a beer and a plate of calamari in the Bar Jandilla next to the Corral del Carbón, not far from the office. He'd lost his breaded cutlet and didn't want to explain anything to the widowed barman about the gauze and medical tape crowning his head. This morning I left my house ready to close a good deal at the train station, then eat my sandwich at the office and catch up on some work, he said. We blew the sale at the train station, we had a good laugh, and I got hit in the head with a rock. It could've been worse. So instead of complaining, let's order some calamari in the Jandilla, like two gentlemen. Ok, but you should let me pay, I said.

He paid. Vicente isn't tall or short, handsome or ugly, fat or thin. That's why it always takes me less than five minutes to go from scorning him to liking him, from admiring him to hating him. We were already in the office when Consuelo returned from her lunch break. Vicente brushed off her concern about the attack. You know how it is, head wounds always bleed a lot but aren't usually that serious. Either they kill you outright or they're no big deal. This was no big deal. There was other news in the neighborhood that everyone found much more interesting.

"Marcelo says that our dear León has a beautiful, rich girlfriend." Vicente's voice shot through me like a bullet. "Life is so unfair. I have a horrible day and lose a sale, while León shows up at the Café Lepanto with a beautiful, rich girlfriend."

❧

Rolling on top of me and across the bed, Consuelo reached for the book I'd borrowed from her. She took it from the nightstand and tucked it under her pillow. The sun was coming up. I'd barely slept. Each night has its own personality, like each person. Nights can be calm, peaceful, bellicose, unfriendly, happy, profound, and monotonous. People depend on their friends, the night depends on bodies, with all that's hidden inside them. Tell me who you keep company with, and I will tell you who you are. Tell me what kind of darkness is hidden in your body, and I can tell you how your life goes and how you spend the night. The shifting darkness of the night is born of the body. Your worries sink in overnight before they surface to your brow.

It was my happiness that woke me up. But if you think about things too much, handle them too much, get them dirty, you end up perverting them. Or maybe you end up understanding them. I'd just experienced one of the best nights of my life. I'd enjoyed a jealous Consuelo, an ironic Consuelo, a queen-of-roleplay Consuelo, a homebody Consuelo, and a naughty Consuelo. We emptied the fridge of food and beer in a joyous meal. Then she asked me to stay the night. I succumbed to sleep curled around her body like a wild animal in its den. I was not a dog tied to a tree, at the mercy of a cruel boy from the projects. Nor was I some pastor's dog, condemned to suffer the revenge of the mayor's arrogant son. I was in a safe place, next to the light of my life, exhausted, emotional, ready to hibernate.

But my happiness woke me up, or maybe it was a sense of unease that I was slow to understand. Some forms of happiness are really just foreboding that you haven't deciphered. You go along, live your life, the days flow by, sediment builds, and only later the heart interprets more precisely and with more wisdom what your worried brain could not. Finding the reason behind your sadness can take a while. Life is not a single road or a straight line.

As soon as Vicente said goodnight with his briefcase and his bandaged head, Consuelo stood up. She conjured up the theatrical expression of a betrayed woman, looked me in the eyes, and asked me about this rich and beautiful girlfriend. She was teasing and I was about to join in by inventing some corny details worthy of a romance movie. But I decided to tell her the truth. She was not my girlfriend, but the cousin of my roommate Jacobo's girlfriend. Consuelo's role required that she act suspicious, demand the woman's name (She's called Elena), to ask what she studies (She's going to start philosophy and literature this fall), and to push me to confirm that she was beautiful and rich (Yes, she is beautiful, and also tall, and I don't know if her family is swimming in wealth, but I suppose so because her father is a notary). The interrogation was easy because all my answers were true. I started to enjoy myself. There was no danger in it, although I would have given anything for Consuelo's jealousy to be real.

Then she asked if Elena and I had kissed. For a moment, I wasn't quite sure of the best way to tell the truth. I didn't want to lie. If I said we hadn't kissed, I'd be hiding that Elena unexpectedly sought my lips as we were saying goodnight at her front door. If I confessed that I'd walked her home and she'd kissed me before disappearing inside, I was practically admitting that yes, she was my girlfriend and that the story the widowed barman had invented to tease me, and that Vicente had repeated throughout his short, ugly, and impoverished day, was true. The scene was classic, the young suitor, kissing his girlfriend goodnight at her door. In that sense, saying that we hadn't kissed was closer to the truth.

"No, we didn't kiss."

"Then why did you just hesitate?"

"I didn't hesitate. I just like to see you jealous. Even though it's all an act."

"Actually, I am a little jealous."

"Well, you have no reason to be. That whole girlfriend thing was a lie, and you're the one who's making me spend time with my school friends. You want me to meet girls my age and not think about you all the time."

We left the office together. There was no question that I had permission to accompany her home. She wanted to continue questioning my sudden romantic escapade with the notary's daughter, making it into a big produc-

144

tion. I was just thrilled to be with her like this, like a married couple who's gone to the movies and is walking home together. The seasonal change in the light was palpable. The sun was setting earlier, bathing the city in a lovely violet glow. In the mornings, clouds parted to reveal unexpectedly crisp skies framing the view of the Alhambra and the Sierra Nevada from the empty lots around the train station. We didn't talk about Elena, the false girlfriend, or Marcelo's fibs in the Café Lepanto. Consuelo was leaving all that for later. As we crossed Calle Ganivet, the Plaza del Campillo, and the Carrera de la virgen, she asked me to explain in detail Vicente's head wound. I didn't hesitate to confess my admiration for the way he'd handled himself, his courageous calm. By that time, heading into the evening, walking alongside Consuelo toward her house, my feelings toward Vicente had swung again from hate to affection. It was also becoming clear that his indiscretion about my tall, beautiful, rich girlfriend was favorably reshaping my horizons. Maybe it wouldn't be a bad idea in the next phase of my interrogation to mention that Elena also has long legs, large eyes, full lips, and enchanting conversational skills. It's true Consuelo, Elena has long legs, large eyes, full lips, and enchanting conversational skills.

We talked about the slums in the abandoned lots around the train station. I waxed literary with my impressions of the dog tied to the tree, the threat to douse him with gas, the indigence of the small boy, the insolence of the tall boy, and of how the environment of poverty and squalor reminded me of Baroja's trilogy *The Struggle for Life*. People demoralized by the need to seek and resist. Misery, weeds, bad omens, disease, false hopes, excuses to survive. Consuelo told me *The Tree of Knowledge* was her favorite book of the trilogy, the Baroja novel that had influenced her the most. I was too embarrassed to say I hadn't read it, but she noticed and offered to lend me hers.

When we got to the Paseo del Salón, I turned the page to the next chapter of my confessions. I described my ill-fated sales pitch to Ramiro Martínez and his friends, which had devolved into a farce. Once again, I found myself saying nice things about Vicente. If he'd used the meeting to set me up, I could only applaud the fairness with which he accepted my counter-prank. Like for like, don't give it if you can't take it. And if it wasn't a prank, I could only applaud his camaraderie in not reprimanding me in front of our clients for my impertinent and paranoid behavior.

"Wait, wait, wait. You called the railway worker a pretentious baritone?" Consuelo was reacting with excited amusement in an effort to loosen my tongue. No scolding about my professional behavior today, just about my girlfriend. "How did he look when you said that?"

"I think Ramiro was flabbergasted. Vicente didn't stop laughing about it until he got hit by that rock."

"We'd better keep an eye on you. You're capable of sinking the whole business."

"Well, my girlfriend isn't the only thing Vicente's been indiscreet about. He also told me you spoke to Don Alfonso about giving me a part-time contract for the school year." I wasn't sure if I was overplaying my hand, but it seemed like a good time to mention it. We were getting close to her house, and I wanted to put my best foot forward as we headed down Transversal de la Bomba. I wasn't quite on parole, but Consuelo the jailer had decided to be nice to me. "I'm really grateful you thought of me."

"That was before I knew you had another girlfriend."

"I do have a beautiful girlfriend, who is almost tall, and with just enough money."

"I don't know her. What's her name?"

When we got to her house, she sat me on the sofa without letting me embrace her. Her usual hospitality was missing for the first time since I'd entered her private life. She didn't bring out the two beers that normally contribute their friendly and domesticated foam to our conversation. Instead, she went to the bookshelf and took down two books: Baroja's *The Tree of Knowledge*, and *Locked Up with Just One Toy*, by Juan Marsé, a young writer from Barcelona, I wasn't familiar with. You have a lot to learn, Consuelo said. At that moment, I didn't get the connection between the toy in the novel and my own life. I thought about the tree of knowledge though, what you learn when you eat the apple, and how you make decisions about good and evil. I took Baroja's novel with me to bed when we decided it was time to sleep after having dined together like a pair of newlyweds who've gone to the movies, come home, made love in the living room, scoured the fridge for something to eat, turned on the reading lights by the side of the bed to read together, to be together, to enjoy the wonderful closeness of the routine. But the thing that kept me awake at night, and that later transformed into a strange sense of unease, crystalized in the fear that I was turning into a toy, Consuelo's toy.

After she gave me the books, she sat down on the sofa next to me and continued the interrogation. Names, details, dates, a summary of the facts. Jacobo, Mariví, Elena, last Sunday morning, the tram ride up to the Sierra Nevada, great snacks prepared by the heiress of the Pastelería Pintor Velázquez, sandwiches, pastries, the river, the light sparkling on the river, the bodies and the conversations by the river, Mariví and Jacobo disappearing into the woods, Elena and I, talking about literature, Spain, the world, the obligations of the intellectual, the prestige of being a writer in training, clouds passing overhead, time passing, the tram back to the city, a sandwich in the Lepanto, Jacobo's desire to be alone with Mariví, my orders to accompany Elena to her front door, the Gran Vía, the trees along the Avenida Calvo Sotelo, her doorway, the farewell, Elena's kiss, the summary completed.

"And then the two of you kissed?"

"She gave me a quick kiss."

"On the lips?"

"Yes, on the lips."

"Shameless hussy."

Further exposition of the facts. My scarce interest in going on Jacobo's excursion, my melancholy on catching the tram so near to Consuelo's house, my feeling like an imposter as I was talking about literature and becoming a writer, the lies about my important role at an important publishing house on the recommendation of an important and very famous professor of literature, my confusion about why I really wanted to take everyone to the Lepanto for sandwiches, my need for Marcelo, the walls of the Casa de Socorro, and the lobby of our office building to see that I had a life beyond selling encyclopedias on the easy installment plan, Manolo the bootblack's jokes about the respect due to señoritas of good—meaning rich— families, my genuine sense of solitude, the reality that I'm not

147

from an upper-class family, nor am I old enough to handle a relationship with a thirty-seven year old woman, the sad and sweaty face of nineteen sixty-three, the disillusioned and fearful breath of the coming school year which will begin in October nineteen sixty-three and end in June nineteen sixty-four, my lack of interest in holing up in my student apartment to study, the walk with Elena, and the shiver of the unexpected kiss at her front door.

"Shameless hussy."

At that moment it began to rain. The drops beat against the terrace and the windows with the joyous pulse of the water through the pipes. The mayor's office thinks it's a good idea to continue the drought restrictions a while longer. The reservoirs are still very low after so many dry months, but at least the city is starting to breathe in the new season. The rain, and a forecast for more, hinted at a time when we might forget about the shutoffs and the burble of the water returning. But I don't want to forget the sound of water announcing its arrival, and its solidarity in provoking Consuelo's nakedness, my giddiness, our temptation. When I heard the rain on the terrace, I thought of fall's arrival, and of winter and the possibility of spending the months of cold and snow seated on the sofa in that apartment, to leave behind everything beyond these windows, to raise a wall between fearful reality and desire. The rain gave me an idea. We could celebrate the sound of water a different way, backwards, by going outside. I told Consuelo we should pretend that the rain was the water running through the pipes, and that the terrace outside was a big shower, and that we should open the door and step out to let the water soak us, falling and falling over our bodies. But she said no. She had another idea.

"You need to be punished."

She rose, took my hand, and led me to a corner of the living room. Up against the wall, she said. Arms out like a cross, she said. I obeyed. I was happy to play along. Playing games was a special part of our intimacy, I was used to it. It took me a minute to get into position, *The Tree of Knowledge* in my right hand, *Locked Up with Just One Toy* in my left hand. I was a student being punished by the teacher. Don't turn your head, don't move, don't lower your arms. No talking, no protesting, no begging for mercy.

148

Her high heels click-clacked toward the bedroom with decisive authority. Her bare feet padded out of the bedroom, across the living room, and into the bathroom, where she turned on the shower. I imagined her underneath the falling water. The rain was pounding on the terrace and on Consuelo's body. Consuelo, the city, and my disciplined silence were being cleansed all at the same time. No tricks. Don't turn your head, don't look, don't move, don't lower your arms. I waited as the city searched for a towel to wipe dry the vulgarity of its citizens, its offices, years of bitterness, and differences in age. Consuelo's hair was clean and dry. Her shoulders, breasts, and thighs were clean and alive. I was excited, committed, ready to obey, to wait not questioning orders, to receive my punishment which was my just reward.

I heard her leave the bathroom, come close to me, kiss me carefully on the back of my neck. I felt flushed with the humid heat of a summer storm. The shower was silent, but the rain continued to pound on the window in its effort to glimpse Consuelo's naked body standing behind me. I felt her kiss and her hands unbuttoning my shirt, caressing my chest, carefully, so I wouldn't drop the books. Don't move, don't talk, don't lower your arms. Whoever drops the books loses. Punishment is punishment. My Aunt Rosario never punished me. Consuelo is nothing like my Aunt Rosario. Consuelo's hands were on me, caressing my belly, finding my belt buckle, unbuttoning my fly, she pulled down my trousers and my underpants. No protesting, no moving your arms, no dropping the books. Consuelo's hands lifted one foot; there we go. Then the other foot, there. Pants are liberated.

She stepped back, looked at me, came close again, slowly pulled me away from the wall, leaving a space between my body and the corner. She inserted herself into the space, and I felt myself become a toy in time and space, that was the fact of the matter, a toy in her hands, in her mouth, which was moving down my chest, down my belly, overpowering me, don't drop the books, don't lower your hands, don't move, don't protest, don't pull away, don't resist, don't object. Do succumb, do abandon yourself to complete defenselessness, to the end of the rainstorm, the departure of the clouds and to the power of that miraculous absence of mercy.

Afterwards, we went to bed, and I thanked her for my punishment. You can punish me as often as you like, I said. I made love to her, we felt hungry, improvised dinner, and she asked me to stay the night. I read a while at her side, with her head resting on my chest, before turning out the lights. But my sorrowful happiness kept me awake. You can turn things over and over in your head so much they change their meaning. Or maybe it just takes me longer to understand reality. I didn't want to be a toy, Consuelo's secret, an obvious and wanton folly between a twenty-year-old boy and a thirty-seven-year-old woman. I didn't want to be caught in this passionate, demented, and indecent convergence of a young man who needs to lose his innocence and a mature woman taking advantage of the train passing right in front of her door. I didn't like Consuelo's false jealousy, her cooling off plan, her jokes about Elena, her strategy for building a clandestine hideaway, her project to schedule secret meetings week to week, month to month, with pleasant afternoons followed by shameless acts, while outside the world continues its routine, and I perform my role as a nothing, or as Jacobo's roommate who goes on excursions with Mariví and her cousin Elena.

I woke Consuelo and told her everything. I wanted fewer games and more of a genuine life of love with her. She rolled across the bed, reaching over me, grabbed and then hid the Pío Baroja book. I don't think this is a good book for you, she said. It ends with a suicide. I didn't play along with her joke this time and repeated my concerns. I had a very bad night, I said, dealing with one of those darknesses that emerge from your own body. She changed her tune. But I think she misunderstood me.

"I made a mistake. Forgive me." She closed her eyes as she spoke. She looked beautiful, younger than ever, with her head on the pillow and her voice lost in a confession that was only partly directed to me. She seemed to be talking to herself, clarifying something personally. "I'm ashamed of my behavior yesterday, I'm sorry. You're right. I wasn't trying to be indecent with that game...."

"Consuelo...."

"Wait, let me finish. I do take you seriously. I like you, but our relationship can never be, we simply can never be. It's the age difference, it's my life, it's other things much more complicated than you can imagine. Give me time. I confess that I care about you, that last night's little game was me

150

trying to deny to myself that I'm in a serious relationship with you, a real relationship, but one that cannot go on. I hate it that there are beautiful, rich women around you. But that's the way it is. It's the way it should be. It's all my fault. We need to end this."

And then she added:

"It's hard to endure evil in the world. But it's equally hard to endure innocence."

We talked a lot more without saying anything new. She kept coming back to the idea that our relationship could never be. She even confessed that she loved me, but at the cost of insisting with ever greater conviction that our relationship could never be. I couldn't convince her. The only thing I did achieve, for the very first time, was to make her late for work.

Don Alfonso invited me into his office. Vicente had let me know ahead of time that the boss was going to be there. By mid-morning it was time for a coffee break and fed up with myself and tired of answering phone calls and trying not to look at Consuelo, I got up from my desk to keep my regular morning appointment with the widowed barman. But Vicente said we needed to wait for Don Alfonso. This was it. The opportunity we'd talked about. He might be about to ask me to stay on and work part-time into the fall. September was putting its best foot forward, with lots of rain and new orders. The Universo Encyclopedia company was promising a bright future to families across the city, available with easy payments on the installment plan. The encyclopedia offered knowledge, education, culture, and dreams that could open the door to hope, all for just a modest cost, a modest amount of your day-to-day savings as an investment in your future, an investment in your son's confidence if he had at his fingertips information about the Caroline Islands, the capital of Sweden, and the meaning of antithesis. But I didn't have it in me to make fun of such naivety today. I thought about the pride with which my parents awaited my University graduation picture. They were already planning where it would hang in the living room, a family trophy.

Don Alfonso's arrival wasn't the only surprise of the morning. As the clock's hands were approaching ten-thirty and I was battling my dismay at being frozen in time, three days gone by without speaking to that evasive Consuelo, things between us still unresolved, my literature professor Ignacio Rubio called. He was back from his vacation in Santander, and a short trip to the Escuela de Altos Estudios in Paris. His courtesy and kindness had me beaming. I was especially grateful for the invitation to visit him, that very afternoon, in his home. He wanted to hear about my work at Universo, my writing progress, and my plans because he had a proposal for the coming year. I was thrilled to know he was counting on me and couldn't wait to hear more. Yes, of course, you can count on me, nothing would please me more. Could he give me a hint over the phone? No, just be there around seven in the evening. It's just a little project, he added, in French. Ignacio Rubio likes to adorn his memories, conversations, literary theories, and meetings with students with a garland of French culture.

The city had returned to its routine. Jacobo had spent the last several days declaring himself useless for studying law and making plans with Mariví. Jesús, my other roommate, had let us know that he'd be back the next day, ready to make himself into a rich and religious doctor, the two values that define the profession in these times. His bragging about the certainty of his future, never noticing the contradictions, drives me crazy. He doesn't get the hypocrisy of his shuffle between pragmatism and spirituality. The only one still resisting a return to the autumn routine is Don Alfonso. He showed up in the office, but only in passing. After taking care of some business in Granada, he's on his way triumphantly to Madrid, to polish up the final details and then sign the contract with the Ministry of Education and Recreation. He told us all about it in his office, after a quick summary of his beach holiday in Torremolinos, the amazing opportunities that emerge in such a perfect location to collect business contacts, and the great results you can get when you know how to mix an irresistible cocktail of business, party chatter and ocean breezes. Not all the words are gone with the wind, he declared with pride. I should know, he said, since I've spent my working life pitching words from bars to trenches and back again. It seemed to me he gave Consuelo a special look as he said this, enjoying his own joke.

Don Alfonso had run the numbers and had good news for everyone. He asked for our complete discretion because he didn't want the employees at other regional Universo offices to get jealous. And there was definitely something to get jealous about. It was a huge deal, he said. He was pleased to confirm that we would receive excellent commissions. Vicente and Consuelo would receive thirty thousand pesetas each. A fortune! He wanted to reward them for their hard work, their years of experience, and their willingness and efficiency in managing the office during his long absences. You can't attend mass and ring the church bells at the same time, you know, and someone who's out fishing on the high seas can't be seated at his desk in the office. Don Alfonso likes to mix his metaphors and fold them into his briefings and instructions with a precise pinch of his own personal philosophy.

I'm getting a tidy sum as well. I'm part of the company, like everyone else, though I would never want to force things or draw comparisons. It makes sense that I should get less than Vicente and Consuelo. That said, a fortune is about to fall on my juvenile head, a jackpot for the philosophy and literature student and relatively recent arrival in Granada and Editorial Universo. Twenty thousand pesetas, that's what Don Alfonso is going to drop in my pocket, in addition to other commissions and my regular salary. Don't go wild, Don Alfonso said. The company looks bad if its employees get involved in any scandals.

When Don Alfonso told us about his upcoming trip to Madrid and our bonuses, he also confirmed that I'd become a permanent employee of the company with a half-time contract. He'd called me to his office. Studying philosophy and literature shouldn't be too time consuming, he declared brusquely before I could even sit down in the chair that he offered. It's not a difficult major like Medicine or Engineering. It should be easy to study and work at the same time, earn both a living and a degree.

"You need to take advantage of all your youthful energy, use the impertinence of youth to break down barriers. The world is all about youth and violent creativity." He was repeating the word youth so many times that I took another look at him to guess his age as he spoke. His grey suit, white shirt, and dark tie made him look older. When I first met him in August, my emotional anxieties about him and Consuelo along with his more casual summer clothes made me think that he was seventeen years older than Consuelo. Thirty-seven plus seventeen equals fifty-four. Now I calculated his trimmed mustache, his hair dyed an intense black and combed back over his head, his wrinkled skin camouflaged by a timid tan, befitted a man of sixty. "A man can never allow the flame of his youth to extinguish. Then he's lost, some other macho will come along and take over the pack. Do you have a girlfriend?"

"No sir."

"Marcelo told me you were at the bar with Pedro Salinas' daughter."

"She's starting at the University this fall, studying philosophy and literature, like me."

"Of course, that's a girl's major. I told you. You're not a queer, are you?

"No sir."

"I guess it's ok for some, but it would be a disgrace for you if you were. It's better to be the top dog. Work, study, take advantage of your youth. Vicente and Consuelo said you definitely made the grade. So, I'm offering you the chance to continue working with us half time. It's better for us if you can work in the mornings, but if that's a problem for you at the University you can come in the afternoons. You'll be responsible for occasional home visits on weekends. Vicente will let you know. I suppose you agree to all that?

"Yes, sir. Thank you very much."

"Your parents will be pleased. It's not a huge salary, but the work is part of your education. Now we're going to call Vicente and Consuelo in. I have good news for all of you."

The generous commissions were indeed welcomed news, and I was the happiest of all that good luck had struck the Granada delegation of Editorial Universo just as I had been accepted as a full-fledged member of the firm, someone who could be trusted with secrets, receive a sealed envelope and go to the office every day to enjoy being an employee, moving around the city, on and off trains and buses, patiently watching the clock in the office and finding occasions to see Consuelo in private while trying to still the vertigo that defines our relationship. Because behind each piece of paper, each telephone call, and each minute in the office, is the apartment at Transversal de la Bomba.

Maybe I could ask Ignacio Rubio for advice. I could even leave my journal with him so he could understand from the inside my crossroads of love and uncertainty. I think there's some good work on these pages, transparent sincerity, justifiable concerns. And he's treated me as a friend, invited me to have coffee at his house, and now he has a project for me. But leaving my notebook with Ignacio would be to betray Consuelo, an unjustified act of madness. I have no right to open the doors to our intimacy, the doors to our office when we are alone, the doors to her home, to her shower, to the terrace overrun with the geraniums and ivy, and to the bedroom where I learned about her body, my own body, the value of pillow talk, the words of two naked lovers when they discuss the world, what it means to make love, to surrender to another with joy, enthusiasm, sadness and fear.

It would betray Consuelo and also Vicente because I've recorded too many of my opinions about him. Just now, as I'm writing to fill time before I meet with Ignacio Rubio, I'm going to record something else I've seen, a discovery that makes me sad. My feelings have changed about this man who is neither tall nor short, fat nor thin, handsome nor ugly. He's a good colleague, loyal and contradictory. I've seen him play the fool then emerge as a hero, feign aloofness then become precisely efficient, understand nothing and everything at the same time. Summarizing his contradictions in my journal every day has made me feel closer to him. I've kind of started to like him, and I realize there are things that I don't really need to know about. And this is one of them, damn the luck.

Becoming a certified member of the glorious Editorial Universo means you have to watch your step, earn your commission, and go out to buy cigarettes when Don Alfonso asks you to. All young encyclopedia salesmen are also office errand boys. So, when the boss asked me to go out to the tobacco stand and buy him a carton of Goyas, I smiled and did it. I took the stairs two by two, got to the street, inhaled the fresh air like a melancholy lover, and, walking like the owner of a small fortune I was, went past the Bar Jandilla and onto Calle Reyes. When I was almost at the tobacco stand, a surprise left me paralyzed. Life has many twists and turns, more than you

155

could imagine, even with an overheated imagination like mine. They didn't see me, but I saw them, a couple coming toward me along the sidewalk. Because they were a couple, a woman grasping the arm of a man, a typical married couple, veiled in routine, two people speaking intimately, walking down streets they know intimately. He wasn't wearing his uniform, but he was handsome and pretentious. It wasn't hard for me to identify the sound of his voice, the syrupy warmth of a baritone accustomed to seducing. She was tall and also handsome, unexpectedly lovely, the dark-haired beauty no one would believe was married to Vicente, the discreet and betrayed office worker of Calle Lepanto.

Ramiro Martín and Marisa were walking arm in arm along Calle Reyes Católicos. It goes without saying that I followed them. When the poison of detective work enters your veins, it's difficult to break the addiction. I'd spied on Consuelo's building, and successfully followed Vicente and Marisa through the nocturnal streets of Granada. I had even more reason to follow my friend's wife and the railway worker. It was a piece of cake to blend into the crowds at the stoplights, taking advantage of the morning rush to keep a safe distance. The stores, cars, buses, pedestrians, and traffic cops were all busy doing their own thing, they didn't care about uncovering possible secrets in their midst. But I kept my eyes fixed on the false couple as they moved through the indifferent tumult of the city. It was a short pursuit though because when they got to the Gran Vía, they crossed over toward Calle Elvira and entered a building near Plaza Nueva. Without a pause, they disappeared through the front door. No sign indicated what kind of building it was, but it wasn't a hotel, and it didn't have any offices. There was no doorman to ask, either. Maybe Ramiro Martín lived there, though his name wasn't on any of the mailboxes. Maybe Vicente was being betrayed here by his wife, that dark-haired beauty I could now imagine next to the sad, pale, and defeated flesh of my colleague. I had noticed at the train station that Vicente knew Ramiro from somewhere, but where? A friend of a friend? The relative of a neighbor, the coincidence of a wedding reception, the luck of a random encounter, an apparition that remains forever and unpredictably stuck to existence?

Vicente would have the answer to that question, but now I know more than he does. Marisa, his wife, had fallen into the arms of the baritone. She secretly belonged to an alternative reality, a long way away from her husband, where her nakedness sparkled in another mirror, in other sheets, in other bedrooms where someone would make her play or get angry, sing or stay silent. This was the family crisis Consuelo referred to, the reason for Vicente's grief-stricken visits to her apartment, the danger that was threatening the marriage. Whoever saw Ramiro and Marisa together in the streets wouldn't hesitate to applaud nature's balance. A handsome man and a beautiful woman, a perfect pair. Life is like that, joy seeks joy, grief seeks grief. By the time I got to the tobacco shop, I was filled with fury, on the warpath against logic and perfection in the world.

"Finally. I thought you'd taken off with the tobacco money. Where've you been?" Don Alfonso scolded my tardiness, but he wasn't angry.

"A car hit a motorcycle at the corner of Gran Vía. I saw the crowds and had to go and look."

"Anyone die?"

"No, just one person injured."

Don Alfonso celebrated his departure for Madrid and his stopover in the office the same way he did in August. No one works this afternoon, he announced. Tomorrow is another day, and the clients can wait. We went down to the Café Lepanto, had a beer, and celebrated Manolo the boot-black's joy as he enthusiastically seized on the boss's shoes. After two and a half months out of action, he had every right to take his position at Don Alfonso's feet and enliven the conversation with his polish, his brushes, and his impertinent commentary on the fauna of Granada. See the director of Editorial Universo, a vision of happiness, his foot on Manolo's shoeshine box, his hand around a glass of beer, a plate of shrimp on the bar, and all his employees gathered around him, celebrating the luminous possibilities of life.

I couldn't look at Vicente or speak to him. I was afraid he'd see in my eyes the shadows of that deceptive night along the bridges, gardens, and streets of the city, when I followed him from the movie theater to discover where he lived and spy on his wife, who embraced him and kissed him and rested her head on his shoulder while gazing in a shop window or respond-

157

ing to a whispered confidence. Now I was afraid that he would see in my eyes the image of Marisa crossing the Gran Vía on the arm of Ramiro, the baritone friend Vicente had laughed at so long and hard when I mocked the railway worker's air of a seducer. Ramiro's suspicion that Vicente and I knew something may have been behind his look of panic that day. My colleague's spontaneous, irrepressible laughter after we left the station was rooted only in innocence. Innocent laughter cut short by a rock to the head.

There are blows to the head, and then there are blows to the heart. I can't let Ignacio Rubio read this journal, for Vicente's and Consuelo's sake, and for mine. And I better watch what I say to Ignacio tonight.

$$\sim\hspace{-0.5em}\circ$$

I've been to Ignacio's home before. He lives in a spacious apartment with balconies that overlook the Plaza de la Trinidad. His building is easily identified by the tumult of birds in the linden trees at sunset. The fascinating chaos in the trees matches the chaos of the books in every room of Ignacio's apartment. They don't fit in the bookshelves that cover every wall, so they accumulate in the corners, on top of tables, chairs, and the sofa in his home office, at the base of lamps, spilling out into the hallway in an escape toward the living room and the bathroom. His wife, Ángela Domínguez, a history professor at the University afflicted with the same malady, doesn't complain. As a result, it's difficult to find a place to sit or a surface to put down a serving tray. Ignacio Rubio's house is a riot of birds and books.

The classes I took with this man really made my whole first year. I admire his knowledge, his command of language, his ability to pick out a detail and weave it into a storyline with suspense and a surprise ending. There's always something that I need to know about, that can sharpen my idea of myself. His commentaries range from literature to life, veer into history, pause on a soccer field or a radio news broadcast, then swing back to literature to declare a poem definitive or a novel or an essay must-read.

Other professors may be good, bad, or indifferent, but they all belong to the same world. So, as a student, you leave your village, you burst into the city, you start your university study, you submit yourself to the logical evolution of things, life goes on, the years go by, habits and responsibilities adapt themselves along the way. The cycle continues, everything follows a predestined path. But suddenly, along comes someone earth-shattering, who cuts time in half, transforms your perspectives, and defies normal evolution, unleashing a different world to pull us outside of ourselves. For me, that person was Ignacio Rubio. I identified with him from day one.

"Come in, come in. You look good. I can't believe it's been two months since we've seen each other. Le temps passe très vite."

In Ignacio's classes, I've always identified with the writers he talks about. He loves to ignore the syllabus, vary the discussion, and bring an author to life through biographical anecdotes, details about their passions, their most dramatic encounters, and their disputes. If the lives of poets and novelists are like novels themselves, it's because biographies are novels, and that includes your own lives, he tells the class. I want all of you to think about your lives as if you had to recount them in a biography or in class. Above and beyond any novel is history, an all-encompassing plot that allocates our places in life. We all contribute to that single text that is History. That's where our responsibility begins, he concludes.

One day when Ignacio paused during a lecture on epic poetry and El Cid Campeador to talk about Espronceda in Paris, I started to think about the novel of my own life, and I found it wanting. No youthful conspiracies against the king, no storms at sea, or barricades in the streets of Paris, no mad elopement with the daughter of a rich merchant. If exile was the mark of a great liberal writer, my biography had a long way to go. On the other hand, I have become the protagonist of a romantic episode, a complicated story of a woman seventeen years older than me, a love that's changed my life as much as literature and my classes with Ignacio Rubio have. Difficult love affairs can enrich silences, just as beautiful verses can or affirmations that are released to float around the classroom like trial balloons that everyone can take home and study.

As a student, I've taken home many verses, a few biographies, and a vocation. One day, I will find Collioure, the village in France where Antonio Machado is buried. One day, I will have a home overrun by books, and I will allow history to intersect with my personal experience, upending everything including the tables and chairs, the furniture in the living room and in the office, until it puts me where I'm meant to be. And that's why I'm learning to see, to doubt, to invent, to use irony and distancing, learning to develop my own personal style, like Juan Ramón Jiménez and his manic obsession with using the *j* to write *antholojy*, or like Valle-Inclán and his groupings of three consecutive adjectives to describe devotion to a complicated, powerful, and inevitable woman. Three cheers for Valle-Inclán.

After finding a spot for the tray with two cups of coffee and an ashtray, Ignacio asked about my job at Editorial Universo. I searched for the right words. I wanted to demonstrate my gratitude and my intelligence as I commented on most of the same things I'd already told him in my letter; that I was happy there, that it'd been an enlightening experience. In order to write, you have to live, interact with people, experience being alone in new situations, face events as they happen, make decisions, discover the truth. Now I'd come to know the pulse of the city that assembled and disassembled itself every day far from the insular world of the University.

He asked me about Vicente. I sketched the profile of a man whose appearance is deceptive. At first glance, he seems to be a caricature of the faceless office worker, cannon fodder, the apathetic man who just wants to avoid problems, who breathes whatever air circumstances allow, is content to not be a bother and not be bothered, who doesn't miss poetry or harbor ambitions. But little by little, after sharing experiences with him, you end up respecting his silences, his cautious approach, the fatalism with which he mops his brow, or drags his pinching shoes through the streets. I told the story of the tied-up dog, the rock thrown by the gang of boys, and their state of misery and cruelty worthy of Baroja's *The Struggle for Life*.

He asked about Consuelo, and I offered him a half truth. I told him that getting to know her had been a revelation. She was an unusual woman, highly educated, someone I could talk to about literature, complain to about the mediocrity and hypocrisy of our society, and with whom I could even share my hopes for a different future, a future awakened in me by the boldness of my dreams. Consuelo viewed the world with keen, untamed eyes. You can tell she has a degree in Romance languages and literature.

We read Pablo Neruda together, she lent me books, she helped me a lot at work. Thanks to her suggestion, Don Alfonso offered me a part-time job selling encyclopedias for Universo during the school year.

He asked about Don Alfonso. I'd only seen him twice, but I had a pretty good idea what kind of character he was. Marcelo, the owner of the Café Lepanto, helped me understand the type of guy that hangs out at bars and beaches in Torremolinos. A lot of talk, a lot of charm, and an instinct for business deals and for taking advantage of the intricacies of the Franco regime. He's the kind of person who keeps a low profile during war, but afterward knows how to get his hand in, put everyone ease, allow the boot-black, the women, and the government ministers to adore him.

Ignacio's smile confirmed that he'd enjoyed my portrait of the boss, which encouraged me to say more. I told him about Loja, Motril, Maracena, unexpected births, impoverished slums, the Guardia Civil station, the empty lots around the train station, festivals celebrating saints, and the suspended calendar at the Café Lepanto. Now, I have a very different relationship with the city. I learned to see as I walked along the Paseo del Salón, through the half-built suburbs of Zaidín, or along the sidewalks of the Gran Vía. I've discovered many things in Granada, I told him, quoting in my best French:

—*Paris change! Mais rien dans ma mélancolie*
N'a bougé! Palais neufs, échafaudages, blocs,
Vieux faubourgs, tout pour moi devient allégorie,
Et mes chers souvenirs sont plus lourds que des rocs.

"Baudelaire, 'The Swan,'" I said, proud that I remembered the verses I learned in Ignacio's class that day he leapt from a lecture on suspended time in the sacred poetry of Gonzalo de Berceo, to the melancholy reflections of Garcilaso, to wind up talking about the devastation caused by the rush of modern and anonymous cities.

"Everything changes, but memories remain," Ignacio said. "Buildings go up, suburbs spread, vacant lots are paved over, but you'll always remember the geography of this summer. Reality is an allegory for memory. That which touches us stays with us, even though it may be lost in time."

I thought about Consuelo's body at thirty-seven: firm, white, mine. An inevitable presence, fixed in time, *plus lourds que des rocs*—heavier than rocks. I will age. She never will. Years may go by, but she will remain unchanged, immutable, identical to the way she was that first afternoon, lying naked next to me in the summer of nineteen sixty-three when a prolonged drought led to water rationing and to the sound of the pipes announcing that a young man of twenty and a woman of thirty-seven had seized the day, abandoned themselves to desire, beyond ages, conventions, fears, and hostile looks from the neighbors. Age doesn't matter ... Ignacio's question broke the silence of my reverie.

"Have you read about the French Resistance to the Nazis? I wanted to talk to you about that."

My relationship with Ignacio during my first year followed a ritual of encounters in stages. First came my quick questions after class outside lecture hall number three in the main campus building, where, amid a tumult of other students leaving the room, I sought clarification of one idea or another that he talked about in his lecture. I'd use any excuse to approach him, doubts about a point of fact or a request for a book title would do. After that, there were visits to his office, for closed-door conversations about the University's program and literature in general, his gallery of preferred authors, recommended reading, and advice to a future writer and current student frustrated by some of his other classes. One of those conversations ended up in the department café over two coffees and some confessions about my life in Granada, reality in Villatoga, my family situation, the history of Spain, censorship, and intellectual mediocrity among the many professors who still embraced the bellicose spirit of the Crusades or who navigated carefully through the humbled and fearful post-war.

Then, after the classroom questions, the office visits, and conversations in the café, came the invitations to his home. This implied a level of intimacy and preferential status that I accepted as a form of personal recognition. Without a doubt, it was a path that brought me closer to his library and his own perspectives. As our confidence grew, I was able to speak frankly about my disappointments and my need for radical change. That was the moment, just at the end of the school year, when Ignacio spoke to me about Editorial Universo and the possibility of working there during the summer. It would allow me to stay in Granada, have some new experiences, and avoid going back to Villatoga. And I hadn't let Ignacio down. The fact that Don Alfonso had asked me to stay on meant that my work had fit the bill.

"The Nazis were defeated in France. Some of Spain's Republican fighters took part in the French Resistance." Ignacio was speaking in his customary tone, but I noted a twinge of doubt in his voice, as if he were broaching a confidence with a sense of uncertainty. Not just for himself, but also for me. I recalled how fragile a door-to-door salesman with a guilty conscience feels when standing before a difficult client. I still didn't know what Ignacio was going to say, but I didn't want to make it more difficult for him. I accepted a third cigarette. "In Spain, the dictatorship still exists. We need to organize a resistance movement."

"Some of the other students have been talking about that. We've discussed it."

"The most serious opposition to the regime is the Communist Party's clandestine political organization in Spain."

"You mean the ones who kidnapped Di Stéfano in retaliation for Grimau's assassination?"

"No, I'm not talking about guerrillas, or kidnappings or armed conflict. This is a new kind of resistance, one that creates the foundations for an opposition political party inside this country. We must nurture a culture of democracy among workers, professionals, students. It's what I'm doing."

I knew instantly what he was proposing. He allowed the weight of his intentions to settle slowly amid the cigarette smoke, and I embraced them with decisive commitment. "You can count on me."

"It'd be good to have someone who could help work with the students, someone who could contribute to a new direction for Granada."

"I am ready."

"You should be aware that it means joining the Party as a student liaison."

"I agree." Rather than trying to express any opinions about a reality I was only beginning to comprehend, I wanted to make very clear my desire and intention to identify myself with his way of life and thinking. "You can count on me," I said again.

"The previous leaders of the Party were arrested a few years ago. They're all in jail."

"I know, I read about the trial in the newspapers."

Ignacio was warning me that the step I was about to take wasn't a game. It was a dangerous thing, involving police, judges, jail sentences, prisons and sometimes worse. It wasn't armed conflict, but risk would become a daily companion, getting up, leaving the house, going to the University and to the office. My life could get really complicated. He looked me in the eye. He paused, as if offering a chance to reconsider.

"Do you want to think about it?"

"I don't need to."

"Well, I've thought about it a lot. I've had these contacts for some time, I've been to Paris, I've been evaluating it all for quite a while."

"I've decided, Ignacio." I started to feel a pang of fear from the seriousness in his voice, but I was determined not to turn back. No, it was better not to think, not to doubt. "If no one steps up, nothing will ever change here. I hate indifference," I told him.

"The day after tomorrow we're all going to meet at the Cubillas Reservoir. It will appear to be a casual gathering, a group of friends on a Saturday morning excursion to the countryside. We're going to elect a new party leadership. Do you want to come with me?"

"Yes, I will go."

The only plan I had for Saturday was easy to cancel. Jacobo had arranged for us to go to Mariví's family farmhouse in Huétor Vega, a village just south of Granada. It was no problem for me to shift gears and postpone my roommate's enthusiasm, the boxes of food from Pastelería Pintor Velázquez, and the conversation with beautiful, tall, and rich Elena. Any excuse about my job and working on the weekend would do the trick.

"You can think about it. If you change your mind, just let me know. But there is something you must promise me. Whether you decide to come or not, you mustn't speak a word of this to anyone. Not your friends, not your family, not your co-workers at Universo. No one. This is a clandestine

meeting and if you let it slip out, you could put us all in danger. So, no one.
Do you promise?"

"I understand. I promise."

"Ok. I'll see you Saturday at noon. Meet me here."

I left Ignacio's house feeling surprised. I'd thought he was going to offer me a project at the Department. Something to do with Universo or maybe research for a book. I never imagined that his political ties were so serious. People talked sometimes around campus about his commitment or his lack of commitment, but it was all just rumors, and truth be told I'd always suspected that his ideas never reached beyond the literary circle of his classes and his office.

But suddenly, we'd entered a world of grown-up words, and I'd entered a state of fear. I needed some time to take stock of this new reality. In the plaza's trees, the birds slept.

⌒⊙

I caught up with Consuelo as she was leaving the office, but we didn't go to her apartment. We'd made a pact to have coffee in the Café Suizo. Since our last conversation, she'd avoided being alone with me. Suddenly, she didn't seem to have time for anything; she always had something else to do. Her commitments took her here and there, appointments with friends, family duties, phone orders for Don Alfonso, shopping, hurrying, fibbing, and always away from me. And, if I was able to take advantage of any slips on her part and break through her defenses, she was always able to deploy her art of being affectionate and elusive at the same time. She never let me doubt her feelings for me, her dissatisfaction with our situation, her love for me, or that she was not going to let me visit her at home. As soon as Vicente left the office for the day, she would stand, answer my questions with delicacy, then with a quick kiss on the lips she said goodbye and rushed out to some urgent appointment.

This afternoon it rained again. Once more, I gave thanks to the weather for shifting the dimensions of our intimacy. Consuelo opened an umbrella in the doorway of the building and handed it to me. Here, you carry it, she said, and took me by the arm. The dimensions of the umbrella forced us to huddle close together. We walked past the Café Lepanto like any normal couple, continued along Calle Mariana Pineda, and came out onto the Plaza del Carmen under the solidarity of the rain clouds. As long as the rain doesn't gush and the wind doesn't howl, umbrellas create a separate world, a submerged reality. Consuelo and I sheltered together underneath an umbrella and an intense whisper of raindrops. On the other side of the wall was the rest of the world, people running and the traffic of the city.

We got to the Olmedo Department Store, and giving into the temptation to be an idiot, I turned toward the Fuente de las Batallas, following the evening path we often took that ended at her apartment on Transversal de la Bomba. But Consuelo pulled away from my arm and the umbrella, halting my intentions. I don't want to get my hair wet, she said, I just had it done.

I hadn't said anything about her hair. When she arrived at the office that morning, her hair was cut short, and she was again wearing the glasses of a submissive office secretary. She preferred her hair short so she wouldn't have to deal with it all the time. That made sense, but it bothered me: why hadn't she trusted me to talk about such a big decision ahead of time. She looked strange, older, colder, almost distant. She had looked at herself in the mirror and saw a way to create a distance between us. Since Vicente was, as ever, steeped in his indifference and said nothing all day, I was able to wallow in my own sullen silence. I don't need to know about that, Miss Submissive Secretary, Vicente's mutism suggested, the motives for your new look and your short hair don't affect me. But my lack of interest must have communicated something different to Consuelo because at lunchtime, she announced that she had the evening free and proposed we meet for coffee.

Fridays in the office are torpid. It's hard to work because the exhaustion of the week has accumulated, and the clock maximizes its sluggishness to delay the joy of departure. I, of course, was anxiously anticipating our coffee date, but I distracted myself by fantasizing about my new short-haired ally. I imagined Consuelo naked, without her long tresses. In the shower, her head on the pillow, her body next to mine, in the kitchen, on the terrace with the geraniums, summoned by the water in the pipes or the rain on the roof, her short hair and her nakedness facilitated my endless fantasies. The earrings that my lips had often sought through the strands of her hair now trembled brazenly before my eyes. I was quick to acknowledge that I had no right to question her, that she had no obligation to seek my opinion before making a hair appointment. And then I started to imagine the new Consuelo, as she walked around her house, as she moved from room to room, as I lay down next to her, on top of her, underneath her. And so on, this accumulation of images kept me going all afternoon.

"You haven't said anything about my new look." She reproached me as soon as the waiter left. She'd ordered a café con leche and a slice of butter cake in honor of her mom. That's what the two of them would always snack on right after going to the dentist. I had a café cortado, but no food since I felt no need to trigger a memory. "What do you think?"

The Café Suizo, with its wooden chairs and marble-topped tables, is spacious enough to accommodate many memories. It's an institution in this city. People talk about afternoons at the Suizo, the potato salad tapas at the Suizo, the waiters at the Suizo and everyone knows what they mean, as if the words drew a picture of daily life and special occasions in that unique atmosphere. The murmurs that grip this place doesn't come from the conversations or the tinkle of tiny spoons against espresso cups. They emerge from Granada's secrets, from the weight of memory forced into secrecy. Those who don't belong to this world can feel a strange sense of vulnerability here. That's my case since I hardly ever come. My conversation with Consuelo about our future was about to happen in a place that was solemn, comfortable, and foreign. It belonged to the opposing side. It seems like an apt venue for secrets like my discovery of Marisa's affair with the baritone, but not the right kind of place for a mutually frank and supportive conversation about our future.

"Your haircut took me by surprise this morning. But I'm getting used to it. Actually, it looks like a disguise, like you're trying to camouflage yourself."

"So, you don't like the way I look?"

"I don't like you turning into a traditional type of woman or adding years to the way you look. It seems like you're trying to push me away."

"I don't need to add years. I'm seventeen years older than you."

This was not the way I wanted this conversation to start out. I'd admitted that I didn't like the new look, and she instantly trotted out the same old theme, the damned difference between our ages. We weren't going to get anywhere this way. I tried to learn from our previous arguments. I stopped thinking about myself and tried to think about her feelings. How many times had she left the living room and gone into the bedroom or the bathroom to look in the mirror, contemplate her face, reflect on her body, her life, her heart, her job? How many sleepless nights did she spend, tossing and turning, before deciding that a change of image was the thing to do, and calling to make an appointment to cut her hair?

There are many ways of being alone, but solitude always ends up filled with strange elements, whether people or rumors, obsessions or roommates. The previous night I'd felt very alone in the company of my two roommates, one who was obsessed with arranging outings with his girlfriend and her cousin and the other ready to organize everyone's lives to ensure a future of certainty, judicious devotions, and rapid personal financial growth. Jesús had come back from summer break with an insufferably assertive and propagandistic sense of determination. And then we argued about the landlady's rent hike for the new school year. She wants to charge us four hundred and fifty pesetas each, including the weekly cleaning fee. I'm not so worried about overspending my parents' monthly allowance anymore, but our landlady's out of control. The calculations of a carefree lifestyle, the constant excursions, the Law, Medicine, and the daily demands on the pocketbook, were building up to an unbearable combination ahead of the new school year. It was difficult to find time to write, or even think about Ignacio Rubio's proposal, and the hardships that awaited my new commitment. Although in the end, I had to admit that Consuelo's silence and her decision to distance herself were the things that bothered me the most. It didn't diminish the significance of my political transition, but last night the state of my love life was bothering me more than my anticipation of Saturday's excursion to the Pantano de Cubillas. The conspiracy would come later, on the other side of Friday and Consuelo's evasive eyes which were waiting for me in the office the next day. Jacobo wouldn't forgive me for ruining his weekend plans at the farmhouse in Huétor Vega. He took revenge by barging uninvited into my room, leaving the door open, talking about money, love, criminal law, and arguing about everything and everyone. He was there until two in the morning.

Having company would have assuaged Consuelo's loneliness in her apartment. So, I tried to understand her. I forgot about her short hair and her nakedness and used my imagination to connect with the fears a thirty-seven-year-old woman in a relationship with a much younger man might feel. It actually wasn't difficult to understand her anxiety, the threat of rumors, the potential storm of negative opinion. But I could also sense something deeper, more important, an intimate uncertainty, a fear of hurting and of being hurt, the responsibility of a relationship that could negatively affect another person's life, the dread of abandoning herself into the hands of an immature, unstable, fragile young man. I told her all of it. Although at that moment she was finishing off her butter cake with the irresistible expression of a greedy young girl, I explained to her that I had put myself in her shoes, that I thought I understood each and every one of her thirty-seven years, her maturity, my insecurity, her fears, my anxieties, her situation, and mine. I told her that I understood everything, and that we had the right to seek out opportunity, our opportunity.

"Ok then, let's talk about it. If it's true that you understand me, you'll have to accept some things. They aren't rules, just realities." As she spoke, she looked at me with touching seriousness. I had the instant impression that we'd broken through a barrier. "Let's have lunch tomorrow. Come to my place, and we can talk."

Damn the bad luck. Like a rock to the head. Consuelo was inviting me to her home for lunch on the very day of my commitment to join Ignacio Rubio. At any other moment, any other day, rain or shine, I would have dropped everything and run like a loyal dog to her call. But on Saturday I had to be at the Pantano de Cubillas. My relationship with Consuelo and the promise I made to Ignacio were in fatal conflict. You can count on me, Ignacio. You're the only thing I care about, Consuelo. I don't know how I'm going to break myself in two. And worse, I can't tell the truth, I can't look the other way, I can't stay silent. I can't just apologize to Ignacio. Sorry about that, I'm having an affair with Consuelo, the secretary at Universo, and she's invited me to her house to talk about our future, which is even more difficult than a political revolution. I can't just apologize to Consuelo. Sorry about that, I know I've been begging to come to your house to talk about our relationship, and I want to be there, I wouldn't miss it for the world, because I know that finally we'll really talk, that we'll take each other seriously, and then I'm going to ask you to play a game with me, to punish me, to turn my fantasies into reality with your short hair and nakedness. But, sorry about that, it turns out that I have to go to an important meeting, my first clandestine meeting, and I can't miss it, and furthermore, I can in no way justify, reveal, or explain any of it to you. After pursuing you like a madman, I now have to make my excuses and lie to you.

"It's just that tomorrow my parents and my Aunt Rosario are coming to Granada, and I have to spend the day with them. Couldn't we meet on Sunday?"

"Well, that's a coincidence. If you want, we could meet up and you could introduce me to them, and we can all have lunch together."

"My parents don't ..."

"We don't have to say that we're lovers or that you're planning something crazy like moving in with me. That's not what I'm saying. You just introduce me as a colleague from work. If you want, we can show them around the office."

"I feel a bit embarrassed." The tragedy of my endless bad luck was crushing me once again. I was on a dead-end street. I had no choice but to betray my parents. "But my parents are villagers, and I would feel uncomfortable. Can't we just meet on Sunday instead?"

"So, it turns out that I'm the one who embarrasses you. You're afraid of letting your parents see you with an older woman. That's it, isn't it? 'Papá, Mamá, this is my girlfriend. She's really old, but I love her truly.'"

"Consuelo..."

"I'm old enough to be your mother."

Her torture was driving me to the of point surrender, of singing like a canary, pushing me beyond my capacity to resist. There was no way I was going to allow Consuelo to doubt, presume, believe, imagine, or suspect that I was ashamed of her. It would be too unfair. But what was I supposed to do? Invent another lie that would just make things worse? No, that was no good. I was going to do it, to betray Ignacio Rubio and some comrades I hadn't met before even making it to the first meeting. Some problems are unsolvable. Not even literature can help. Imagination, triads of adjectives, and distancing are useless. Everything's become too literal. Bad days are really bad. Dead-end streets with no way out. You're transformed into a creep without really being a creep.

"Consuelo, look..."

"Don't worry. I get it. That's life. On the one hand, there's what we feel. On the other, there's reality. Sometimes, the two can never marry."

"Consuelo..."

"Hush. Never mind, don't worry about it. We'll have lunch on Sunday. But now you understand our situation, right? Now you get it?"

The word Sunday appeared like a miracle on Consuelo's lips. I thanked her. I asked her to forgive me. Inside her apartment, I would find a way to make amends. After this Saturday, I hoped to have more information so I could stop fumbling for words and discover a way to move forward and remain loyal. Consuelo had calmed me with a smile and the word Sunday. She was there with me in the Café Suizo. Behind her was a huge mirror: in it my reflection trembled as did the marble-topped tables and the mysterious, relentless hum of the city.

Ignacio was waiting in the doorway to his building. He looked like a hiker about to plunge into the darkest forests of the Sierra. Hiking boots, thick sweater, a red flannel shirt, and corduroy pants that to me looked like a bit much for a mild morning toward the end of September at the Pantano de Cubillas. I thought of my father who went to work in the fields each day wearing his canvas shoes and no coat, even well into winter. I assumed Ignacio's excesses had to do with the need to disguise our appearances for the clandestine meeting, but I couldn't help feeling a surge of campesino pride. My coarse clothes would be much less suspicious to the police than this

171

mountain climber kitted out to conquer the Himalayas. For the first time since I arrived in Granada, I felt comfortable with my memories, not of trams and city streets, but of irrigation canals, farm fields, olive orchards, and the village lanes of Villatoga. Of course, I said nothing about Ignacio's get up. I simply gave myself permission not to feel embarrassed by my shirt, my jeans, and my shoes. Manolo the bootblack would have his work cut out for him on Monday thanks to this conspiracy.

Ignacio had parked his two-horsepower Citroën in front of his building. As we made our way through the city toward the highway to Jaén, he again asked me if I was sure of my decision, if I understood the seriousness of the step I was taking. He again insisted on complete secrecy, it was critical not to trust anyone, not to talk about these meetings even with your most intimate friends. It's as if we were writing a novel, Ignacio said, a novel of suspense and we must ensure that no one can guess the outcome until the very end of the story. We passed by the Hospital Clínico, the soccer field, the prison—there's an omen for you—until we finally made it to the highway to Jaén. I was able to tell my professor of literature—and politics—that yes, I was capable of silence. I could say to the passing trees and the car's shifting gears that my very presence here, stuck as we were behind the truck that wouldn't let us pass and was forcing us to go thirty miles an hour, was proof that I had renounced a date with Consuelo in her apartment, and I had done so without opening my mouth, without saying a word about the meeting, without confessing the true motive for my absence, and instead improvising an excuse which triggered all sorts of misunderstandings and unfortunate consequences. My first sacrifice.

Riding along next to Ignacio, I realized that I hadn't told Consuelo about my discovery of the previous day. The secret became intertwined with the lie. Our conversation in the Café Suizo had taken such an unexpected turn that I forgot all about the affair between Marisa and Ramiro Martín, the reason for Vicente's personal drama and the dark circles under his eyes, his sad handkerchief, and his pinching shoes. In life, as in any relationship, people are affected by things they don't even know are happening but are there, camouflaged behind the strife of routine. I forgot to tell Consuelo because I was so focused on our own situation, the missed date

172

in her apartment, the possibility of seeing each other on Sunday despite the secrets. I admit I felt very uncomfortable about Vicente's misfortune. My daily contact with him, the little details, his behavior toward me, and his attitude toward life had consolidated my friendship with him in these last weeks. I preferred not to reveal anything that would hurt him.

The water mark around the edge of the reservoir revealed the drought's advance. The level was very low, and traces of earth and reeds poked through the surface of the water. Ignacio commented that the water shortages would continue through the fall. It didn't matter to me, though I didn't say so to Ignacio, concealing my debt to the drought. We passed the main entrance and took a small road to the right that circled the reservoir. A narrow bridge provided access. The difficult journey through the thick pine groves reminded me that I was penetrating an unknown world. Looking out the window of the bus on the highway, I'd always seen the reservoir as just another chapter in the journey between Villatoga and Granada. But this country road, the proximity of the water, the scent of humidity, and the silence of the trees surprised by the sound of the two-horsepower engine announced a new reality. I was about to inaugurate a different phase of my life.

New reality? Different phase? Yes, but no. My imaginings about the group of conspirators that I was about to meet were quickly surpassed by the only surprise that I never could have imagined. I thought I might encounter a familiar face or two from the University, other tenured professors who were friends of Ignacio's, or maybe a student from one of the upper classes. But that was not the scene that destiny had prepared as the culmination to my strange and decisive summer of nineteen sixty-three. The climax instead was a very different one. Ignacio drove into a small clearing in the forest that surrounded the reservoir and parked next to a grey SEAT Seiscientos. As we walked toward a group of hikers that were occupying a stone table near the shore, a strange and disorienting sensation began to grip me. I had no idea how to interpret the scene unfolding before my eyes, Ignacio's greetings, the reality I was stepping into, a situation that was new, but not different. I felt paralyzed, ashamed, overwhelmed by the turn of events, as if my life had departed from the logic of the normal world. Everything was spinning out of control. I lit a cigarette to create a pause, to give me time to come up with some kind of explanation. I studied them with my eyes, to see how they studied me. The tobacco was making me dizzy again.

Consuelo's short hair, her earrings, her white-rimmed glasses, her hiking pants condemned me to a confusion I was incapable of hiding. She was taking two bottles of wine and some dishes wrapped in paper out of a basket. I felt more scrambled than the eggs and potatoes in a tortilla. Consuelo didn't look too comfortable either. She glanced at me with a timid smile and said hello. Consuelo was the only one in the group who seemed flustered. It showed. Except for me in my surprise and humiliation as the Convidado de Piedra, everyone else was smiling.

"How are you, Ignacio? Aren't you hot in that getup?" Vicente Fernández Fernández made no effort to hide the irony in his voice when he saw the literature professor disguised as an alpine adventurer. Cool and confident, he seemed determined to celebrate the situation. "Next time we'll meet in the Alps."

"Ay ay, Nature divine!", a good-humored Ignacio pronounced in English, happy to laugh at himself and his own eccentricities.

"L'habitude est une seconde nature. Nature humaine!" responded Vicente in French, then added "You're obviously not used to walking in the woods." With that he called an end to the hellos and the jokes. "Ok, let's all take a seat. Thanks everyone for being so punctual."

I was thinking the whole thing must be a joke, like hazing the new kid in school. Ignacio and Vicente had pulled Consuelo into the prank as a spectacular farewell-to-summer and welcome-to-employee-status-at-Universo event. A surprise picnic! But the other hikers weren't writers, or Café Lepanto clients, or Don Alfonso's party friends. None of them were connected to Universo, but I knew all of them through my work as an encyclopedia salesman. There they were: Juan Benavides, the lotero from Motril; Pablo Aguayo, the farmer we visited the morning of the unexpected birth by the Corto de Loja; Antonio Mendoza, the mechanic from Maracena; his friend Antonio Cid, El Colorao; Marisa, Vicente's wife; and her secret companion, Ramiro Martín, the pretentious railway worker. No, no, this was impossible. It couldn't be a joke.

174

Everything fell into place only later, after Vicente and Consuelo explained the plot of this tangled turn in my life. The process required a very long walk filled with my questions and complaints, and their answers for me to understand what was going on. But in the end, my humiliation turned into solidarity, and eagerness to absorb all the details. I came to understand that for the last three months, I'd been participating, without knowing it, in the organization of the Party in Granada. I was in the play without realizing I was on stage. I was in the spotlight but ignorant of the plot.

Consuelo first came into contact with clandestine Party members in Madrid through Alberto Toledo, the painter she dated for four years. But her world view had already been transformed by her university years. Little by little, she had stopped being the obedient daughter of a military officer addicted to the Franco regime. She stopped being the naïve Consuelo who'd spent her childhood and adolescence in Granada without ever doubting the good intentions of the military saviors of the nation. While her first boyfriend shared her political misgivings, the painter brought her into the Party. It was because of him she traveled to Paris, where she first made contact with some of the leaders and learned a different way of life. When she and her artist boyfriend broke up, he sought tranquility in Mexico and she returned to Granada, but not to her previous innocence. She kept her membership and collaborated with the Party, discreet and vigilant while continuing her peaceful routine as a secretary in the Granada office of Editorial Universo.

Life can take many turns, but some people choose to follow a straight line. Consuelo's father, Captain Astorga, decided to retire and move to Madrid with his wife. Consuelo also considered moving to Madrid and applying for a library job with the Education Ministry. But the Party asked her to stay in Granada to act as a liaison between the two cities. She was the daughter of a military family, and worked for Don Alfonso, an old hand in the Falangist movement, so she didn't raise any suspicions. When the Party leaders were arrested, and the Party decided to send Vicente to Granada to evaluate the situation, Consuelo let him know about an opportunity for a sales job that had just come open in the office. Vicente wasn't really, as he had told me, a long-time employee of Universo who'd been sent by the company to Granada; he was a Party member who arrived from Paris in nineteen sixty-one with orders to rebuild the local clandestine organization.

A discreet word from Consuelo, and Don Alfonso was convinced of Vicente's merits as the best candidate for the job. The Granada office wasn't too much work anyway. All Don Alfonso needed was one efficient secretary and a salesman who could respond to requests from distributors. He never really paid much attention to his own role as editor, appropriately enough, and was happy to trust his diligent secretary, the daughter of a close friend and a discreet woman who, for some time, had been taking care of his business anyway. The introduction of the installment plan for the purchase of Editorial Universo encyclopedias meant that the salesman could start selling to individuals and visiting homes in addition to handling distribution to institutions. This new sales strategy required a salesman with new skills. It didn't take Vicente long to turn himself into that very salesman.

And that's how he began his job. He sought out old contacts, made new ones, mended previously broken threads of relationships. Ignacio Rubio was among the first of his targets in Granada. The fact that one of Ignacio's books had already been published by Universo facilitated matters. Coincidence, quiet effort behind the scenes, and the new sales requirements at Universo conspired to make the office a perfect cover for traveling around the province. Right underneath Don Alfonso's shifty, tidy mustache, the melancholy fans, and the bureaucratic shadows of number seven Calle Lepanto, a new resistance to the dictatorship was being organized. At the end of the last school year, Ignacio thought of me as a possible intermediary to other students and they decided to offer me the three-month summer contract. Vicente wanted to get to know me, to test me, to be sure. He preferred to tread carefully when it came to approaching university students. You never know, he said, and he was right.

I didn't need to know about all the details that Vicente and Consuelo shared with me later on our long walk, to understand that my three-month job this summer was in reality a trial period, a lab experiment to decide if I would be invited to join the organization. Logically, I was most concerned about Consuelo. How far did her role as Party informer go?

That was the wound stinging me most when Vicente asked us all to sit and began to talk.

"We're meeting here on the thirtieth day of September of nineteen sixty-three to constitute a new leadership group. The members are: Pedro Aguayo, who from now on will be known in all Party documents and reports as El Pájaro; Juan Benavides, will be known as El Justo; Antonio Mendoza, El Automovilista; Carlos Cid, alias Cándido; Ramiro Martín, El Barítono (if you'll forgive the joke); Marisa, La Guapa; Consuelo, La Maestra; Ignacio, El Francés (if that's ok with you); León, will be embraced by this group as Pío Baroja; and myself, I will be known as El Perro, in honor of the liberated dog. The first item on the agenda: procedure to follow in case of arrest.

"That's a terrible way to start." Juan Benavides was the only one not respecting the solemnity of the moment. He'd been listening to Vicente with a look of amusement and didn't want to jinx things by talking about the worst that could happen.

Vicente cut him off. "The important thing is how we finish, not how we start. So, procedure in case of capture: speak your name, your real name, with pride. Declare without fear that you belong to the leadership of the Party. And that's it. No other names, no other information, no other details. Nothing else."

"Just the will to survive when they beat the shit out of you." Benavides just wasn't going to shut up.

I was worried about Consuelo's nombre de guerra: La Maestra. What did Vicente mean by naming her The Teacher? I needed to know if she had used me somehow. I did finally understand the reasons for her reticence, the illogical rhythm of her trips to Madrid, the true reason for Vicente's nocturnal visit to her apartment, and the distancing project she had forced on me. But I wanted to know to what degree our love story might have been just another episode in a political plan, or if it really meant something more, a relationship that appeared by chance, a shortcut off the map that Vicente had drawn up.

Fortunately, holding a meeting in the forest makes it easy to break off into side conversations. And my friends had a lot of explaining to do.

When the meeting ended, Vicente and Consuelo invited me to walk with them along the reservoir's shore. They wanted to share the details of their Party activity and the strategy they had developed to use Universo as a cover. Now, as I write in my journal about my surprise and disconcerting entry into this clandestine group, I have to laugh at myself when I remember Vicente's prudence, his desire to be invisible, my irritation with his apparent indifference, his insistence that: "I don't need to know about that." Watch out for the humble office worker! Now I understand a lot. Whenever he sent me ahead to buy train or bus tickets, he really wanted to stay behind to speak alone to his contacts. The sealed envelopes from the office with explanations about how to buy encyclopedias from Editorial Universo on the installment plan hid documents and reports from the Party. I also understand that he was nervous in Maracena because he was afraid of what Antonio Mendoza and Carlos Cid might do. And those funny incidents, like Benavides' comments in Motril or the scene with Ramiro Martín behind the train station were not pranks dreamt up in Vicente's head but a dual reality, of which I was completely unaware, and which had created inevitable confusion, a clash of normality and innuendo, of appearances and secrets. Now, it all falls into place.

"There are two more things I want to talk to you about." Vicente bent down to pick up a stone and launched it into the water, the waves rippling along the surface. "Consuelo and I have decided to donate part of our commission from the Education and Recreation sale to the Party. We're each keeping five thousand pesetas and donating twenty-five thousand. This way, the Franco regime's money goes to its political opponents. What do you think?"

"How much should I give?"

"I think it would be good if you gave half. You keep ten thousand, and you donate the other ten. You can be sure that your contribution will be very much appreciated."

"Ok."

"One more thing. La Guapa really is my wife."

"I know."

"And I know that last Thursday you saw her walking with Ramiro, and you followed them to Plaza Nueva. Marisa spotted you. They're not lovers. They went into a building to throw you off the track."

"I'm glad for you."

"A pair of lovers walking along a city street might invite envy, but not suspicion of illegal political activity. Such are the intricacies of clandestine life. It helps them move easily through the city. They were on their way to Telefónica to make a phone call, helping to prepare Benavides' trip. Before coming to Granada, el Justo went to his wife's village. In theory, he's still there. I'm grateful that you didn't say anything about this to me, or, even more importantly, to Consuelo. I think I can guess the significance of your silence."

With those words, he turned and left us alone. Consuelo turned around and walked away from the group and warned me that she wanted to set a few things straight. She came straight to the point, taking refuge in the spirit of synthesis and her white rimmed glasses. She deployed the same dizzying resources as that afternoon when she got mad at me because I was jealous of the boss. Honestly, it seems like three months can contain a lifetime. This time, she wasn't indignant and happy but seemed timid and relieved, ashamed and committed, just like the strange situation we were living through. She summarized it all in six points which she launched without giving me a chance to speak. One: comrades are even more puritanical than priests, so it wasn't a good idea to confess our relationship to anyone. Two: what happened between us and what might happen in the future is only between us. Consuelo considered it a happy disruption of the original plan, but any ill-timed indiscretion would bring an abrupt end to a possible future relationship. Three: Vicente started to suspect something when she told him I'd spotted him going into her building. She had to reveal my spying for reasons of security, but his concerns had abated. Four: she couldn't care less about the neighbors and their conventions. She'd been a political operative for too long to care about things like that. Our age difference wasn't a question of honor, but one of biology. We will see. Five: her restlessness and mood swings in the last few weeks had to do only with the impossibility of telling me about her participation in the Party, her busy schedule of obligations, and her meetings. Now that's taken care of, and everything would be easier. She wasn't going to bother worrying about any tomorrows. And six: speaking of tomorrow, she expected to see me at her apartment for lunch.

"Just out of curiosity, on Friday when you invited me to lunch for today, did you already know that I had agreed to come out here with Ignacio?"

"Of course."

"And then you offered to join me and my parents for lunch."

"And you were crushed. I felt so bad. I'm sorry. But a girl likes to know how far she can trust ... both a comrade and a lover. You got a very good grade and graduated with honors. Which is why I agreed to change our date to Sunday."

"La Maestra?"

"Vicente likes to pretend he knows more than he does."

"Don't play any more games with me."

"Only if you start to get bored with me."

"Never."

"You know, your face is starting to look more mature somehow, sort of like a grown up."

Who was it who said that a man is the age of the woman he holds in his arms?

Last night, I stayed up late writing. My silent, comfortable bedroom seemed like a crystal palace. But this morning I woke up realizing I have to destroy everything I've written. I'm drafting my final entry in this journal with the sole intention of closing the doors behind it, of shutting down my summer of nineteen sixty-three. I went to sleep feeling like there was justice in the world. Things had turned out well. I have no complaints and I need nothing else from life. My friendship with Ignacio, my relationship with Consuelo, my decision to commit myself to the resistance; everything had unfolded in the right direction. But then, I woke up worrying that this journal, my apprentice's workshop toward professional writing, a laboratory for my fantasies, ironies, distancing, adjectives, and truths, is incompatible with my new situation. You can't live a clandestine life with a pre-published confession. This journal is a full-blown indictment of Vicente, Ignacio, Consuelo, and my new friends. I will now proceed to erase myself. I'm going to live on the other side.

Jacobo is spending the weekend at the farm in Huétor. Jesús is heading out at eleven-thirty so he can go to mass at the sagrario church. When I hear the door shut behind him, I'll get up, tear out the pages of this journal and burn them, one by one, in the bathtub. The last bit of flame from each page will light the next. And so on, until there's no trace of my story. Then, I'll walk to Calle Transversal de la Bomba to have lunch with Consuelo in her apartment. And whatever happens there, I'm not revealing any more.

My literature professor thinks that writing is a form of militancy. Seeking out important books, reading them and studying them are useful ways of participating in a resistance movement. It depends on the books we choose and the ideas we're capable of defending. Conditions in Spain today are as horrific as a police station full of prisoners. We need to seek out other words, other perspectives, other emotions, even if later we have to burn them all. Ignacio explained all this on the drive back to Granada, trying to help me understand my new situation. Some of the others in the group went on foot to El Chaparral to catch the bus. Some rode in the SEAT Seiscientos with El Automovilista. Ignacio and I drove back in his Citroën. El Francés and Pío Baroja began to speak.

"Politics is an extension of your commitment to literature."

He said this in the hope that my new responsibilities wouldn't lead me to neglect my studies or abandon my vocation as a writer. I will go to the University, I will work each afternoon in the office, I will study every night and I will go out to visit our clients on Saturdays. Everything's in order. But I do need to burn this journal because it's an unnecessary risk. If it fell into the hands of the police, no one would believe my excuse that it's just fiction. The trips, the work meetings, afternoons of amor, names, rebuilding the Party, fear, jealousy, misunderstandings, confessions, a clearing in the woods, geraniums in pots, the drought, the customers in the Café Lepanto, and the conspirators are nothing more than literary resources, fragments of an apprenticeship.

All apprenticeships are destined to burn. In the hands of the police, there's no such thing as an innocent life. The times are not in our favor, as my father says. But these flames aren't an escape. They're a commitment, a way of seeking and offering warmth.

My father's prudence? Let it burn, along with the cowardice of the indifferent, the arrogance of the Villatoga mayor, and the brutality of his son. Pedro el Pastor, my Aunt Rosario, my mother? Let them burn. Consuelo Astorga's nakedness, our pillow talk, her long hair, her records, her earrings between my lips, the commitment of two bodies embraced in joy and in sadness. The memories of the know-it-all who spent three months without a clue. Let it all burn.

The Café Suizo, the Cine Aliatar, the Realejo neighborhood, the kiosk at Calle Reyes Católicos, the melancholies of the widowed barman, the Fuente de las Batallas, the Jardinillos del Genil, the tram station, the fourth-floor apartment at number four Calle Transversal de la Bomba. Burn. I will not leave any clues for the enemy. Let Elena burn.

Let everything burn now, right now. Although…maybe I should wait a few days, and maybe before I burn it, I'll lend it to this person I know. I'm interested in their opinion, and I know I can trust their discretion. They're part of the plot, too.

My literature professor always insisted it's important both to live and to write. After we parked, and he invited me in for a glass of wine, and we went up to his apartment, and he swapped the mountaineering gear for his usual attire, and we found a space amid the books to put down the tray with two glasses and an ashtray, and we talked about Collioure, and Federico García Lorca, and the Juan Marsé novel Consuelo lent me, and the poet Jaime Gil de Biedma, and after all that, Ignacio asked me, once more, very serious, very contrite, looking me in the eye, to consider everything carefully. I could still back out.

"Really? It's possible to go back?"

"What do you want?" he asked. "That's what counts."

It seemed like the right moment to give him an answer that was symbolic, literate, and reassuring.

"I want to go to Paris."

Swan Isle Press is a not-for-profit publisher
of poetry, fiction, and nonfiction.

For information on books of related interest or
for a catalog of new publications contact:
www.swanislepress.com

Someone Speaks Your Name
Designed by Marianne Jankowski
Typeset in Adobe Jensen Pro